THERE'S A SOMEBODY

A NOVEL

To Michael Brewton for this conversation so far — thanks for this house & so — let's make more —

THERE'S A SOMEBODY

A NOVEL

BY STEPHEN W. LONG

A Hand In Hand Book, co-published by A Vireo Book

A Vireo Book
453 South Spring Street, Suite 531
Los Angeles, CA 90013
rarebirdbooks.com

FIRST TRADE PAPERBACK ORIGINAL EDITION

Set in Garamond
Printed in the United States of America
Distributed in the U.S. by Publishers Group West

10 9 8 7 6 5 4 3 2 1

Publisher's Cataloging-in-Publication data

Long, Stephen W.
    There's a somebody : a novel / by Stephen W. Long.
    p. cm.
    ISBN 9780988931299

1. Trucking—Fiction. 2. Fatherhood—Fiction. 3. West (U.S.) Fiction. 4. Travel — Fiction. 5. Western stories. I. Title.

PS3612.O527 T4 2013
813.6 –dc23

There's a somebody I'm longing to see
I hope that she turns out to be
Someone to watch over me

—Ira Gershwin (1926)

CHAPTER ONE

"M r. Stovall?"

At first I don't know she's talking to me. For one thing that isn't my name. For another I'm not looking her way. I'm standing with my hands shoved in my pockets, staring at a painting on the wall. The scene is three ducks on a pond and another one in flight, wings flared, legs stretching for the water. In the foreground are cattails and lily pads, and in the distance a forest. It's only motel art, but the whole thing upsets me to the point I taste pennies in my mouth.

"Mr. Stovall?"

I turn and see it's a nurse. She's in the doorway, unsure, it seems, whether or not to come in.

"If you want to welcome your baby into the world, better hurry. Put this on and follow me."

She crosses to where I'm standing and hands me a paper mask with elastic straps. The mask is pale blue. The duck painting is hung on a beige wall. I'm standing on a gray carpet. Ever since I stepped into the hospital all the bright colors have washed away. Worse, my vision is shrinking as if I'm looking through a tube.

I've experienced this before when I was ten or twelve and an altar boy. I fainted dead away on the altar steps before communion. There is every possibility I will do the same here.

I look at the mask and then at the nurse. She circles her hands over her ears, pantomiming how to place the straps. She must think I don't know how to put on a mask.

When I still don't move, she says, "It's all right. Lots of new fathers are nervous. Just join us whenever you're ready." She points out the door. "Up that way to the first corridor, then right, to the end. Your mother-in-law is already in there with your wife. You'll see us through the glass."

She leaves and I toss the mask onto a chair. I look at the duck painting once more and now see clearly what I only sensed before: None of them have a chance. They're all going to drown.

I walk out the door into the hall, but turn toward the exit instead of following the nurse. As I push the bar to open the door, I tell her, though I know she won't hear me, "She's not my mother-in-law. She's not my wife."

OUTSIDE I SIT IN the car, convincing myself this is best for everyone. I make a good argument and find I'm not hard to persuade. After all, I have the past to predict the future. People who count on me suffer. People I'm supposed to protect die.

So it's not that I'm selfless by nature, or that I'm crazy in love with the baby about to be born. How could I be? I don't know it. But one thing is easy enough to figure: it deserves better than me. Allison does, too. Allison is my girlfriend. Ex-girlfriend I'm sure, as of ten minutes ago. She's wonderful. The best. She'll do a great job raising the kid. And she won't have to do it alone. Her mother and father will help. Also I know that because Allison is so pretty and funny and smart, she'll get a new guy in nothing flat.

The thought of her with someone else pushes me over the edge. I rake crazily at the door handle, not making it in time. I throw up on the closed window, the door, the car seat. I feel better now. My face is damp and cold, sweat runs from under my arms, but at least my vision is returning. I take this improvement as the positive consequence of doing the right thing.

I look around and from the back seat find a sweatshirt to clean myself. I wipe my hands, my pants, the door. When I'm as good as I'm going to get, I put both hands on the wheel and stare out at the overcast sky. "June Gloom" they call it here in Southern California. I can barely make out the white shale cap on Mount Baldy only ten miles away.

June, I think again. School and graduation. If I'd stayed in class three more weeks, I'd have coasted to a diploma. Allison made it, and she was big as a house. But I couldn't stay on track. I couldn't hold a thought long enough. My refuge was physical work, where I didn't have to think at all. Just lift and tug and carry and walk.

I start the car and drive south on Garey, toward the freeway. This is a commercial area with flower shops, a tux rental, CPAs, the hospital's billing office. But down side streets are the old houses with orange California poppies and purple lupine in the yards. I take comfort in seeing things grow. In seeing color again.

I head west toward the school, my old life, but pull off before I get there to park in front of our apartment. Inside, I pop open two paper grocery bags and toss in clothes: five pairs of jeans, five white T-shirts, five pairs of white socks, my good Reeboks I wear only in the gym, three jocks, a fistful of underwear, a toothbrush and a razor. I change my shirt, then wet a towel to wipe down the inside of the car.

But before I leave, I take a last look around the room. On the little round breakfast table there's a Michelob bottle with a candle sticking out, various colored waxes running down the sides. Behind the ratty couch is the bullfighting poster we stapled to the wall. Across the room, a bookshelf made of cinder blocks and bare plank boards.

More importantly I see what isn't there: Sunday mornings, reading the paper with Allison snuggled against me on the floor. Us watching old movies late at night, or drinking coffee and hitting the books for school. I see us making love everywhere, as if we had to mark every inch of the place with our combined scent. I see her belly growing, me thinking she is the most beautiful girl in the world.

I return to the car with my clothes, leaving behind all the furniture and dishes, not that there's much. But they're the things Allison and I bought together like we were really building a future. Although technically, I guess, I bought them because I'm working and she isn't. She had a scholarship and plans to be a shrink. A marriage and family therapist, I can hear her correct me. She'll be good at it, too. I should know. She's worked on me enough. We called it her homework.

"Your sister's death wasn't your fault," she has told me a hundred times.

What I could never make her understand is that *not guilty* is a world away from *innocent*.

FROM THE APARTMENT I drive to Corey's Diner. I order coffee and a pastry, trying not to think of Allison and her mother and the baby. Trying not to roll around in my head how by now they're back in Allison's room, talking about me, saying how much they hate me. I pick up a *Greensheet* and turn to the rentals, looking for something cheap and closer to work. At least that's what I tell myself, though it doesn't make much sense. I'm paying for the apartment we're in now, so surely I could keep paying for it. And our place is only twenty minutes from work, not exactly an excessive commute. But I know I can't be at our place when Allison comes home, and I can't be there when she's gone either. I have to be somewhere new. Somewhere with no history.

While I'm looking through the paper, it strikes me I'm always moving away from something old, rather than toward something new. Two days after my high school graduation I moved from Iowa to California. More than that, I moved from James or Jimmy to Jim; and still farther from Bassovich to Bass. Jim Bass of Pomona, California, that's who I am now, not James Bassovich of Benton Junction, Iowa, which I was for eighteen years.

"Hey, Marie," I say. "Got a pencil?"

The waitress has two, one behind each ear. She slides out the one on the left and hands it to me. I circle four listings that have potential. One, a converted garage, sounds so derelict and depressing it's perfect. Two of the possibilities list the monthly rent plus fees, but two don't. I'll call those from work, which is just up the street, then I'll go visit each of them and pick one.

"Bass," Terry says when I get to the terminal. "Hey man, what's up? You aren't scheduled today."

Terry is in the shack in the middle of the dock. He's our dispatcher, probably my age, though he's already married and has graduated from ASU, so maybe he's a year or two older than me.

I smile back and shrug. "Thought I'd use the phone, make a couple calls if it's all right. Allison is moving back to Illinois now that school is over. I don't need our big apartment, so I thought I'd find something smaller." I hold up the *Greensheet* as proof I've been looking, though I have no idea whether she's actually moving or not. We talked about so many possibilities over the last several weeks, just never the one that actually happened.

I take a step toward the phone, but Terry doesn't move aside. He cocks his head as if he's trying to work out whether I'm telling the truth or blowing smoke up his skirt. "I've got one for you," he says.

"Got one what?"

Just then the forklift rolls by, banging over a dock plate into the back of a trailer. One of the old-timers is breaking a load of toilets and sinks from Universal Rundle. If one of the boxes slips off the pallet we'll have shattered porcelain six ways to Sunday, but the driver bangs back onto the dock with not so much as a jiggle.

"Owen," Terry yells at him. "Careful, man."

Owen shoots him a lopsided grin. Owen's the best man I've ever seen when it comes to pushing freight. He's a machine, built like a bulldog and never seems to get tired. And he has that attitude where nothing upsets him. If I was ever in real trouble, he's the one I'd want on my side. On the other hand, I've worked at Southwest Trucking nearly a year now and I'm not sure he even knows my name. Whenever we talk, he calls me Chief or Ace or Sport, whatever comes to his mind. The worst thing he's ever called me is College Boy.

"Got one what?" I ask Terry again.

He looks at me like I'm coming back into focus, like he forgot I was there. He even shakes his head to clear his thoughts. "Actually it belongs to my uncle. He has a little trailer for rent. Small as a hat box, but dirt cheap. It was the guard shack on his construction sites, but he closed the business down."

"I'll take it," I tell him.

"Maybe you oughta look first."

"I said I'll take it."

Terry starts to backpedal a little. "It isn't especially closer to work than you are now."

He doesn't understand. I don't care if it has furniture or running water or a toilet. I don't care about anything except that it isn't my old place. "Trust me," I tell him. "It's perfect. Call your uncle."

And so he does.

When the deal is done, he hands me a slip of paper with the address. "My uncle says the lady next door has the key and the address where you can send the rent."

I fold the paper and slide it into my pocket. I figure I'll check out the place right away, but then Terry asks, "You feel like sticking around? If you'd break out the load Owen's working, I can get him out on the road for pickups. Which reminds me, when are you going for your license?"

I hired on as a swamper, but for six months now I've been spotting trailers, plus hooking up the interline rigs at night. I've serviced the tractors, and one night one of the long-haul drivers spent hours showing me how to back a set of doubles. So I feel pretty confident handling the equipment. The only thing I haven't done is drive out on the street, but around the yard I can handle a ten-speed Road Ranger and a twelve-speed Spicer. There's no reason not to get my license now. I know I'm never going to be a draftsman. And I sure don't have anyone waiting for me at home.

"No time like the present," I tell him. "I'll go this week."

IT'S STILL LIGHT AFTER work, so I go to the address Terry gave me. It's a quiet little street below Mission, on the eastern edge of Pomona. The neighborhood is so old there are no sidewalks. Most of the homes need paint, at least, and many could use a new roof, or a new porch, or a screen door that isn't falling off its hinges. But down at the end of the block, next to the empty lot on the corner, is a two-story home that looks like a picture from a gardening magazine. The title of the article might be "Cottages—Cute 'n Cozy." There are flowers and hedges and statues in front, and a picket fence surrounding it all. The paint is fresh, with a couple of contrasting colors accenting the trim. The style is Craftsman like most of the houses on the street. But as much as the others are rundown, this one is as crisp and inviting as freshly laundered sheets. I can almost smell how clean it is from inside the car.

It takes me two passes to find what I'm looking for because I don't see any house numbers on the property, and also *my* trailer is sitting back from the street and sort of fades into the landscape. The trailer itself is one of those little teardrop shapes with fake silver wings attached to the rear, as if it's a vehicle Mercury would travel in. I consider the possibility that even the few things I've brought with me won't fit. The trailer is clearly used and clearly old, but there's something about it that attracts me powerfully. Maybe it's that I could hook it to my car and take off in the middle of the night and still have my home. I love it.

Since the lot is on the corner, the only house next to it is the neat-as-a-pin house. This makes me happy, too. I park on the dirt verge of the road, between the asphalt and the chain link surrounding the corner property, and walk to the neighbor's. My thought is to introduce myself, get the key, and then go find something for dinner, probably a cheeseburger. I know the best thing is for me to keep busy until I can't hold my eyes open so I won't think about what happened at the hospital.

I let myself in through the little gate and I'm walking toward the porch when I hear a chicken squawking, and then a *thunk*, and then nothing. I've heard those sounds before, in that order, and my heart pounds. I haven't made it to the front door yet and now I'm not sure I want to.

"Hey?" I say tentatively, so softly, in fact, I doubt anyone could hear. I consider turning around and leaving, but I've got nowhere to sleep except my car, which is not comfortable and still smells from my earlier sickness. "Hey? Anybody home?"

I say this louder and now hear a scrape as if someone set down something heavy and metal. There are footsteps on gravel and then a woman appears from around the side of the house. She's short and trim. Her long black hair is threaded with silver. She's probably my mother's age but moves as if she's younger. She's carrying a headless chicken by its feet. The animal is squirming and flapping like it might yet save itself if it could only get away. The woman shifts the bird to her left hand so she can offer me her right.

"Irma Garcia. Mrs.," she says. "You're Bass, I know. You doan need to tell me nothin'."

I shake her hand and wonder how much chicken blood got transferred.

"How did you know my name?"

"I got a phone, doan I? Mr. Herman who owns the trailer, he call to tole me. He says you work for his nephew. He says you're hokay, but to keep an eye on you anyway. You hungry?" She holds up the chicken, which has mercifully slowed its twitching, if not its bleeding.

I don't answer quickly enough, or maybe I don't answer at all because she says, "Hokay. Geeb me one hour. You go get some beer and I'll do the ress." She looks across the yard to my car. "I doan figure you got much of anythin' with you. Clothes only, right? So what happen? You break up with your girl?"

A shiver goes through me and I have the premonition this won't be the only time she pegs me exactly. I believe I know how the chicken felt.

BEFORE I GO, SHE gives me one key, which fits both the padlock on the big rollback gate and the padlock on the trailer. I wonder if the heavy hasp on the door is preemptory or if the trailer had been broken into on a jobsite at some time and this was a sort of barn-door-after-the-horse-is-stolen kind of thing. But the door frame doesn't look jimmied, and the aluminum skin is undented. I go inside expecting gloom and musk, but the trailer is surprisingly clean. There's a tiny table, a two-burner stove, a fridge about three feet tall, and in back a potty and shower, which is a fiberglass closet barely big enough to turn around in. At first I see no bed, but then I realize it's the wide plank folded against the trailer's front. I unfasten two stays and the bed hinges down, held horizontal by a chain at each end.

I bring my things from the car and find cubbyholes to store them in. I also take a portable tape player I always carry in the car, and install it on the counter beside the stove. I plug it in and push play. Etta James sings "At Last," and I feel really happy for the first time in a month.

I lock the place up and drive to Lou's Liquor on Holt. From the cooler I pick up a six-pack of Bud because it's such a popular brand I figure there's a good chance Mrs. Garcia will like it. Then I put it back because I personally hate Budweiser. It gives me heartburn. Instead, I pick up Corona because it's my favorite, but I immediately put that back, afraid she'll think I'm stereotyping her. I'm pretty sure Guinness doesn't go with chicken or anything else, so I don't even open that door. I also pass over Jet malt liquor, Coors, Heineken, Pabst, and Miller. There are suddenly more choices for beer than I ever imagined, and none of them seem right. Too snooty, too cheap, too plain, too weird. Finally I get Newcastle, hoping she's never had that before and will believe it's exotic without being pretentious.

By the time I'm back it's been forty-five minutes since I last saw her. She said to give her an hour, but I don't know if that means sixty minutes or just some period of time. I'd like to take the beer to the trailer and put on one of the compilation tapes I've made and start drinking, but I can't show up with a six-pack with a bottle missing. That's like showing up with a wedge out of a cake. All things considered, I'd rather drink than listen to music, so I park the car inside the gate next to the trailer and walk over to Mrs. Garcia's house in the darkening evening.

"It ain' locked," she calls out as I climb the steps.

I let myself into a front room that seems to have come from a museum. It's dark, both because it's unlit and because the furniture is heavy and brocaded. Everything is clean, but there's too much of it. There are pictures and knick-knacks on the tables, in the two hutches, on the shelves, on the walls.

"Put those in the fridge so they doan get warm."

I can only think she's talking about the beers. I come into the kitchen, which is no less crowded but more inviting than the front room because a huge circular fluorescent light is humming away on the ceiling. She has pots and pans hanging over the stove, canning jars on the counter, dishes stacked, canisters open. There is the smell of wet chicken, or dead chicken, or chicken feathers—something from before. But now that odor is mixed with spices and herbs and frying smells, and somehow is not at all unpleasant.

"Might as well open a couple of those," she says, still not looking at me.

Without turning from the stove, Mrs. Garcia pulls open a drawer and hands me a bottle opener. I flip the cap from one and ask, "Do you want a glass?"

"Naw," she says, and I hand her the bottle. Still without looking, she swigs it down and says, "Newcastle. So what are you? A big shot?"

I'm deflated beyond reason.

The fridge is an old, rounded Kelvinator. The handle reminds me of a handle you'd pull to open the emergency door of an airplane. Inside there is so much food I don't know if the four remaining bottles will fit.

"Are you expecting company?" I ask.

"You never know who might stop by," Mrs. Garcia says. "I got kids, and Mrs. Horvath down the street. You would think none of them ever have a bite 'till they come see me. They're like camels filling a hump. Me, though? I doan eat much. Where would I put it?" She turns and holds her arms out to her sides. Indeed she is as lithe as a teenager.

In the kitchen light I look at her more closely now. I thought she might have been my mother's age, forty-five, and that still could be the truth. But if she said she's sixty-two, I'd believe her. Her skin is nearly leather, and her hands look like a workman's. By contrast, she moves like an athlete in a hurry, so I just don't know.

"I been gettin' your mail," she says.

This seems impossible, as I haven't yet spent a night in the trailer. No one even knows I've taken the place except Terry, Mrs. Garcia, and of course the fellow who's renting it to me. Her comment reminds me, however, there's a mailbox beside the gate.

"If your name is Occupant," she continues, cracking herself up. "Nothing good yet. Only pizza coupons an clean your carpet. Three rooms for ninety-nine dollars. As if you got carpet, right? I been inside that box on wheels an I can tell you the best thing would be cut a hole in the floor so you could just hose it out."

I realize then that she must be the one who's kept the place clean. Mrs. Garcia is the reason the trailer is so livable.

"Thanks," I say.

"For what?"

I'm not sure how to tell her. It seems she has anticipated me and it makes me feel more welcome than I can express. Not *home* exactly, since I wasn't at all comfortable there. And of course not like I'd been with Allison. I want to say *appreciated*, though that doesn't make much sense either. In answer to her I mumble something she accepts as adequate.

When the meal is ready, we sit at a small Formica-topped table in the kitchen. Seeing it, I realize her furnishings are from every era since the twenties. This table is mid-century, gray Formica with those boomerang shapes in red and green. It looks like it might have come from the Cleavers' television home.

I cut a slice of the meat on my plate and say, "I didn't know you were allowed to keep chickens in town."

"Who's gonna say anythin'?" she answers, giving me a look so innocent the challenge is unmistakable. "Anyway, I geeb away most of the eggs to keep folks quiet. Sometimes cops come up the street, but they only care about shootins an drugs. Chickens they got no time for. Lucky me. I put the shit on the vegetables. Makes everythin grow like crazy."

The meal, I have to say, is fabulous. Like nothing I've eaten before. There are hints of cilantro and rosemary, and other herbs I can't name. I put out of my head that an hour ago our meal was walking around the back yard. Besides the meat there are roasted peppers and grilled asparagus, steamed rice and handmade tortillas with butter and honey. I get up and get each of us another beer, thinking, if the guys on the team could only see me now.

"About the chickens," I start again. "I don't mind a bit. In fact I like them. I just meant it's unusual. And my guess is we're eating some of the vegetables you, uh, fertilize."

She laughs. "You din know chicken shit could tase so good, huh?" For a moment she looks down at her plate and I think she's gone somewhere in her mind. "If I had the land, I'd have me a cow or two. I'd grow wheat an oats an every vegetable you can name. An flowers. An…"

When she doesn't finish there's a silence until I say, "That would be a farm, then. Not a house with a yard."

"Tha's my dream."

When we finish eating I ask if I can help her clean up.

"Go to bed," she says. "You got work in the mornin'."

From the look of her place I'd bet she never stops working, but I don't argue, just smile and thank her for her hospitality.

Back in the trailer I put my Cole Porter tape in the machine. "I've Got You Under My Skin," "Night and Day," "I Get a Kick Out of You." Along with the Gershwins and Hoagy Carmichael, Harold Arlen and Yip Harburg, Porter wrote the best music ever.

I'm tired, and the clean bedding is inviting. But before I climb in, I take the last two items from my paper sack luggage. The first is a photo of Allison I shot when we walked to the horse stalls on campus. She's leaning against a corral, her right arm up on the railing and the toe of one foot crossed over the instep of the other. She's got a long piece of straw in her mouth and is mugging what she thinks is a cowgirl look. But she's wearing a white sleeveless blouse and sherbet green shorts, and looks like a city girl entirely out of place in the scene. The second item is the T-shirt I wrapped the picture in. It's Allison's, and I hold it to my face, breathing in her scent before I turn in for the night.

CHAPTER TWO

I ONLY HAVE TO TAKE the written portion of the test for my Class A because Terry signs an affidavit saying I know how to handle the equipment. The test is long compared to a regular license test, but it's not especially difficult. I've been taking tests for sixteen years now and I know how to do it. My favorite question is this:

Q: What are the only two items that may legally fall from a moving vehicle?

A: Water, and the feathers of live birds.

The first delivery Terry assigns me, the first time I'm out on the road by myself, I have half a trailer of book matches for a restaurant supply company and half a trailer of experimental gasoline for environmental testing. The matches are in cardboard cases, and the gasoline in drums. I suppose it's safe enough, but I'm not comfortable. I don't know if this is a joke or S.O.P. Maybe it's a sort of test to see how compliant I am, what kind of a team player I'll be. In any case I don't say anything and just take off toward San Bernardino, and then out to Adelanto in the desert. An hour and a half later I'm back, feeling like a hotshot and ready for the next load. If this was a test, I aced it.

WHEN I WAS GOING to school, I scheduled my classes for early in the day so I could be to work by noon. Midday there's less activity on the dock, and often it was just me and Terry and sometimes Al Barnes, our terminal manager. I'd break a trailer while they hung around the dispatch shack talking and drinking coffee. But now that I have my license, and especially because I'm permanently out of school, they've changed my start time to eight.

At first I assume I'll get off at five or six, giving me an hour or two of overtime. But most days I work until seven or eight, and sometimes it's nine or ten. It's like they're so used to me being around in the evenings they forget to send me home. I work this schedule all summer and put a ton of money in the bank. My rent is next to nothing, and during the week I don't have time to buy anything even if I wanted to, which I don't.

A month after the baby was born, I sent a check to Allison at our old apartment, but it came back as undeliverable, with no forwarding address.

Although I'm working like a fiend, so constantly damp from perspiration that my clothes start to fall apart, I don't lose any weight. Instead I get tougher. I can pick up a La-Z-Boy chair and toss it shoulder high on top of a stack of canned goods, or tilt a fifty-five gallon drum of oil onto its rim and roll it the length of the dock, hand-over-hand like turning a steering wheel. At night I'm so tired I sit in my car in the terminal's parking lot, waiting for the energy to start the engine. But the next morning I'm up and raring to go. I like this life.

Every couple of weeks I have dinner at Mrs. Garcia's place. I find out the title *Mrs.* is open to interpretation. She's married, but only because she's never been divorced. Years ago her husband went back to Mexico, remarried, and raised a separate family of five children.

"He's a stupid man," she tells me one evening. We're sitting on her back patio, which is a small collection of used bricks laid down in a herringbone pattern. Big terracotta pots with bougainvillea on trellises line the perimeter. On the wall beside her sliding door, one dim porch light provides illumination. "He walk away an leave me the treasures. He doan even know what a fool he is. Stupid, stupid man."

I wonder what treasures those are, if she means this house or what. "You still love him?" I say.

She waves her hand in front of her face as if attacked by a persistent mosquito. Then from out of nowhere she says, "Ah, my Angela."

I don't know what that means. I was raised Catholic, and my default assumption is that as a Hispanic she's Catholic as well. So my thoughts drift to the Angelus prayer and the Angelus bells, neither of which makes any sense.

"Angelus?" I ask aloud.

"Angela," she says again. "My daughter. One of my daughters. Maria Elena, she the oldess, then Angela. Lupe, he my only boy, excep for Little Lupe, *mi nieto.* My granson."

I can't help it. I think of "Little Latin Lupe Lu" by the Righteous Brothers. And then I remember all the photos in her front room; they must be the kids and grandkids.

"Show me," I say impulsively and stand up to go inside. I lead the way, and Mrs. Garcia follows me.

In the front room we stand looking at several framed photographs on a long table positioned behind a couch. The table is narrow but oval. Not really oval but obround, like a vanilla finger cookie. It strikes me as a different style from the rest of her furniture, though what style that would be I couldn't say. The decor is a hodgepodge of time and fashion.

"Is this Angela?" I ask, pointing to a thin girl standing with a young man and two children.

"Yeah," Mrs. Garcia says. "An her husband, Hector. Hector Sanchez. The kids are Little Lupe an Vanessa." She points to another photo. "This one here is my Guadalupe, Big Lupe. An this here is Maria Elena."

Guadalupe reminds me of a puppy dog. He's big and round faced, and looks like he'd never be angry with anyone. Maria Elena is a real beauty, but austere. Angela is plainer. She's pleasant enough but looks wrung out, wan and tentative even as she tries to smile. Her husband is looking off to the side of the camera as if following a voice no one else hears.

"Good-looking bunch," I say, and mean it.

"My treasures," Mrs. Garcia says, a little sadly it seems to me, and I now get her gist from earlier.

She stands looking at the pictures so long I feel I've lost her to them. I consider slipping away, going back to the trailer, when she picks up the photo of Angela and Hector and the kids.

"My other two," she says. "They do hokay. But this Hector, you know, he's a drinker. Not a bad man, but…" She shakes her head. "An Angela is so stubborn. I wanna help but she woan let me. She woan take a dime. I bring clothes for the children from Saint Vincent's, but if it ain a birthday or Christmas, she woan take 'em. I ask to watch the babies so I can feed an clean 'em, but Angela says 'We're fine, Mom. We doan need nothin.' Ay-way," she sighs.

I've never seen her like this before. I wait, not sure what to do or say. So what finally comes out is obvious and trite. "If there's anything I can do to help…"

This sort of talk is easy because, of course, I *can't* help. I don't know these people and probably never will.

She puts the photograph back down and looks at me hard. "Ya," she says, brightening. "Ya, there is somethin'."

Mrs. Garcia is animated again, which makes me happy but also nervous. There's something about her demeanor that's alarming.

"You wanna crash your car for me?" She says as innocently as if she were asking me to stop at the bakery and pick up a loaf of bread.

I laugh. Either I misheard her or she's crazy. And my hearing is pretty good.

For the next forty-five minutes I listen to her plan to get money to her daughter. It seems Hector is a freelance auto body repairman, though "freelance" may be an overstatement. But when he works, he works from home, so I can't think what else to call it. Mrs. Garcia says he has a reputation for good work, excellent work, so much so that he has a nickname—Hector the Bondo King. Her plan is for me to bump my car into something hard enough to cause a small dent, and then to have Hector fix it. I'm still hesitant, but Mrs. Garcia graciously reminds me the Duster isn't all that much to look at even now. "This will be a improvemen'," she says, and gives me three hundred dollars, expecting that this will more than cover the cost of repair. The key, she informs me, is that it's cash.

"Too much he works in trade for car parts an stereos an promises. But you can't pay the rent with those thins." She rubs her thumb and fingers together. "They need money."

It occurs to me I've never seen Mrs. Garcia herself go off to work, and I wonder about the source of *her* income. With what I've learned of her husband, he's obviously no help. But then maybe her hours are similar to mine, so I don't ask.

I get the directions to her daughter's place in Fontana and promise to go as soon as I have time. We say goodnight and, unexpectedly, she hugs me.

WHEN I MOVED INTO the trailer, there was a line from the power pole to a weatherhead on the roof. Now there's a second line. Terry said he might sometimes need to reach me at home, so I told him I'd put in a phone. I don't have it installed more than a week when it rings for the first time. I'm so startled, for a minute I can't imagine what the sound is. I pick up the receiver, and the first words I hear over my new phone are, "You weren't going to tell me I have a granddaughter?"

Several thoughts flash through my mind at once, though I'm able to order these by priority: Number one, I have a daughter. Number two, I never considered that the child affected more than me and Allison, but now I see I was wrong. Number three, I haven't talked with my mother for quite a while.

"How did you get this number?" I ask.

"And hello to you, too."

"You didn't say hello to me."

"Hello. You weren't going to tell me I have a granddaughter?"

It's really more than I can bear, saying that I didn't know myself. So I don't say anything, hoping for more information before I continue.

"Allison and Amanda are living back home with her parents. Mrs. Stovall called to tell me. It was so embarrassing when I didn't know what she was talking about."

Mrs. Stovall is, of course, Allison's mother. Amanda, I assume, is the baby's name.

There seems nowhere to go with this conversation. How can I explain to my mother that after nearly three months it's hard to call her and say, "How's Dad? How's Lucky? And oh, by the way, I have a child, although I don't know the gender." It's hard to tell her anything, so I don't.

"Jimmy?"

"I'm here."

"Well?"

My heart is thudding in my chest. "I gotta go, Mom." She starts to say something, but I beat her to it. "I'll call you."

THE NEXT SATURDAY I pick the rear fender opposite the fuel tank to smash, figuring there's no sense in blowing myself up just so Hector can make some money. The problem is, how do I hit the side and not the rear? I don't want to wrinkle the bumper and have Mrs. Garcia's money go for a new one.

I drive around the corner and down a few blocks until I find a retaining wall made of concrete blocks. This is accessible if I can jump the curb, so I drive slowly past, reverse, and bounce back over the sidewalk. I scrape along the edge of the brick at an angle, which makes a horrible sound. When I hop out to check the damage I see a woman has come from her house across the street. She looks at me, shakes her head and goes back inside.

"I'm fine," I holler at the closed door. "Don't worry about me."

I suspect I've broken three or four laws, so I hope she doesn't call the police. I don't stick around to find out.

I drive out to Fontana, and though it's officially summer the day seems like the best day of fall. It's warm but not hot, clear, with a view to Mount Baldy, Cajon Pass, and over to Big Bear. As I watch the scenery, I concoct a story about the accident because I know I'll be asked. I imagine scene after scene, but nothing rings true. I keep coming back to skidding on ice, but I know that won't work because this is, after all, Southern California, home of the perfect Rose Parade, where every year there is only sun, no rain, and no snow for sure.

I trust something will come to me before I see Hector.

At the outskirts of Fontana I drive past big, two-storied homes with ornate porches and colonnades of cypress, or rambling bungalows with conical towers. I know the city has been trying to bring up its image (who wants to live in a place known as Fontucky?) but seeing these stuccoed palaces I'm reminded of driving by Nevada brothels that are single-wide house trailers surrounded by Greek statuary.

By the time I get to Angela's neighborhood, the architecture has calmed down, which is not to say it's improved. There are still no sidewalks, but here the lawns are burnt and stubbly, or mostly dirt. If there is fencing it is chain link. Nearly every property has a broken-down car, or broken-down appliances, or broken-down toys. When I come to Angela's address, I see they have all three, and the truck on blocks in the front yard has been there so long a tree branch has grown through one window. Around the tree a small dog is chasing a large one, who is disadvantaged by having only three legs. Under the circumstances I'd say he's doing fairly well.

I park in the dirt next to the asphalt drive and walk to the side yard. From here I look east and north, and see that the land falls away for some distance until it rises again against the mountains. There is evidence the area was once vineyards, but now everything seems dead or dying. Down the hill at the far end of Angela's property is a dilapidated barn, where I assume Hector does his work.

When I round the corner of the house, I suddenly come upon a woman hanging clothes on a line. I pull up quickly, and though she must know I'm there, she doesn't acknowledge me. She is not so much pale of complexion as pale of spirit. Except that she's sort of pretty, she could be an extra in a zombie movie.

"Mrs. Sanchez?" I say. She doesn't answer. "Is, uh, is Hector around?"

When I accepted Mrs. Garcia's proposal, it seemed a lark. A few hours spent getting the car repaired, and a good story to tell afterward. But now I don't want to be here, because clearly life isn't a lark for this woman.

"It's, uh, it's only a dent," I tell her. "I could come back later."

She looks up, but before she can speak there's the noise of a car door banging shut behind me.

"That's him," she says, nodding toward the street.

She clips the last blouse to the line, then stoops to pick up her wicker basket. I realize that there is a child lying in it. The baby is older than Amanda, but I can't help contrasting Allison's situation to this one. I tell myself I'd never let this happen to *my* child. Angela goes into the house, and when I turn, Hector is nearly on top of me.

"Bro," he says, smiling.

The alcohol on his breath is a wave that catches me, and I ride it a step back.

"Hey."

"That your ride?"

I tell him it is.

Hector is carrying two sacks, one from an automotive paint supply, and one from 7-Eleven. He pulls a six-pack of Bud from the second sack and holds it out to me.

"No thanks," I say, shaking my head.

"Up to you, Bro." He shifts the bag to one arm and snaps open the top of a can. Without taking a breath, he drinks what must be half the contents. "So," he says, "not hard to guess why you're here. Nasty dent. Could have frame damage. That could run you, know what I mean?" Like Mrs. Garcia, he rubs his thumb and first two fingers together. I feel like telling him how ironic that is. "Wish I could help, you know, but I'm like, busy," he continues. "Maybe I could squeeze you in next month or so."

My heart sinks a little. I want to just give Angela the money and go. I'm not sure what to say, so I don't say anything, which I believe Hector interprets as negotiation.

He holds up his beer and looks at the can closely, as if he can see through the aluminum to judge the clarity of the liquid inside.

"I've got cash," I say finally. It seems a ridiculous statement since that's how I expect to pay for anything. Still, it gets his attention. He cocks his head.

"When was you wanting this done? Not like, right away?" He doesn't add, "I hope" but it's in his tone.

Nevertheless, I smile absurdly. "Actually, I could wait while you fix it."

"Bro," he says. "You don't know much about body work, do you?"

"I know you won't have to replace anything," I say. "No parts to order. No frame damage." This part I slide over quickly, but I want him to understand I know what's going on. "This job is mostly labor. We could be done this afternoon."

He thinks a minute. "Come on down to the barn with me. Sure you don't want one?" He holds up the five remaining cans of beer, strung together in their plastic net like well-behaved fish. I decline once more and he says, looking out over the fields, "Nice out here, huh? Peaceful. 'Course you can't paint when the wind blows, and it blows a lot. Otherwise I like it okay. Don't nobody hassle you too much. EPA, AQMD, all that environmental shit. Angela though, that's my wife, she don't care for it. She don't say much but she gets, you know, like *moody*, man. Don't hardly talk, just sits and rocks the babies. Looks out the window. Shit like that. This place here," he sweeps his arm over the landscape, "it gets her down. Then she gets me down, and believe me, Bro, I don't need it."

I want to tell him that not eating makes me cranky too, but I figure I'm here for Mrs. Garcia and not to argue.

When we get to the barn, Hector rolls back the big sliding door. By the light filtering through the holes in the roof and the slatted sides, I see there are three cars waiting to be painted, all with primer spots, all with a thick coating of dust. On a shelf above a long bench sit cans of paint and thinner and a tumbling stack of rags. Scattered around the shop are various vises and hand tools, dollies and hammers, a sort of hydraulic ram, sanding equipment. Chaff floats in the striped light. There aren't going to be any show cars painted here.

"Help me push this shit out of the way," Hector says. "Gotta make room for that fine ride of yours, you know?"

I'm not certain when we went from him being too busy to do my job to doing it immediately, but clearly we're there now.

We actually have to push only one car. The others start on their own, and while Hector backs them out, I return uphill to fetch my Duster. As I'm driving in, I see him drinking from a second can, and by the tipped angle I know it's nearly empty. In fact, he drains the can and flings it away so both his hands are free. He steps to the center of the barn, and using both arms, signals me straight ahead as if I'm a pilot bringing an airliner to dock. When I'm in place, he pushes his palms out flat. I'm not out of the car before he throws himself underneath to inspect the damage.

"Hand me that cord," he says.

He springs up and grabs a drill motor from the bench. I fetch an extension cord, and as soon as he's plugged in, Hector dives under the car again and begins popping a series of holes along the dented metal. I'm amazed at his agility and focus. I've seen him drink two beers and I know he's had more, yet he seems completely unaffected.

When he's done with the drill, he springs up like a thing under pressure, something elastic that was stuck to the floor and then released. He's manic, grabbing a slide hammer, screwing it into the holes he's just drilled, banging the hammer backward to pull the dent. Mrs. Garcia appears to be correct about his expertise, or at least about his confidence. Hector doesn't hesitate from one movement to the next.

He gets the metal to the approximate original shape, then begins tapping the outside with a hammer, backing up the inside with a dolly. When the fender is nearly right, he unplugs the drill and swaps it for a sander. Back and forth in sweeping arcs he sands the entire quarter panel. In no time he is covered with paint dust, and his sweat has created runnels of color down his face. He grabs a rag, douses it with acetone, and rubs the area clean.

He jumps up again and goes to the bench for a beer. He chugs it in four or five gulps, then pops open a can of body filler, scooping out a softball-sized dollop onto a piece of cardboard. Over this he squeezes a ribbon of red hardener and mixes the compound together. He opens one more beer, takes just a swallow, and plops down beside the car, holding the cardboard high in one hand like a painter with a palette.

By now I don't believe Hector remembers I'm here. On his knees, he stares at the dented fender and I wonder what he sees there, what he's imagining, if he visualizes the work already completed. For several moments he doesn't move, until suddenly, in a flurry, he scoops the pinkish filler onto a flexible paddle and smears it, strokes it, smooths it onto the damaged area. He spreads the Bondo far beyond the actual dent, and I see now why he's prepared such a large area. The patch is smoothed and feathered so that there's hardly a ripple. When he's satisfied, Hector stands and comes to the bench.

I'm not four feet from him, but he doesn't acknowledge me. I don't know whether I should praise his ability or keep quiet. He may be irresponsible, maybe even a bum, but he's in his own world now and it's a world where he is king.

As the filler cures, he finishes the beer he started and pops open another. I wonder whether I should have accepted his earlier offer, if only to leave less alcohol for him to drink. He mumbles something about *edges*, but I don't think he says it to me. He takes a very long, flexible band of steel with a handle at each end, and to this fits a corresponding strip of sandpaper. At the car, he touches the repair, determines it has sufficiently cured, and then sands the area smooth. With his eyes closed, he once more runs the flat of his hand over the area. Satisfied, he tapes and masks the panel and then the bumper.

Maybe forty-five minutes have passed since I met Hector San-chez. Maybe an hour. I think about how much he's accomplished in such a short time, and translate that into dollars per hour. If only he'd set a firm schedule and complete the work on time, he'd pick up twice as many legitimate customers as the freeloaders he's servicing now. This may not be a goldmine he's sitting on, but it's a long way from the poverty I see around me.

He disappears outside and I hear a compressor chug on. When he returns, he picks up the open can of Bud, shakes it, tosses it aside. He cracks open the sixth and final beer, this time not offering it to me, though he stares me in the eyes.

"Edges, Bro. Got to knock down them edges."

I don't think he's referring to something physical.

Hector takes down a can of primer and mixes it with solvent in a spray cup. He goes to the car, sprays a tack coat, waits a few minutes, and sprays again. He comes back to the bench, where he cleans the cup and empties the beer. Half an hour later he lightly sands the area and cleans it, this time, with a chamois soaked in alcohol.

That's when I feel a rush of panic, thinking about the actual paint. Of the thousands of color choices available, it is unlikely, probably impossible, he'll have the one I need. But as before, there is no hesitation. He eyeballs the car, pours a little yellow into the cup, eyeballs again and adds brown. He stirs this, then dips in his pinkie and touches it to the car. A minute later he wipes it off and adds a touch of cream and a touch of red. To my eye none of these are remotely the correct color, and I believe he has finally and truly lost touch with the world. But he stirs the mixture, dips in his pinky, touches the car, blows it dry, and this time it's such a perfect match I cannot see the spot he's made.

As he goes to the car carrying the spray gun, the vague concern I've harbored for the past hour becomes clear: he should be wearing a mask, if not a respirator. I probably should be wearing one as well, but I'm not in the thick of the fog as he is.

Knowing it's pointless, I start to say something anyway, and then I notice his movements are now somehow different. Slower. Less precise. I wonder if he's overcome by fumes.

"Shouldn't you wear a mask or something? Man, I can hardly breathe and I'm way over here."

He turns to me and smiles. His teeth are the beige yellow color of the car. His skin is a series of sweat streaks: brown, yellow, gray. He shakes his head.

"I'm telling you, Bro."

Before I know it, he's done painting and is stripping off the masking paper and tape. He's got the material wadded in one hand and the gun in the other when he says, "Hunnert dowars."

I miss his meaning. "I'm sorry?"

"Hunnert dowars," he says again, angrily this time. "Thas cheap, man. Goddamn Earl Scheib'd sharge you more 'n at."

I want to give him all the money, not just a hundred dollars. I'm wondering how to accomplish this when he says, "Doan wash it fer a while. Four, five days at lease. You can drive it, but don't wash it." His eyes are sleepy. "An it ain't worth buffin'. It'll only make the rest of the car look dull 'n' shit." He throws the wad of paper and tape toward a trash can by the wall, and misses by a mile. "Shut off the compressor, Bro."

I walk outside, find the tank, and throw the switch. When I come back, Hector has leaned against the barn wall and slid to the ground, looking like he's melted into a puddle.

"Gotta clean up all this shit here," he says, but he's looking through his legs to the floor, and I doubt he can even stand. A minute later I hear him snoring.

I get into my car, struck by how much and how quickly this has all happened. I back out of the barn and do a three-point turn, driving up the path and stopping between the clothesline and the house. After I knock, it takes Angela a minute or two to come to the door. The baby is riding her hip. I dig Mrs. Garcia's money out of my pocket and add a couple of twenties of my own.

"Hector's cleaning the gun and says he'll be up later. He told me to give you this."

Angela takes the money without a word or a nod, and I drive back to my own life.

CHAPTER THREE

B Y OCTOBER I FEEL like an old-timer at work. I'm comfortable with all of the equipment and I know the area. Also,
over the summer a couple guys have been hired, and they
look at me as if I've been here forever. Let 'em think it.

I'm assigned the position of utility driver, which means I
don't have a specified route but pick up the overloads, deliver
the big shipments, fill in the gaps. Some of the guys see this as
an inferior position because the work is harder. As soon as they
get enough seniority, they bid for a route. But utility would be my
preference even if I had the most seniority at the terminal. Mainly
I like the variety; I never do the same thing twice. But I also like
that I drive semis exclusively. Route drivers have a bobtail, which,
God forgive me, isn't as impressive as a tractor-trailer. If I ever
run into someone I know, I want them to see me driving the biggest rig we own.

And one day this exact thing happens.

I have five pallets of books for the student store at Cal Poly.
They don't have a forklift, so I unload the shipment by hand,
which means hand-trucking the cases to the back of the trailer,

climbing down to the ground, stacking the books on the sidewalk, and then climbing up again. It's a workout if you don't dog it, and I don't. Fifteen minutes into this routine I'm sweating like a track star, and there are ten or twelve tall piles of books on the sidewalk. I'm standing on the bed, maybe four feet above ground, and as I've done so often before, I half fall, half leap into space, grabbing the rope attached to the rollup door. This is a slick way to pull the door closed, and at the same time it saves climbing down because the tension of the door spring slows you to a gentle landing.

Or it always has in the past, but this time the rope breaks.

I've done my half turn in the air so that I'm facing the trailer, but with nothing to stop me, I hit the ground hard, moving backwards. Instinctively, I splay my arms to catch anything that will hold me upright, and what I catch are several columns of stacked books. Those columns hit other columns, which hit others, and in an instant all the cases of books have tumbled over the walk.

I lie on the ground, the wind knocked out of me, and watch a cutie walk by.

"Hey, Jim."

"Hey, Sarah," I croak.

THOUGH IT'S ONLY LATE October, a lot of the work at SWT is hauling Christmas merchandise. The stores are stocking up, getting ready. They began advertising for Halloween in September, and now paper turkeys and pilgrims' hats fill the windows, though there are still bags of candy corn and Bill Clinton masks on the shelves inside.

Maybe it's the coming holidays, but Allison and Amanda are on my mind almost constantly. When I see tiny xylophones or ducks on wheels, I can hardly stop myself reaching for my wallet. When I hear a Christmas song, or any song for that matter, I want to get the tape for Allison. I've had no contact at all with her, and I know that's best. Even if I changed my mind about being able to care for them, which I haven't, it isn't fair to be in their lives just a little. For me, Allison is an all or nothing kind of girl, and now with the baby to consider, she has to be nothing. That's what I've picked and I've vowed to stick to it.

But then I get her letter.

It isn't much, just the hi-how-are-you-we're-fine sort of thing. A very, to-a-guy-I-once-knew-but-that-was-a-long-time-ago letter. No Xs and Os at the bottom. No code I can break that says she can't live without me. Which is good because I'd only have to remind her how dangerous it would be to live *with* me. At the bottom of her few lines it says, "I thought you'd like this picture of Amanda." I appreciate that she doesn't say, "I thought you'd like a picture of your daughter," because that also would be difficult—impossible actually—to interpret without hearing her say the words. With the right inflection it could come out heartbreakingly tender, as in *She's the reason we should get back together.* But the same words said differently could sound mean and sarcastic, as in *What the hell is wrong with you and I never loved you anyway.*

One thing for sure, if she'd written, "Here's a picture of your daughter," I would have read it the second way, guaranteed.

In any case, the letter starts me thinking and the thinking is like the first crack in a dam. It's the line in the concrete wall that's always moist. What if I *could* be a parent? I wonder. What if I *could* provide for them and protect them and be with them? What if we had a fairly normal life with scraped knees and measles, but no car crashes or drownings? What if Amanda didn't fall off a roof and break her neck, or contract some rare blood disease so that I'd have to watch her waste away before my eyes? Would that life even be possible?

I want to say, no, it wouldn't, because otherwise it means I'd have to turn around and go back the long road I've traveled already, and truthfully I'm afraid of what I'd find when I got there. I'm afraid what I'd find is that Allison has by now come to see me clearly. I'd find she's figured out she made a mistake in the first place by trusting me, loving me. Believing I'd be as good for her as she was for me. I'd find she's come to realize she can do a lot better for herself and for Amanda, and to that I can only agree.

I know all this, and yet the knowledge doesn't patch the crack that has started to spread.

ONE SATURDAY MORNING I look out the little window of the breakfast nook and see the ground toward the back of the property is darker than I remember. The patch stands out, because today my lot is washed in yellow light except for a stripe of shadow from my trailer to Mrs. G's house.

The day is a crisp fall day, just beautiful, perfect really, so that I get a tingle of excitement that starts in my chest and floods through my arms and into my legs. In a few hours it will be warm enough to wear shorts comfortably, and I look forward to going to the park to play a little ball on the outdoor courts. I'll play until I'm soaked with sweat, until I'm drained. I'll play until late afternoon. But I've got some time before anyone else will be down there, and anyway I want to see what has happened in my own yard.

I put on coffee and pour out some cereal, then slice a banana on top. Next I put a favorite cassette into the player: "String of Pearls," "Perfidia," "Moonlight in Vermont," "Moonlight Serenade." I'm listening to the songs and sipping my coffee when there's a knock on the door.

"Hey, Bass," the voice says. "You got your clothes on?"

"*Pasé*," I tell Mrs. Garcia.

She's dressed in jeans and sandals and a long-sleeved work shirt three sizes too big, which makes her not pretty, but cute. She drifts in like a Hispanic Tinker Bell and I think, not for the first time, she occupies a world of her own.

"How about some coffee?" I say. "I've got some rolls I could heat."

"*¿Por qué no?*" she says.

I pour her some coffee, spoon in the two sugars I know she likes, no cream, and then I place a few sweet rolls on a cookie sheet. Over the last couple of months, Mrs. G has picked up from her work items she feels I need: this cookie sheet, a couple of dishes and cups, some silverware, some towels. I've learned she manages the local St. Vincent de Paul store, which is the source of her own furnishings.

"So whas with the old-time music you listen to?"

"I just like it."

"Ay-way," she says on an escaping breath. She gets a look like I've just told her about planet X, where the sky is red and objects fall up instead of down. "I remember clear back to Perry Como, but he's modern compared to this."

She misses the point, that it isn't the singer so much as the songs. The classics. The standards. But I don't say that to her. What I say is, "I remember Perry Como too. 'Hot Diggity, Dog Ziggity,' 'Round and Round,' 'Don't Let the Stars get in Your Eyes.'" For my sister Kitty and me, Como was our Mr. Rogers. Comfortable in those cardigan sweaters. That soft voice pulling you in and calming everything down. My Aunt Bets had all his records and I sometimes wondered whether it was his voice she liked or that, like us, he was Catholic.

We're quiet for a while then, enjoying the companionship and the music and the bright morning. I can tell she wants to say something, and finally she shifts in the seat. "So what you think?"

I smile blandly, holding my cup in both hands and waiting for part two, knowing there's more to come, though I don't know what it will be this time.

"The yard," she says with emphasis, nodding toward the back of my lot. "I started working it."

I now realize the dark row I noticed against the block wall is tilled earth. "What's up with that?" I ask.

She gets ever so slightly defensive, sitting up a little taller, her mouth just a little pinched. I love to get her goat.

"It was wasted dirt," she says. "You doan want that do you? Waste? Why shouldn't we plant it? Get some vegetables going?"

I want to say, "What do you mean *we,* white man?" but I doubt she'd get it. I know where this is going, or think I do, but I have to poke her a little. "I don't know," I say, drawing out the words. "I'm not home enough to care for anything. You can't just water and weed on Saturdays. Besides the weekend is my only time off. I don't want to spend it in a garden."

I've fed her the line she's hoping for and she jumps right on it. "No, no. You doan have to do nothin'. Lemme. I'll do it."

I try on a skeptical face. "This wouldn't have anything to do with you wanting a farm? I'm not going to come home someday and see livestock out here, am I?"

Now her mouth migrates to the side of her face and her eyes roll to the ceiling. I've given her an idea she likes very much, and I suspect she's wondering how to accomplish it.

MY THOUGHT ABOUT ALLISON and Amanda is this: If I was *some-thing,* something big, maybe I wouldn't feel so powerless to protect them. If I was worth more financially, maybe I'd be worth more in other ways as well. I know money wouldn't have saved Kitty; watchfulness was what I needed. But watchfulness is a hard to thing to measure. It isn't something you can hold in your hand.

And in any case, you can be watchful twenty-four hours a day for weeks, years even, but the first time you blink you could lose everything. But if I *had* something that people could point to, *owned* something that couldn't be taken away. Maybe then…

One day I see Owen has clocked out just before me. He's nearly to the exit, and it's dinner time, but I'm hoping he can spare me a few minutes.

"Hey, Owen."

"What's up, Sport?"

I have to run to catch him, and now we're in the parking lot, heading to our cars.

"Can I buy you a beer?"

This is an odd thing to ask. We're different generations and we've never hung out before. It must seem to him that the offer is completely out of the blue, and worse, to my ears at least, the words sound like a pickup line. For a second I fear he may punch me. Instead he looks at his watch.

"Why the hell not? You want to hit the Whippoorwill?"

The Whippoorwill Lounge is a bar down the street, right at the freeway entrance, so I pass it every day on my way home. I've stopped there a couple of times with some of the younger guys, but it doesn't appeal to me. The word my mother would use is "seedy," and I don't think of myself as a seedy kind of guy. But I tell Owen, sure, the Whippoorwill would be great.

Of course it's dark inside, and smoky. The seat and table of the booth we pick are both sticky, and I leave my jacket on so I can rest the sleeves on the table's edge without getting my skin dirty. We don't say much to each other until the waitress takes our order, but when she does I still don't know how to start. Owen is calm and relaxed. He stretches an arm across the back of the seat and smiles like we come here all the time and he expects nothing else of our meeting. Finally our beer comes and he pours us each a glass from the pitcher.

"So what's on your mind, Ace?"

I start to tell him, except everything comes out in such a rush I have to stop myself and start again.

"I like my job. It's a good job. But as long as I work for someone else, SWT or any other outfit, I'll never be more than they allow me to be." As soon as I say this, I see how he can misinterpret my meaning. If working as an employee is less than I'd like for myself, what does that say about him? Nevertheless, I plunge on. "But I was thinking, what if I had my own rig? I'd do the same work as now, but I'd have more opportunity and fewer limitations. The more I work, the more I make. Plus I'd own everything; the tractor and trailer, and maybe someday a little land. I figure I don't have to make much at first, and I'm willing to learn along the way. My one problem is how to get enough work to keep me busy. I know other outfits have salesmen, but I couldn't afford anyone. And if I take the time to hustle up the business, it means I'm not making the deliveries."

I go on and on, probably repeating myself, but Owen doesn't interrupt. Better yet, he doesn't smile like I'm an idiot. Then, when I finally run out of steam, he takes a big drink, wipes his mouth with the back of his hand, and says, "Getting the work is easy."

My heart jumps.

"Use a broker," he says. "I know a good one. I could hook you up."

It's funny. He says "I *could* hook you up," not "I *will* hook you up." Such a small thing, probably irrelevant, but it worries me.

I say, "But you don't think it's a good idea? For me to go out on my own?"

Just then a woman comes in. Homely as a mud fence. She has to be sixty, sixty-five, but maybe that's generous. She could be ten years older. She's made up like a Spanish dancer with black lace and red trim. She has a tall comb in her hair, and red, red lipstick. The rouge on her cheeks looks like it's been put there with a perfectly round sponge.

"Buy me a drink?" she says to nobody in particular.

I look at Owen, hoping he'll answer for both of us. I'd like him to send her on her way so we can get back to business. Instead, he gives her such a big, genuine smile I'm not sure what's going on.

"You thirsty, momma?" he asks in an inviting way.

His voice is like a homing beacon, and she turns just enough to exclude me from the conversation. Where she was talking to the table before, now she's fixed on him.

"Thirsty for you, handsome."

Owen laughs and pats the seat beside him. "Sit down, honey," he says, "What are you up to?"

"Just looking for a date," she says, sliding in next to him. Her hand disappears under the table and I can just imagine where it goes.

"And what do you hope to get for this date?"

"Ten."

Owen reaches down, takes her hand, and brings it up to the table. "Momma, don't sell yourself short. Why, there's a hundred men'd cut off a finger just so's you'd turn and notice 'em. You're such a beauty. You got it all over the young ones."

She's not a beauty, of course. She's horrible. Her teeth are bad, and there's a musty smell I pick up from four feet away. But with Owen's touch she softens. Her face relaxes, and now she's someone's grandmother, out for a walk and slightly confused. Owen reaches for his wallet and plucks a twenty. He folds it and slips it into her hand.

"Now you gotta promise me something, all right?" She doesn't answer, but looks at him like he's come down from on high and is standing in a pool of light. "You gotta promise me you'll stop this hooking nonsense and start taking better care of yourself. Will you do that for me? You go on now and get yourself a nice dinner, okay?"

He leans toward her and kisses her cheek. It's all I can manage not to wipe my own mouth clean. She slides out of the booth then and floats to the back door. I never see her again. I doubt Owen does either.

"You don't know her," I say, meaning it as a question.

"Just a lost soul. By tomorrow she'll forget all about this and be back here or some other place. It's the way things are."

I can't get her out of my mind, but more, I can't stop thinking about how generous Owen was with her. Not the money, that's easy. But generous to build her up, to touch her out of compassion and not lust. I wonder how long it's been since someone did that for her. I'm so taken, I forget why we're here in the bar, which is why I don't follow what he says next.

"I can't recommend it. It's harder than you think."

"What?" I say.

"Being an O/O. An owner/operator. Maintenance can be expensive as hell. You miss a shift, jerk a sleeve, and there's a few thousand bucks. Then you've got trip permits, road use tax, fuel costs. Not to mention the broker commission, weather delays, customer delays, and asshole cops."

He's shooting down my dream, and I don't like it. "But you can make a lot of money, right? I mean other people do. Southwest does."

"Oh, sure. You can make a small fortune. Trouble is, you got to start with a large fortune to do it. You want my advice? Stick where you're at. You get a paycheck every week, and at the end of the day you go home and play with the dog. Leave the worries to the other guys. You don't need the heartache."

I don't say anything, but in my head I challenge every one of his points. And the more he talks, the more I know I'm going to do it despite what he says. When he's done and we've finished the last of the beer, I throw a couple dollars on the table and we head for the door. I reach my car first, but instead of getting in I hesitate, and before Owen can drive away I holler over to him.

"Just one thing."

"What's that, Chief?"

"How come you know all this stuff? Why do you think it would be so hard for me to run my own rig?"

Owen folds his arms atop the car door and rests his chin on his hands. "It only takes one sip from a pitcher to know how the whole thing tastes."

IT'S MONDAY, AND MRS. G invites me to Thanksgiving dinner. I accept because, well, why not? I don't have anywhere else to go. I don't think about *her* having somewhere else to go, or rather about her having someone else to celebrate with. But three days later as I'm getting ready, I see cars pulling into her driveway and realize that probably all her kids are coming. All her kids includes Angela and Hector. Surely they'll recognize me from the car repair weeks earlier.

I phone Mrs. G to ask whether this is such a good idea, but the phone only rings. She must be cooking or getting herself ready, or both. I'm supposed to be there at three and it's now ten after. I wait a few minutes, phone again, and this time someone does answer, a female, but not Mrs. Garcia. I hang up immediately, then think how stupid that was. I could have asked to speak with her and no one would have known it was me. I wait another couple minutes and call again. Now Mrs. G does answer, but there is so much background noise I'm not certain she understands me.

"Hector is there," I say. "And Angela."

I can almost see her putting a palm over her unoccupied ear and wrinkling her forehead to hear me better.

"Yeah?" she says.

"Maybe I shouldn't come over and, you know, blow my cover."

"No," she says. "Come over an doan worry about nothin'."

I sigh and tell her I'll be right over.

I'm wearing my tan slacks and button-down shirt that haven't been out of the suitcase for nearly a year. They've still got the fold creases, but I don't own an iron, so I hope they'll smooth out as the day goes on. I grab a six-pack of Corona and head out the door, worried about who will say what, and who is angry with whom. But this isn't my show and it's not my family. If Mrs. G wants me there, I'm happy to accommodate.

Hector answers the door and I freeze, but nothing happens. There isn't a flicker of recognition in his face. He introduces me to Angela, in whose eyes I think I see some spark, but she also says nothing. Guadalupe is bigger than I imagined him from his photo, and just as nice as can be. It turns out he was a horticulture major at Cal Poly and knows some of the general ed teachers I had. Now he's a manager at Monrovia Nursery. It's a huge organization, and I feel his excitement when he tells me the things he's involved in. More importantly, I can see his mother in the glow of his personality and in his love of the land and the plants. Who knew such things were genetically transmitted?

Of Mrs. G's three children, only Maria Elena is absent. I learn she called at the last minute to say she wasn't coming, after indicating all along that she'd be here. When we're alone in the kitchen, Mrs. G relates the conversation.

"...so then she toles me, everyone from work is goan a this fancy place at the beach an I'm gonna go with them. So I toles her, then how about after? You could come by later an eat again.

You could see your brother an sister. An me. I doan hardly see you no more. Well, no, she toles me. On account of it's goan a be real late." I thought Mrs. G might cry then, but she only tightens her jaw and goes on. "Finally I toles her, it seems to me family comes before work people. But then she toles me right back, it seems family would understand how important this is to me."

Mrs. G shakes her head for the little lamb who has lost her way.

For an hour the rest of us mill around while Mrs. G finishes the cooking. When we finally come to the table, I see there is an extra place setting meant for Maria Elena. No one has removed the dishes or scooted the chairs closer together to fill the gap. It's as if someone has died. But the oldest daughter isn't mentioned, and in fact the mood is fairly lively.

"So, Bro. I heard you got a promotion," Hector says as he passes a dish of green beans to Guadalupe. "That's good, man, you know? Lots a money 'n all that. Way cool."

Despite the complimentary words, I sense there is tension or history, or at least distance between Hector and his brother-in-law, and I don't know which one I feel worse for. They are nearly the same age, my age, but Guadalupe holds such a clear advantage that it's difficult to find a subject that doesn't call attention to the disparity. Hector, on the other hand, strikes me as a soldier dropped behind enemy lines, so that his entire world is a dangerous and untrustworthy place.

"But you know, Bro," he goes on. "That kinda thing ain't for me. Not something I could do. 'Cause, I'm like busy, too. And you know, the difference between you an me? The difference between me and most guys?"

Guadalupe smiles, waiting to hear the difference Hector has selected to disclose.

"Taxes." Hector sits back in his chair. He spreads his fingers along his ribs, and I think of a fat banker fondling his watch chain. If Hector had a cigar, I believe he'd light it now. "Taxes, man, that's the difference. What I make is what I keep, you know? I deal in cash."

Though we've just started to eat, Guadalupe pushes back from his meal as well. If he stands there'll be trouble, but he only smiles. "I guess that's right. At least for a while. But if they ever catch you, there'll be hell to pay."

"Hell?" Hector laughs. "Man, I already paid hell and got the receipt back, too."

We're all quiet, waiting, I believe, for some escalation. But nothing happens. If there was strain between the two, it seems to have disappeared. Nevertheless, the adults, and I include myself among them, turn our attention to the little ones. First we comment on how nice they look. Both Little Lupe and Vanessa are dressed in outfits I'm sure were supplied by Mrs. G, gotten at a discount from St. Vincent's. Lupe has on a brown suit complete with white shirt and tie. Vanessa is wearing a frilly white dress that is vaguely religious, as if she is to be the recipient of a baby's sacrament. I wouldn't be at all surprised if Mrs. G pours water on her head from her table glass, and then says a word or two while performing a symbolic gesture.

When we've finished the meal, Mrs. G shoos Hector, Big Lupe, Little Lupe, and me into the backyard.

Outside, Little Lupe picks up a ball and says to his uncle, "*Tio* Lupe, watch. I can throw good."

He wings it between Big Lupe and me. We both reach out and both miss catching the ball, which bounces against the side of the house, rattling the window in its frame.

"Whoa, *mijo*," Hector says. "Your *abuelita* going to come get you if you ain't more careful."

"I threw it as hard as I could, Daddy."

His words bring up a memory.

I'm ten years old. My father is bending toward me, a cigarette stuck to his lips, his eyes squinted against the smoke. His right arm is behind his back hiding the ball, and his left, the one with the glove, hangs in front of him describing a small circle. He nods, then straightens, bringing ball and glove together. He checks over his shoulder, holding the runner on base, except there is no runner, no base, just the back door to our little house on Tenth Street. He lifts his leg high, rears back, his throwing arm comes over the top, and the back leg follows up. The ball comes at me so hard I don't see it, not completely. But somehow I get my glove up in time and the ball pops into the pocket. The sting takes my breath away. The force nearly knocks me over.

"Good," he says. "Now toss it back here and we'll try again."

Big and Little Lupe play catch a while and include me, which is nice. I love the movement. I love handling the ball. In half an hour it's getting dark and chilly, and I should go home right that minute, but I don't. When Mrs. G calls from the door, we go inside for pie and whipped cream. She's made pumpkin from scratch, using fruit she's grown herself. The taste is different from what I'm used to, but wonderful. Earthier. Not as sweet.

I finish the pie and believe I've made it through the afternoon and evening without trouble. I've tried not to look Angela in the eyes, but it doesn't seem to have made any difference. Throughout the day she has fussed with the children, spoken occasionally and in short sentences to her mother, but mostly it seems she has drifted in her own world. I suspect she's so tired she'd just like to sleep.

I stand to go and start to thank everyone, but Mrs. G has one more tradition we must fulfill. She brings tiny, delicate glasses to the table and pours in two fingers of sherry.

"To warm our hearts an our souls," she says. She lifts her glass, and then she gives what is more a prayer than a toast. "Firs,

I wanna say thanks to you, God, for all the good stuff you geeb to us. Ain't nobody died this year, leastwise none of us did. An we ain't starving, an we all got roofs an all a that. An also we got these little babies that are healthy. An…"

She goes on and on with this litany. She goes on so long, in fact, that we get tired holding up our glasses and our arms start to droop. Finally she is done and we drink the little bit of alcohol. There are offers to help clean up, but Mrs. G tells us all to go. This is followed by a mild commotion of chairs scooting back and people preparing to leave. I've been sitting with my back to the wall, so now I have to work my way around the table, hesitating just a moment for Hector to clear a path. We're nearly toe to toe when suddenly I see in his eyes a forty-watt bulb blink on, as if the alcohol has put him into a reverse state, cognizant instead of dull.

"Bro," he says, looking at me like I just walked into the room. "I know you. Left rear quarter panel, right?"

Angela has been jerking Little Lupe's arms into the sleeves of a heavier coat. But now, finally, she is on board with her husband. I wonder if he has confirmed a suspicion she's carried all day. Angela gives her mother a disgusted look. She says, "I thought that was a lot of money for a couple hours work. I'm paying you back, Mom. I don't have it right now, but I swear I'm paying you back."

CHAPTER FOUR

THE MONDAY AFTER THANKSGIVING, I tell Alan Barnes, our TM, that I need tomorrow off for personal business. Without looking up from the papers on his desk, he waves his hand to say that's fine. Out on the dock I tell Terry that Alan gave me the okay, and Terry's reaction is pretty much the same. Fine. No sweat. Since I don't have a scheduled run, it's not too hard to cover for me. Besides, Tuesdays are generally slow.

The next day I put on slacks and a button-down shirt, the same outfit I wore to Mrs. G's a few days earlier. As I dress, I review what I know about business. Mainly there's the gozinta and the gozouta, and there has to be more of the first than the second. I learned that in my one business class. I also know I'll need some money to get my business started, but I'm not too concerned because I borrowed money to buy my car and I've already paid that off. I'll just borrow some more.

I pick B of A out of the phonebook because their ad says they're the *businessman's friend* and I figure that's the kind of place I need. I'm standing outside the doors when the bank opens, but I still have to wait half an hour before Mr. LaPorte, the manager, can see me. After I read a year-old *Time* magazine cover to cover, a woman walks me to his office, a glass walled affair at one end of the lobby. She steps aside to let me enter alone, but introduces me by name over my shoulder. Mr. LaPorte stands and smiles and offers his hand. He asks me to take a seat.

"So, Mr. Bass, what can we do for you today?"

He's built like a football player, which, for some reason, makes me uneasy. It's like he should be doing my job and I should be doing his. I take a breath, trying to slow down my heart, and talk as calmly as possible. I want to sound enthusiastic, but like an adult, not a kid wanting a very fast and totally impractical sports car. I want to sound like someone who's a good risk. But by the time I finish telling him my idea, he's stopped smiling and looks like he has to use the toilet.

"You seem young," is about all he can manage.

I tell him I have my Class A license, that I've been doing this work for a while, and then I lie, just a little, adding I'm a college grad.

Oddly, he extends his hand across the desk, reaching for something he surely knows I don't have because he saw me walk in carrying nothing. "I suppose we can review your business plan," he says.

He reverses the gesture when I tell him I didn't actually write anything down. "It's so simple," I tell him, "I didn't think I'd need to. My plan is just to haul freight and make some money."

His smile comes back then, but it's wearing a different set of clothes. A hazmat suit. He reaches into his desk and takes out a legal pad. He clicks a ballpoint pen half a dozen times like he's warming it up, and then settles down and begins to write some notes. Upside down I read my name, the date, SBA, trucking.

"Primarily," he says, "we need to know how you intend to pay back the money."

I don't answer because I'm processing his statement. My problem is I understand the words but not what they mean. It sounds like he's asking if I'll use a check or cash or a credit card. I'm working this out when he continues, "Where will the money come from?"

This doesn't help me. I'd do better if he weren't speaking English, because at least then I'd have a reason not to understand. I want to stand up and leave without another word, but I'm under the illusion he's actually trying to be helpful and that I should try as well. I take my best shot.

"When I get paid," I say, trying not to sound sarcastic, "I'll pay you." I take care not to end on a rising note, so that he knows I'm telling and not asking. But then I add, and this may be my downfall, "from the profit."

At this he puts down his pen, a little disdainfully it seems to me. "You can't pay a loan out of profit," he says. "Profit is what's left over *after* all debts have been serviced."

Again, I know the words. But when I hear *service*, I think of adding oil and changing filters. I hesitate to respond, and Mr. LaPorte's lips pull into a shape I'd describe as a sneer if the expression were on someone's face other than a bank executive. Nevertheless, in that moment it's clear to me this meeting has become simply entertainment for him, like pulling the wings off a beetle.

"Maybe this isn't such a good idea," I say.

If there is any possible bright spot, it is that I haven't mentioned my plan to Allison, and therefore she can't add this latest to my list of failures.

"Give it some time," LaPorte says, standing. The old smile is back now and he shakes my hand. As I clear the door he adds, "Come back in a year or two and we'll talk again."

THOUGH IT'S STILL EARLY enough that I could get in a half day's work, I go back to the trailer and spend the time drinking instead. I feel like I've been kicked in the stomach. I feel, in fact, like I did the evening I climbed back out of the quarry pit.

After a while the alcohol has an effect, but not the one I hoped for. I feel full and I feel sick, but I can't forget every sneer and slight and condescension on LaPorte's face. I invent scenes where terrible things happen to him, but even then I can't direct my own daydreams to my satisfaction. Somehow he always escapes and I'm the one hit by the bus. I put on some songs: "Rainy Night in Georgia" by Brook Benton, "You Don't Know Me," and of course, "Born to Lose" both by Ray Charles. It's music to wallow by, and I'm thinking about what else I can roll around in when the trailer tilts and there's a knock on the door.

"Hey, Bass," the voice says. "You hokay in there?"

"It's open."

Mrs. G comes in, looks at me, and then looks at the bottles on the table. She acts neither surprised nor disgusted, just slides into the seat beside me.

"So whas up?" she says.

Now that I need to think, I do feel the alcohol. My head is stuffed with socks. I try to remember what the problem is.

"Nothing," I say. "What's up with you?"

"*Caca*," she answers. "Excuse me, but you doan lie too good."

Another failure, I think.

"The girl again? Is that your problem?"

I take a breath, which seems to clear my head some. "No. I went to the bank for a loan and they turned me down. I feel like a fool."

Mrs. G is waiting for more, but I don't know what else to give her.

"Thas it? They turn you down, so now you gotta drink? Come here."

We lean toward one another and I think she's going to give me a little kiss, or whisper some financial advice, or life advice, or at least say something sweet and soothing. Instead she slaps my face. It isn't hard and doesn't hurt, but the surprise takes my breath away.

"Hokay," she says, sitting back again, as if the tap was a small chore that needed tending, and now that it has been accomplished we can get down to business. "Two thins. Number one, I doan need no more drinkers aroun' here. I got Hector an thas enough. Number two, one bank? Big deal. You got any idea how many banks there are? An that they ain't all the same? You unnerstan' one doan call the other an say, 'Hey, I jus' turn down that Bass kid, so be sure you do it too'?" She looks at me, daring me to disagree. When I don't, she goes on. "Now, you been to school, right?"

I nod.

"So you're smart. Anyways, smart enough to do this. Hokay. Did the man say how come you doan get the money?"

I tell her about not having a business plan, and about not understanding the banking terminology. When I'm done she lets out a blast of air that flutters her lips.

"*You* doan understan'?" she says. "What about me? This ain the language I learn as a baby, you know. It ain like I was born right up the street here. An I still got loans."

I want to tell her I've gotten loans too, but this is different. I want to tell her this is a bigger deal than she's ever been involved in. On the other hand I don't want to get whacked again, and in any case I'm not sure what I'm thinking is true. So I just sit and listen.

"Hokay," she says, practically rubbing her hands together. "Here's what we gonna do. We gonna write down a story about this business of yours, only we gonna use numbers instead a words. We gonna say, this is what this costs, an thas what tha costs, an we gonna see what everything costs all together. Then in another part a the story we gonna say this is what this guy pays, and thas what tha guy pays, an then add all a *that* up. We gonna take the first part away from the second part an see what we got left, an if it looks good, then we gonna see what you got that's worth anythin so they can hold it for ransom. After all a tha the very las thing we gonna do is we gonna fine you another bank. One where they act more polite."

Even in my foggy state this all seems logical. I'm not sure about the ransom part, which I take as her word for collateral, but I figure we'll cross that when we get there. One thing I can't wait to learn though is why she'd slap me for drinking when Hector is much worse. So I ask her, why doesn't she slap him?

"'Cause," she says, "a slap means somethin to you. You prolly never been slapped before. You'll remember this. But it ain no use with Hector. I could break both his legs an somehow he'd crawl for another drink. Someday it will kill him, an I'm sorry for that. But even more, I'm sorry 'cause it might kill my Angela too."

I recall Hector's *edges* then, and I find I have to agree with Mrs. G. As bad as I feel sometimes, he has to be in worse shape than me.

OVER THE NEXT SEVERAL evenings I write down everything I can think of as far as expenses and revenue. On the sly I ask Terry what various parts cost, and I'm shocked at some of the prices. Five hundred dollars for a fuel pump, four hundred for a tire. Delivery charges are printed on the freight bills and I used to think the company was stealing money. Now I wonder how they get by. Even so, when I get all the numbers collected, and I've fudged other estimates to my disadvantage, and I've allowed for down time due to repairs or simply no freight to haul, it still looks like I could do better than I'm doing now. And there are two other advantages: There'll be no one to tell me I have to go home at the end of the day, so I can work as much as I want. More importantly, my name will be on the cab door. If Allison sees that, who knows what could happen?

I assemble all the papers, which have now grown to a sheaf of graphs and spread sheets and supporting documents. I don't want to get caught short like before, so I go to step two, which is determining what I own that a bank might be interested in. It doesn't take long to add that part. I've got my car, a beater if I'm honest, and some money in the bank. And though a month ago I thought it was a small fortune, against the cost of a new rig and insurance, permits, and some sort of cushion, it's laughable. I review my options but quickly decide there aren't any. I just don't own anything of value.

For three days I hesitate doing what I know is the only possibility, until finally, on Saturday, I decide to call home. But even then I don't reach for the phone. Instead I stand at the sink drinking milk from the carton. I put on, what is for me, inspirational music. "White Silver Sands"—Don Rondo. "Sail Along Silvery Moon"—Billy Vaughn. I dig my basketball from the closet and spin it on my finger. It falls off and bounces away, and when I look down I see the floor has a spot of tar I've tracked in. For five minutes I consider going out to buy some solvent to clean it. Instead, I dial.

"Mom?" I say when she answers. It comes out like a question, though there is no doubt who picked up the phone.

"Jimmy? Oh, how wonderful to hear from you."

In the years since Kitty died, my mother has clearly rebounded, though I can't say the same for my father. He was quiet before, but now he is sullen and withdrawn. The few times we've talked, he is either angry or absent. One of my greatest fears is that I will become him.

For a time my mother and I talk about nothing—the weather and that sort of thing. We both avoid the subject of Allison and the baby. At last, when I have nothing else to say, I bring up the real reason I called. In vague terms I tell her all the positive stuff, how I've worked out a forecast, and how I'm not afraid to do whatever it takes to be successful. I avoid specifics because, frankly, I don't think she'd get it. She listens but doesn't say anything, and I feel she knows what I'm leading up to, or at least that I'm leading up to something.

"The thing is," I tell her finally, "I don't have any, you know, *assets*." I hate this, this begging. "So I was wondering if, well, if you and dad would cosign the loan, which might mean pledging your house. It isn't like you'll make the payments or anything, I'll do that. It's just like a, a backup."

Mercifully she doesn't ask why the bank needs a backup if the business is such a good idea. But that doesn't mean she's without inquiries. She asks intelligent questions about costs and revenue. She doesn't use those exact words, but she certainly has the gist. The great thing is that now I can just talk without holding anything back. I tell her all I've learned about freight rates and maintenance and permits. I tell her about the brokers, how they arrange the loads and collect the money. She takes all of this in more or less silently, but then when I'm done she asks if I have a name picked for the company.

"Jim Bass Trucking," I say.

As soon as the words are out of my mouth, I regret it. Understandably she's never approved of my name change. I know she sees it as a criticism of her and my father, which isn't the case at all. But I've said it now and can't take it back. I can only wait to see what happens.

"Well," she says, "it's nice and short." I'm relieved and about to agree, saying something about my new name being part of a marketing strategy, when she adds, "This is all so exciting. I wish your father and I had been a little more adventurous when we were younger. I always thought, 'Oh, heck. Let's give it a try.' But Emil, I guess he's what you'd call a Doubting Thomas. He wanted guarantees about the future, and of course that's not possible.

"One time I wanted to start a laundromat, where the women could play bingo while they waited for their clothes to wash. I thought it would be a big hit, something more exciting for them to do than reading old magazines. But your father said bingo would be gambling and illegal. When I told him we didn't have to play for money, maybe just a free wash cycle or anything fun to make the time go faster, he said in a few years everyone would own their own washer and dryer and we'd be out of business. He was sure we'd be stuck with those big machines that no one would want."

I never knew that about Mom. That she had ideas, big dreams. I'm quiet for a moment in case she wants to say more. I wait, not wanting to push, but then end up doing exactly that because it seems she's gone permanently silent.

"So what do you think?" I say.

"About?"

"About cosigning a loan. And pledging the house."

There's another long pause, and when she speaks again it still isn't to answer my question. "Your father always has a reason *not* to do something. Here it is, eighteen years later, and not everyone has their own washer and dryer, not by a long shot, mister. Young people just married, or families traveling. People in apartments. Don't they need a place to wash their clothes?"

"I'd say they do, Mom. In fact I use a laundromat."

"Well, then, there you are. My point exactly."

I don't sigh out loud, but it seems we've come to the end of our conversation without a resolution. I'm thinking how to tell her goodbye without sounding too disappointed.

"Jimmy?"

"Yes, Mom."

"I don't want to miss another chance to be part of something."

"No," I say, agreeing with her, though I'm not quite certain what it is I've agreed to.

"Can you give me a title? Something with letters?"

"Letters?" I ask

"Like you hear on television. CEO, or CFO, or CSO."

I find I'm shaking. If I understand correctly, mother has just made my worries disappear. "You can be anything you want, Mom. But what's a CSO?"

"Oh, I don't know, but it doesn't matter. The ladies at church won't know what I'm talking about anyway. Maybe we could make something up. Chief Supreme Officer? Central Social Organizer? Oh, no. Not that one. That sounds Communist, doesn't it? You just come up with something, Jimmy, and tell me what it is later. But make it sound good so I have something juicy to tell my friends. Won't they be jealous?"

We end the call on the best note in years. Mom is happy, and I'm happy. We're both looking forward to something, and I think things are really turning around. I'll have this business I can pour myself into. I can be *significant*. Not rich. I've never wanted that. I just want somehow to matter. Because maybe from that I'll believe in my heart my sister's death wasn't my fault. And if not that, then at least mistakes I made before don't mean I'll go on making them forever.

I go to sleep that night dreaming of Allison, which I do most nights, but this time she doesn't hate me. This time it's wonderful.

I'M IN A FIELD that shows the first signs of spring. The snow has melted and the puddles are dried, but you can see rivulets in the soil where water has recently flowed. If you kick at the earth, you will find dampness. Scattered and clumped are the brown husks of last year's reeds and grasses. They lie around like broken bones, but up through them grow tender new shoots, unembarrassed and eager as children.

It is into this season, and onto this ground, that I walk.

The sun, I notice, is bright and hopeful, though not yet warm. It shines down on building materials strewn about the lot, casting chunky shadows. I pick my way through leaning stacks of pallets, piles of concrete blocks, a tangle of lumber, plywood. There are sacks of cement for building, but also a deconstructed framework as if demolition were in progress. There are mixers and equipment, but no workers. Not a bird or chipmunk. Not a soul. Not a sound.

I walk with purpose toward an uncertain goal, confident only that upon arrival I will understand and be satisfied with the discovery. I come to a deep hole in the earth. It is precisely square and lined with gray block. Nothing of it shows above ground, but when I look over the side I see the structure goes deep and is shored inside with crisscrossed braces and scaffolding—metal Xs and wooden planks.

Cautiously, I approach the brink. I squat, then ease myself over the edge, swinging a foot into the void. My hands grip the perimeter block, elbows bent. I hold myself suspended for an instant, and then drop onto a wooden walkway. By swinging from the bracing and sliding along the planks, I make my way well below the rim of the foundation.

I sit there and dangle my legs over the edge of a springy board. I look up and see a neat square of blue sky. Below, the bottom is fathomless; it grows darker and darker until the pit is liquid black without end.

Allison sits beside me. At first I don't see her, but I know she's there because I feel the warmth of her body beside mine, from foot to shoulder. It is a comfort too great for speech. In that moment I understand I am both lost and saved.

She takes my hand and together we stare ahead into nothing.

A WEEK PASSES BEFORE my mother calls to tell me about the progress of the business loan. She starts with, "I'm so sorry, Jimmy," and after that I don't hear much for the next few minutes. Later when I reconstruct it all, I realize she really tried to help. It was Dad who didn't want to take the risk. When Mom told him *she* believed in me, Dad said that was fine, *she* could believe all she wanted, but the mortgage was in *his* name and he wasn't signing anything.

"I am so, so disappointed in him," Mom ends up saying. "He's just an old black hole sometimes."

I can tell she's been watching PBS.

"It's okay," I say. "More than one way to skin a cat."

"When I stood there listening to all that negativity," Mom continues, "I thought, what a bumpkin I've been. His name on the mortgage. His name on the car registration. I never cared before, you know? It was always *us*. Emil and Paula. Him being first seemed natural, the right way to do things. After all, I was the Missus. The mistress of the mister. HA!" she says with more venom than I can remember. I like her tone.

"Mom, really, it's fine," I tell her. "I'll figure out something."

I deliver this with more enthusiasm than I feel, but strangely I am encouraged by my own words. I start to think of alternatives, possibly Aunt Bets and how she might help, though that seems unlikely. When I don't come up with anything more solid, I decide that my mood, which is not ebullient but still miles from despondent, may be the result of some sort of chemical imbalance, because for whatever reason, the situation doesn't seem hopeless.

Since there is nothing else to do, she agrees and we leave it at that.

Later, I'm in the trailer wondering what songs will make me feel better, and my choices surprise even me: "Stormy Weather," "Summertime," "Old Man River,"

"Lush Life." They're slow and could be sad or even disturbing, but I don't see them that way. I see them as solid and rich, like the black earth Mrs. G has tilled up in the back.

The trailer door is open and I sit on the floor of the entryway dangling my feet outside, letting the Santa Anas wash over me. The rest of the country, most of it anyway, is in the freezer. But here, late fall and early winter are week after week of Indian summer. It's the best time of year as far as I'm concerned. I open a beer and look to the mountains.

What to do? I wonder. Who to ask? But most of all, is this even what I want, and therefore worth the trouble?

I answer the last question first: yes. I want to own this business. Partly because it's a means to an end, and partly because I can't think of anything else I'd rather do; but nevertheless, Yes.

The image of LaPorte is still in my mind like a bad taste, and I don't want to go through that humiliation again. But without anyone to back me up, I don't know what to do except go with what I've got, which is a plan and a little money in the bank. I'm just hoping Mrs. G was right, that I got a bad apple last time.

I finish the beer and pull in my legs. There's a directory sitting beneath the old rotary phone, and under *Banking* I find a dozen listings. I choose the smallest advertisement, which is P.I.B.—Pomona Independent Bank. I like that they don't say they're the biggest or the best or anything like that. Just that they're FDIC insured and that they've been around since 1953. Also they're open on Saturday—today—so I won't have to take off from work. I figure if they won't give me the money, I've got ten more tries.

ONE MORE TIME I dress in my slacks and good shirt. If this keeps up I'll have to buy some new clothes. I drive downtown feeling calm in a relative sort of way. I've prepared as well as I know how, so now I'll just roll the dice and see what turns up.

The parking lot is only half full and I get a spot near the door. In the middle of the lobby is a half-round desk that I suppose serves as a work station, but also for information or a reception-ist. The young woman sitting there is attractive, in that she smiles and looks approachable. I see her dress is fitted with shoulder pads, and for a moment I think of Lauren Bacall in *To Have and Have Not*, which is not a bad thing to think. When I ask if I might see the manager, she looks up and my heart skips a little. Maybe she's even prettier than I thought.

She has me take a seat while she checks with whoever she checks with, and then she comes back and says to follow her.

The manager is tucked into a little space defined by those gray, movable, upholstered walls everybody hates. There's a name slid into a holder on the outside of the wall—Frank Foote. He doesn't stand when I come in, but it's because he has a dachshund on his lap.

"Hey," he says. His voice is nice and fat, like a praline. He's from the South, somewhere.

"Hi," I tell him.

"Excuse Bingo here," he says. "My wife's dog. She dropped him off an hour ago and said she'd be right back. You can see how that's working out."

I tell him, "No problem. I like dogs." I think about my own, Lucky, and miss him more than I have in years.

"So what brings you in today?"

This time I've got a folder full of charts and spread sheets, and maybe most important, a letter of intent from an outfit called Continental Brokerage. Among other things it says that their intention is to provide Jim Bass Trucking with "general cargo trans-portation obligations of a regular and sufficient nature." This is gobbledygook and in a pinch doesn't mean anything. It's an un-witnessed handshake in a world of airtight contracts and go-for-broke lawyers. But it helps back up the numbers I've provided, and it gives me a place to start talking.

I open the folder and present the documents one by one. Af-ter he absorbs the first, I say, "The trick is to never stop moving. Keep rolling and hold down expenses. I know how to do both those things." One of the papers I give him is a sort of resume, and although mine is short, I list all the jobs I've done for SWT and hope this carries some weight.

While I talk, Mr. Foote reads down through the papers and makes some notes in pencil. He does this with the dachshund poking up through his arms and sniffing the papers, as if there's a rabbit hidden somewhere inside. I see Foote circle Cal Poly, and I wonder if he's going to check up on me, or if maybe he went there himself and feels some sort of connection.

I talk for ten minutes straight until I finally run out of steam. I try to think if I've covered it all, and I believe I have. Gozinta and gozouta. What's the total, what do you get to keep? It seems simple enough.

When he's read everything, Foote asks, "What kind of money you figure we're talking about here?"

I give him my number. He laughs. "That ain't gonna happen."

Maybe I overshot, I think. Or maybe under. Which way am I off? Maybe none of what I've said makes any sense, but so far he's been too polite to throw me out.

He says, "Before I say what we *might* be able to do, tell me a little about your personal assets and liabilities. I didn't see those listed. Eventually you'll have to formalize this on a financial state-ment, but give me a feel. Jesus, dog!" The animal is circling his lap like he's beating down a clump of grass, getting ready to settle in.

With the question about assets, I figure I'm sunk. Embarrassed, I tell him I own my car and that's about it.

"House?" he says. "Savings? Investments? Got a stash of Krugerrands in the attic?"

I don't even have an attic. I don't tell him this, but I give him my bank account total.

"Really!" he says. "I can tell you aren't married."

"No, sir."

"Well, we'll want those savings of yours deposited here, as you can understand."

I had figured the conversation was over, but now I'm not so sure. "Of course,"

Now the dog is nosing into his shirt. I can imagine what that wet, black dot feels like on Foote's stomach.

"That's it," he says. "Off you go."

Foote stands and walks to a pile of blankets next to a file cabinet. He puts the dog down and it circles again, finally settling into a brown ring—nose to tail. When the banker comes back to his seat, he's brushing invisible hairs from his shirt front.

"Obviously, you're way the hell undercapitalized," he says to me as he sits. "And given this is a start-up, you don't have sufficient assets to justify our risk. The big hit outa the gate, of course, is your equipment, though I suspect we can wrangle some sort of financing you can live with. That, and your insurance, and naturally your salary, are all fixed costs, while most of this other here," he waves his hand over the papers like shooing flies, "is all variable, as you've indicated. Comes and goes with how busy you are. But the fact that you live as you do and have managed to put away a respectable amount of cash is greatly to your benefit.

"Tell you what," he goes on. "The proper structure here might be a line of credit for your operating expenses, plus an equipment loan. We could use the truck and trailer as collateral on itself, and hold the cash in the form of a CD against the credit line. Large withdrawals would be subject to review, since you'd be able to cover only a portion of the total."

I can barely keep up with what he's saying. It's like he knows my business better than I do, which I suppose is the truth. "You'd do that?" I ask him.

"Slow down, son. You aren't out of the woods yet. This still has to go to committee. Not my money," he adds with a wink. He hauls some documents out of his desk drawer and slides them across the table toward me. "But I feel good about you. I expect you and me had some of the same profs over to the school there. How're you liking their football team this year? Sorry collection of horticulturalists and English majors if you ask me, but that's what you get. Anyway, you start working on these, and we'll nail down the loose ends as they pop up. Oh, and get that savings account over here, that'll help."

I pick up the papers and stand, not sure what to do next. "Thanks," I say. "Thank you very much."

"Nothing to it," Foote says. He shakes my hand and adds, "Assuming this goes through, I'll want you to stay in close touch with me. Something comes up, I want to know, okay? I don't like surprises." He sits down again and I figure we're done. But he has one more comment. "Think about getting yourself an accountant to keep your books. If you don't know any, check with Niki out there. She'll set you straight."

I DON'T HAVE AN answering machine so I call the bank twice a day until Wednesday. Every time, I talk to Niki, the girl, the woman, I met Saturday. I know if I'm going to be a businessman, I have to start getting that girl/woman thing right. To me every female is a girl. That is most females. My mother isn't a girl. Mrs. G isn't a girl. The third time I call, Niki laughs and says I'll have to be patient, but she says it in a nice way, a way that doesn't make me feel like a kid about to wet his pants waiting for Santa.

Friday I work late and when I get home, I can hardly believe my eyes. It's dark, of course, but my trailer is lit up like a, well, like a Christmas tree. There are strings of lights outlining the shape, including the drawbar. Lights wrapped around the propane tank. Lights around the door. And they're not a hodgepodge of leftovers—some blinking, some not, too many greens and not enough yellows. Nope, these are all the same, the tiny red ones, and it makes the trailer look like a confection. I don't know what to say.

I do, however, know who to thank, and I go next door as soon as I park. When Mrs. G opens the door I say, "You've been busy."

A smile breaks out on her face, the smile made bigger because she's trying to resist. She doesn't admit to anything but steps back from the door and says, "You hungry?"

We sit down to bowls of gazpacho, which seems strange for the time of year because it's served cold. But the taste of the vegetables is wonderful, and besides, she has made a couple dozen flour tortillas and they are steaming hot. Onto them we drizzle a combination of melted butter and honey, and rolled up they serve as a second implement to the spoon. Instead of drinking beer tonight, Mrs. G has made tea. This also seems like an odd choice, but it goes down perfectly. When I can't eat anymore, I push back from the table and hold my stomach.

"Thank you so much," I say. "That was wonderful."

"Not too bad, right?" She has matched me bite for bite but doesn't act as sluggish as I feel.

"What do I owe you for the lights?" I ask, thinking she went out and bought them. "Not to mention all the work."

Mrs. G stands up and takes our bowls and plates away. "No charge," she says. "Only just something I wanted to do. Makes the neighborhood a little brighter."

I suppose she's right, given that until today her house held the only holiday lights on the street. By comparison my trailer looked a bit forlorn; small and alone. The last puppy at the pound. Now it looks great, or at least as good as a little trailer can look. The color reminds me of cinnamon Red Hots, and cinnamon reminds me of baked apples. Baked apples remind me of Christmas, so it all sort of works out.

"I talked with the bank today," I tell Mrs. Garcia.

"An?"

I shrug. "Nothing yet, but at least it's not a no."

She wags a finger at me. "Din I tole you?"

"You did tole me," I say. And then I have a thought. "What would you like for Christmas?"

I expect her to dismiss the idea. *You doan need to get me nuthin'.* Something like that. But she stops and considers for a moment before she shakes her head, sort of sadly, and says, "What I want you got no control over."

She doesn't elaborate, and I don't pry. I thank her again for the lights and the dinner, and then I go home and crawl into bed.

MONDAY I'M OUT ON a run that takes me near P.I.B. It rained earlier, and it's still breezy and cool. I'm wearing an old canvas work jacket with frayed cuffs and a grease stripe across the belly where I lean against the fifth wheel. I don't look like an executive.

Niki looks up when I come in. She had her head down and was scowling at a paper, but she sees me and brightens more than strict customer service calls for.

"Hey," she sings. "Look at you. A working man."

I hold out my arms for a mock inspection and see the line of grease continues up one sleeve. "That's me," I tell her. "Nose to the grindstone."

"Your timing is fortuitous," she says. "Let me see if Mr. Foote is available."

She turns and walks away from me, and I can see the full length of her back. She's wearing a knit dress, beige, and it clings nicely to her shape. She's tall and lean, and I wonder if she might have played volleyball. If so, I think I'd like to play it with her. She looks like she could really spike.

Thirty seconds later she's out from Foote's cubicle, but doesn't cross the lobby to fetch me. Instead she crooks her finger for me to come there. When I do, she stands aside without a word, letting me enter. But she gives me a smile that Mom would say is the cat that got the canary.

"Jimmy!" Mr. Foote says. We shake hands and he motions me to sit. "Son, you've just crossed mile one of the marathon."

My heart sinks. I imagine more paperwork, more time lost. Come back in a year or two.

"Now the real work begins," he says. "The day-in, day-out grind. Making your plans reality."

Niki again appears at the cubicle entrance and hands Foote a manila folder. It's an inch thick. He hefts it and laughs. "It'll take a minute or two to sign all this crap, and I imagine you're on the clock. On the other hand, what are they going to do? Fire you?" He gets a big charge out of this.

It actually takes twenty minutes, because he has to explain the two loans, and what I can and can't do. Also, in between each subject he reminds me to keep him informed. Good news or bad, he wants to know what's going on because he's a bit out on a limb here.

I hear him and I don't. Mostly I'm signing where he points, plus I'm distracted by a scent in the air. At first I think it's my imagination brought on by this heady occasion. Then I realize it's Niki's perfume lingering after she's left. I'm so happy with everything that's going on I feel like the guy in the World War II photo who grabs the girl and bends her back and plants a big one right on her lips. I think about doing that to Niki out of sheer joy. Then I consider *that* thought and wonder what it means, if anything. I conclude it seems like not such a bad idea.

When I've finished with everything, Mr. Foote separates the documents into two stacks, originals and copies, and slides my half into a big envelope. He hands me my package and says, a little gravely it seems, "I expect good things from you."

On the way out of the bank, I walk slowly past Niki's desk. I feel she must sense the thought I had earlier, and that she must feel something similar. At the very least she must wish me the best of luck with all her heart.

But her head is down and I have to say, "See ya," to get her attention.

She does look then, and she smiles. But all she says is, "Congratulations."

I FINISH MY SHIFT without doing anything else unusual. I mark my time at the bank as my lunch and clock out at six. I think about asking Alan Barnes for another day off so I can go look for a rig, but instead I decide I'll wait until Saturday. I don't know if it's cold feet or what, but now that I've got the money, I halfway feel like giving it back. Sort of like catch-and-release fishing. I just wanted to know I could do it.

But Saturday comes and I'm up and ready to roll by seven, though I doubt any dealerships open until ten. I drink one pot of coffee and then another. By nine o'clock even Sarah Vaughn can't calm me down. I know where I want to start looking and decide to go despite the hour.

In the last several years the term *rush hour* has lost its meaning because the freeways can be crowded regardless of the time or day. If there's an accident or a big league game at Anaheim or Dodger Stadium or the Forum, forget it. But today the traffic is moderate, and the low clouds and overnight rain don't seem to have caused any problems. I drive straight to Ricky's Truck Corral, a place in Santa Fe Springs I've passed a hundred times and always wanted to visit. I exit at Carmenita, which, after stopping at the light at the end of the off ramp, deposits me into the dealer's parking lot. I pull up to the concrete bumper and see before me a brown sales trailer. Beyond that must be three acres of asphalt, all of it covered with rolling stock. Before I can get clear of my car, a fellow is waddling down the trailer's metal staircase and heading toward me. From the pavement to the button on his ball cap can't be four and half feet, and he walks with a bowlegged, rolling gait like a sailor or a cowboy. Or a physically impaired truck salesman.

"You want to use that old boat for a trade?" he says.

I've seen this guy on television, and he's no less animated in real life. I feel I'm meeting a celebrity. A minor one.

"I'll need a car," I tell him. "I can't take a tractor to the grocery store."

He slaps his pudgy fingers against both knees as if he's never before encountered such wit.

"Okay," he says. "A tractor. You can see I've got some choices. Whaddya have in mind?"

"A conventional," I tell him. "Sleeper with a shower. Dual drivers and adjustable fifth wheel. It's gotta have power, and most of all it's got to be reliable."

"Brand preference?"

"I'm thinking Kenworth, but I'm not married to it."

Ricky squints and I think of Billy Barty or Popeye. "I've got fifty-eight tractors on the lot today, but I'm only going to show you one." He points his forefinger at me and hammer-drops his thumb. If he says, *this is you, kid,* I'll walk.

"Let's talk price," I say. "I'm on a budget."

He droops his head and shakes it, like he's heard this too many times before, which no doubt he has. "Too poor to paint, too proud to whitewash," he says. "Misguided thinking, young man. My advice is, buy the best. That way you only cry once."

I want to tell him, "Of course you'd say that. You're the one selling." But I don't say anything, and he goes on.

"It all starts with the right horse. After that, things take care of themselves." He holds his finger to his eye, then points to the sky as if he's just remembered something. "I knew I was saving this beauty for someone. Now I know who. Come on. Lemme show it to you."

As I follow his pitching stride, it strikes me he walks using his shoulders as much as his legs, hitching both together like a marionette. We pass a half dozen white utility vans with the name of a bakery in blue on the sides, and next to those a wrecker with a crane and hook. *We don't want an arm and a leg,* the tag line says. *We just want your tows.* Down another aisle are three or four brown UPS tractors, and beyond that, rows of green Ford bobtails. We pass the mid-sized utilities, the Hinos and Grummans, until finally we're into the tractors. There are Marmons and Whites, Volvos, Peterbilts, Freightliners. Ricky has them all.

I'm beginning to think he should use a golf cart, given the size of the lot and his difficulty walking, but we turn one more corner and he stops, holding out an arm as if we've come unexpectedly across one of his children and he can't wait to show her off.

"There she is," he tells me. "That's the one you want."

Indeed, it seems to be. A long-nosed KW, red as a broken heart. In gold leaf on the driver's door, the name *Buttercups.*

"How many miles?"

"Practically new. A touch over three hundred thousand."

The truck appears in pristine condition and the mileage is low. I figure the owner put on maybe seventy thousand per year. Why would someone want to get rid of such a thing?

"Any problems?"

"Just one," Ricky says. "She needs a loving home." I laugh and he gives me the story. "A nice lady brought 'er in. Bit of a cupcake. Never before married and past the age of having kids. Out on the road one day she meets a sugar daddy, snags him, and he doesn't want her driving any more. That was all she wrote. Let's have a listen."

He reaches out to what for him is head high and unlatches the door. Somehow he manages a hop and a hoist, and gets his foot onto the first rung of the cab's ladder. From there it's three steps up into the seat. He fiddles with the compression release, turns the key, and the tractor starts instantly, settling into a sweet rumble.

"Whatcha think?" he hollers down.

"How much?" I holler back.

"Take 'er for a drive."

"No sense if I can't afford it."

"What's your budget?"

"What's the price?"

Ricky shuts down the motor, and then, like a combination gymnast and fireman, swings to the ground using the assist handle. "Forty-seven five," he says.

I tell him I believe I can do better.

"No," he tells me, "you can't. What you can do is cheaper. But sure as Christmas, you aren't going to do any better. The thing you gotta understand," he says in a way that makes me believe, "is that I'm not running a warehouse here. I don't make a dime 'till they roll down the highway. I don't price 'em so's they'll sit." He lets this sink in a minute and then he says, "Now Son, you want to drive 'er or not?"

I AM HOCKED TO the gills.

Two days ago I owned nothing and I owed nothing, and showed up on nobody's radar. Now I am buoyed by the knowledge that if I croak, someone will be out thousands of dollars, and therefore they wish me well. I have value because I have debt.

At work I tell Alan Barnes that I am leaving, and I tell him why. I was wrong to anticipate his disapproval; he seems genuinely pleased and wishes me the best. He asks if I want to give two weeks' notice and continue working during that time, or take off right away. My choice. No hard feelings either way. I tell him I don't think I'd be much good hanging around, that I'm so nervous and excited I can hardly contain myself. He laughs and shakes my hand and says if I ever need anything, just ask. And he says to come around once in a while just to visit. I appreciate him more than I can say.

Terry, too, wishes me well, but is more reserved in his farewell. He won't meet my gaze, but instead looks at the floor as we talk. Maybe, I think, there is real emotion here. Maybe he will actually *miss* me. I find I miss him already.

Most of the other drivers treat me as if I'm a fellow prisoner at the end of my sentence. I'm being released and they are not. Their words are the right words, but the delivery is grudging. Why you and not me, they seem to mean. You're young and I'm not, and yet I'm still here and you're leaving. They act as if I've let them down, sold them out.

In the yard I come across Owen, who is fueling and checking his rig. All the Southwest tractors are cabovers, and he has the cab of his rig tilted, exposing the whole engine. He's standing between the frame and the front tire, wiggling an electrical connection.

"Hey, Owen." He looks over his shoulder at me. "Did you hear I got my own rig?"

He grins at me. "Sucker."

I say, "Maybe sometimes I could call you for advice. You know, suggestions."

He pulls the engine's very long dipstick through a rag, pushes the stick back into its tube, then pulls it out again. "I had one suggestion and you turned that down."

We're both quiet a minute. I don't want things to end like this.

"Still using oil?" I nod at the stick.

"Couple quarts. Not bad."

He climbs out and releases the catch, easing the cab down slowly until it clicks into place. In the damp air there is the sweet smell of diesel and the feeling of winter. The light, which would be low anyway, is further diffused by clouds. From the far end of the property we hear the yard goat, pushed up against the governor, revving for all it's worth.

"Must be Dale," I say.

"That boy couldn't pour piss out of a boot if the instructions were on the heel."

Owen stands beside the tractor, wiping his hands on a shop rag, anxious to go, not wanting to be rude. I hold out my hand to him.

"Stay well," I say.

He takes my hand, smiling. "Make 'er sit up and say Mommy."

Suddenly in the pit of my stomach there is a homesick feeling, as if I've headed down a lonely road with a hobo's bundle slung over my shoulder.

CHAPTER FIVE

ONRAD VEGA, WHO OWNS Continental Brokers, rents me a forty-foot flatbed. This saves some cash, which makes Mr. Foote happy. Besides the money, Foote tells me, it helps bind my company to Continental. They'll want me to succeed so I can keep paying the rental, which means they'll keep feeding me work.

The first load Conrad gets me is twelve big harrows made in Tulare and sold to an implement shop in Red Bluff. I leave my house around midnight and crest the Grapevine at one. Snow flurries swirl in the headlights. I hope I don't have to chain up, and fortunately the temperature warms a little as I drop down the other side of the pass. I sip coffee from a Thermos and listen to Dean Martin sing "Sway" and "Just in Time." Sinatra may have been more famous, but for my money Dino had the best voice of the Rat Packers.

I pull into the fabricator's yard as they're opening up the next morning. The trip uses a good share of my legal driving hours, but the time loading doesn't count against me. Which is a good thing because the guys are in no hurry to get started. But then neither am I. I haven't had breakfast, so I accept when they invite me in for coffee and fresh donuts.

Inside the break room I stand alone near the door, while the other fellows punch at each other, lick the sugar from their fingers, spill their drinks, and shake the liquid from their hands. They seem like good guys. Finally Ed, an older guy, says they need to get to work.

"Let's load this kid up," he says and starts to pull on more clothes.

Appropriate to the weather, the other fellows also don jackets and boots, with canvas overalls on top of everything. They have gloves poking from hip pockets and pull sweatshirt hoods over their seed caps. This preparation takes another ten minutes until finally we go back outside.

As we approach my rig, Ed, the leadman, tells me, "We'll handle this. Just stay out of the way." He says it matter-of-fact, not bossy.

The drizzle blowing against my face feels like needles, but I don't want to sit in the warm cab while they're out in the weather working. So I stand beside the truck with my hands tucked in my armpits, rocking from foot to foot as two of the fellows jump up onto the trailer bed and another directs Ed, who is operating the forklift. It's obvious they've done this sort of thing a hundred times, and before I know it I'm loaded and ready to go. I chain down my load, sign the bill of lading, and climb into the tractor. Before I can pull out, one of the fellows comes back and points to the door.

I roll down the window.

"Buttercups?"

"I'm changing that," I tell him.

I head north on 99 and cut west on 198, toward Hanford. At I-5, I turn north again and off to the west watch the soft, round, feminine hills roll by. This is the start of my career, I think, and it seems to me a good one.

TWO DAYS LATER I'M home. I park the rig along the fence in front of the property and let myself in. It's two in the afternoon. I'm tired but content. It seems the most natural thing in the world would be to call Allison right now and tell her what I'm doing. I feel maybe things are changing for me, and for us. Maybe it's all going to work out.

I get cleaned up, then pack my dirty clothes in a pillow case. I figure later I'll go to the laundromat and catch up on my washing. For now I make a sandwich and pour a glass of milk. I'm at the table, eating, bringing my logbook up to date, when the phone rings. I'm thinking it's probably Conrad with another load, but I'm hoping, though it makes no sense, that Allison has found my number and for some reason is calling.

But it's neither of those people. It's my mother.

"Jimmy?" she says. Her voice is throaty but not strong. At first I think she has a cold. "I've left. I'm gone."

This makes no sense to me. "Left what? Gone where?"

I don't know what she's talking about, but I do know my mother, so I can guess the source of our misunderstanding. Here's the problem: She has thought about whatever this is for a long time, and then has made her lists. Then she's thought about it some more, changed things around, and let this new version steep. Now, by the time she shares any of it with me, she has lived with the thought so long she believes the information is common knowledge. That I'm already up to speed. Normally I'm not, but also normally I can catch up. Here, I don't know where to start.

"Help me out, Mom. What's going on?"

"Well," she says, surprised I have to ask. "I've left your father."

Left my father to go to the market? To go to church?

"I don't understand," I tell her.

Over the next half hour I learn more about my mother than I'd learned in the previous twenty-two years. She tells me of un-realized goals and the disappointments she's felt. She says she's always thought of herself as a seed waiting for the right soil, but instead she fell on hard ground. (No doubt a biblical influence here.) She says she's getting old and regrets wasting so much of her life, but then she adds, "The only thing worse than wasting forty-five years is wasting forty-five years and one day." (This part, I suspect, comes from Doctor Laura.)

I don't mean that her feelings are superficial. Of course I've seen her upset before, though even when Kitty died she held her-self together better than this. Certainly she's never had such an extreme reaction. Leaving home? I mean, how bad can things be?

Now Mom is crying, and I picture exactly what she looks like. She's in a phone booth at a Dairy Queen or a Kentucky Fried Chicken somewhere on an interstate. I can hear the cars swish by. She's got one arm folded across her stomach and tucked under the arm holding the phone. Her eyes are puffy and red. Her hair is a mess. I want to hold her and tell her it will be all right, exactly the way I couldn't do when Kitty died. Exactly like I can't do now, either.

As I'M DOING MY laundry I think that, all things considered, her plan isn't a bad one. Mom will be living with her college friend. She'll be in Maine, a place she has never been before, but to hear her tell it, that's one of the appealing aspects. She's starting over. Starting fresh. She *wants* things to be unfamiliar.

Before I hung up I made the mistake of asking how she'll live, what she'll do for money. Mom answered, understandably irritat-ed once I think about it, "I'll get a job. I'm not stupid, you know."

I know she isn't stupid. It's just that I've never before considered the possibility of her being alone. On the other hand, I wonder what my father will do without her once he runs through the food she has prepared for him.

I contemplate these things while I sit on a bench with my back against the laundromat's picture window. Light comes over my shoulder, and a shadow on the floor in front of me reads *coin-op*. Two children, Hispanic, chase back and forth in front of the driers. The air is warm and moist, and the drone of the machines nearly puts me to sleep. When I close my eyes, my body quivers like a dreaming dog. I've driven fourteen hundred miles in three days, and I think I'm still on the road.

THAT EVENING I CALL my father. He's always been the hard guy, but maybe Mom is right. Without her to lean on, there's a good chance he'll fall apart.

"How are you doing, Dad?"

He says he's fine. We haven't talked ten times in five years, but he doesn't acknowledge that the call today is out of the ordinary. After he says he's fine, he doesn't go on. The line is silent.

"I just thought, you know, with Mom gone and all...I just wondered."

"Your mother is a grown woman," he tells me. "She can do as she pleases." Dad says he's long suspected she wasn't quite stable and now he hates to see he's been right all along. "Anyway," he says, "nothing I can do about it."

You could ask her to come back, I think.

"I got that rig I told Mom about. I've made my first run already. The tractor's a beauty. Cummins engine, Allison trans, Jake brake." He's never been a motorhead, but I'm hoping he'll at least recognize the brands and appreciate the quality. Maybe he'll ask me to send him a picture. I'll take some as soon as I get the name on the door changed.

"Allison," he says finally. "Isn't that the girl you knocked up?"

CHRISTMAS EVE I'M ALONE. Mrs. G has gone to Big Lupe's, and I don't really know anyone else nearby. At least not in the come-over-for-Christmas-and-have-a-drink kind of way. I microwave two frozen burritos and put on a holiday tape I've made: Teresa Brewer, Buddy Clark, Johnny Mercer and the Pied Pipers. When I hear Bobby Darin's "Christmas Auld Lang Syne," I get such a lump in my throat I almost can't breathe. If it were snowing I could be exquisitely miserable, but the weather is warm enough that earlier I washed the truck in my shorts.

I check directory assistance for Mundelein and find Allison's phone number, or rather her parents' phone number. I get the address, too. But I don't call for two reasons; the first is that hearing her voice sweet and loving toward me, would push me over the top. The second is hearing her voice not caring for me, or angry with me, or perfectly happy *without* me, would also push me over the top. As it is, I'm too near that precarious edge to risk any sort of push at all.

Around six my mother calls and I am unbelievably grateful to hear from her, to have someone familiar and with whom I share some history.

"Mom!" I say. "Merry Christmas!"

"And you," she says.

She tells me she's really settled in her new home and couldn't be happier. The place is an upstairs condo not a hundred yards from the beach. She says she can see the water from the front window, and her voice is as full of gratitude as that of a person who's seen a stream after only living in the desert. Which, in a way, is the case.

And she has a job.

Mom giggles, "Jimmy, it is *the* most exciting thing to get a paycheck, knowing someone thinks enough of what you do to give you money. Not a relative, not a friend. A stranger gives you money simply because you're worth it!"

I ask the particulars of the job, and she says she works in a service station. She rings up customers and stocks the shelves of the minimart. She wants me to come visit, and I say maybe. When things are slow. When I'm more established. The truth is I can't imagine the circumstances that would get me there.

And then she says, "I was so upset when I called before, I forgot to tell you I stopped to see Allison and our little Amanda. Oh, Jimmy, she's precious. Such a little marshmallow. Six months old, you know."

She says this like I might need reminding. Like I could ever forget.

I don't say anything, and for a moment neither does she. There is a vibration on the line between California and Maine. It's a tension. An expectancy. It's generated by her wanting to say the very thing I don't want to hear.

"Jimmy," she starts, then hesitates. "I want you to know I understand, or at least I understand in *part*. I know that young people have certain *desires* and that certain things *happen*. And these things that happen, sometimes have more to do with," I know she wants to say *lust,* but instead she says, "the physical, rather than the emotional. But you know, people, men especially, have certain *obligations*. Obligations before the fact, and obligations after the fact. Which brings me to the part I simply don't understand, and especially after seeing the child."

I mumble something in response, but it isn't what I mean. Because what I mean is that my actions are precisely in line with my obligation to their safety and happiness. I don't say this because

Mom wouldn't understand. There is no way she could because I don't either. I just know it's true.

Before she hangs up, Mom gives me her phone number and address in Maine. She makes me promise to stay in touch with her, to write.

And later that evening I do write, but not to Mom. I write the baby. I tell Amanda, "Merry First Christmas." I relate different Christmases I shared with Kitty, and different gifts we gave and received. I tell her about buying my mother a silk scarf five years in a row after she helped me pick out the first one. I tell her about getting my dad a ball mitt that fit me and not him. I say last year I got your mother two complete outfits and more; skirts and blouses, sweaters, a coat, a fur hat. I was so in love and she was so beautiful I couldn't stand it. I would have bought out Macy's if it were possible. I ask Amanda what she might get her mother someday, and I offer suggestions. I sign off using words like *goodnight my marshmallow*, and *love*, and I write *Daddy* at the bottom.

Then I tear up the letter and throw it away.

CHAPTER SIX

I N SPRING A YOUNG man's fancy turns to thoughts of gardening. At least mine do, because one morning I look out the window and see a green haze where Mrs. G plowed and planted earlier. I go back by the block wall and find sprouts of something I can't identify, but I see she has staked strings to the ground and made inverted Vs by attaching the middle of the strings to the wall. So I assume these are pole beans. I look down the rows, and for the first time notice there are a variety of leafs and nubs, all green but in ten different shades.

And there is something more; she has tilled a new patch equal in size to the first. The cultivation now nearly reaches my trailer. She's left paths between the mounds to negotiate the area, but otherwise the ground is planted.

I don't care, really. It's not like I was doing anything with the property. Sometimes I drop the flatbed on the street and pull the tractor inside, in front of my trailer to wash it, but that's in front. The land she has cultivated is in back, so I suppose she can have it if she wants it. I mean, it *is* mine, and she hasn't asked, but why not give it to her?

I go next door to talk with her about it.

"Hey," I say when she opens the door. I say it light and friend-ly, not Heeey, spread out so that it's an accusation. But it doesn't matter how I inflect the word.

"Doan start with me," she says. "You wasn't doin' nothin' back there anyway. Why not put it to use? Why not grow some food?"

I hold up my hands like she's a bandit and has the drop on me. "What did I say? I didn't say anything."

"You had that look in your eye," she says, then backs away from the door. "You wan coffee?"

In an instant all is forgiven. I follow her into the kitchen. The smells of coffee and fresh baked biscuits fill the house, and I have to wonder if this isn't a calculated, preemptive strike. I wonder if she has anticipated me and is saying, I took something from you, so here's something from me in exchange.

While we eat, she starts a story that seems to have no point, but I should know better by now. She tells me she knows a guy, a Mr. Pennybaker, whom she used to work for. He owned apart-ments, lots and lots of apartments, and whenever a tenant moved out, Mrs. G cleaned the place in preparation for the next occu-pant. Mr. Pennybaker paid her the complete cleaning fee he had charged the previous resident. Sometimes the places were a mess, but often they needed only minimal work. Scrub the bathtub, vac-uum the carpet, wash the windows. She wasn't responsible for repairs, but she'd nevertheless paint the scuff marks on the walls so the place looked fresh. Sometimes she could be in and out in two hours, and for this she received a hundred dollars.

"Fifty bucks an hour," I say. "Not bad."

"Sometimes nobody moved out for two weeks or a month an I'd get pretty hungry. But sometimes I'd get three apartments a day for a week. Summers were best. The kids get outta school an the parents doan feel bad about taking a new job far away." She takes a bite of her biscuit and washes it down with a sip of coffee. "So anyway, thas how come I know Mr. Pennybaker."

I'm thinking, okay. I'm thinking, this was a nice break. A little snack. A little conversation. But I've got things to do, like going to the park and playing ball. I haven't been down there for a week and I'm stiffening up. My jumper will be a brick. A frozen rope, as Chick says.

"Which is how I come to know about the property."

"The property?" I say.

"On Baseline. Up by Angela."

I wait. Pushing her works as well as pushing a string.

"I figure, you know, it's good for a person to work. Good to be busy, right? You make a little money, an you get some time by yourself."

What she's doing is handing me a puzzle one piece at a time. My job is to take those pieces and see how they fit. Try to put them together in a way that makes a picture. Whether or not it will be the *right* picture, time will tell.

"So there's this land," I say. "And there's a job, or a potential job. Or something."

"A vegetable stand," she says. "'Cause we gonna have all this produce an you know as well as me we ain't gonna be able to eat it all."

"Probably true," I say, thinking that in an entire summer I couldn't eat the vegetables from half of one row. And we, she, must have twenty rows.

"An we doan wanna waste nothin', right?"

"We wouldn't want that," I agree.

"Well, there you go."

Here's what I have so far: there's a vegetable stand. The stand is on Baseline Road in Fontana. The vegetables in the stand are the ones Mrs. G has grown on my land. There's definitely a picture forming, though it's still out of focus.

"So, this land," I say, trying for clarity, "belongs to Mr. Pennybaker?"

"Din I just tole you that?"

"You did. And he's going to rent you this land? Sell you this land?"

She shakes her head like I better shape up and start paying attention, because next time she comes down my row and stands by my desk she'll be carrying a pointer, with which she will smack my knuckles if I don't get the answer correct.

"LOAN," she says. "Whas he doin with it anyway? Nothin'. It's goin' to waste."

"Like my yard."

"Exactly."

Now she's satisfied. I'm not, but then I don't have to be. Whatever she has in mind affects me only in that it involves the property I'm living on, and therefore impacts me very little.

Of course, I'm wrong.

"So, you gonna help me or what?"

It's pointless to answer otherwise, so I say, sure, why not, although I have no idea what I've signed up for.

THE FOLLOWING WEEK I have three short runs, one to San Diego/ Calexico, one to Palm Springs, one to Goleta. Among California's inherent advantages is that it's a long state, north to south rather than east to west, and of course that it's on the coast. The result is great topological and climatological diversity. *From the mountains to the sea*, and all that. In the course of three days I drive the desert, the cities, the mountains. On Friday I drive the coast. I'm glad to have Goleta as the last run because it's near the southern end of the Central Coast, which I believe is the prettiest region in the state, though there are so many choices I could change my mind in a hurry.

From L.A. to Oxnard there's fog on 101, which slows the considerable traffic even further. But once I'm over the hill, things clear up. The day is cool, and past Ventura a breeze starts to blow. In Carpinteria I pull off the freeway to stop at McDonald's. I park the rig in the Von's parking lot and walk a hundred yards back, up Casitas Pass Road, where I order a couple Quarter Pounders with cheese, some fries, and two shakes, one vanilla, one chocolate. I can hear Coach Kennedy saying, if the fire's hot enough you can burn anything. Right on, Coach.

I make my delivery by one o'clock, call Conrad from a pay phone, and he gives me a pickup in Ojai.

"A hundred cases of wine," he says.

"Not exactly flatbed cargo," I tell him. "You don't have a van in the area?"

He says I don't have to get it if I don't want to, but I know he'd like to impress the customer who called just an hour ago. I tell Conrad no sweat, I'll throw a tarp over the load and rope it down. I believe he appreciates the effort, but all he says is, "See you back at the barn."

I run the wine to a distributor in San Bernardino and I'm home by six. Easy money. It's Friday night, and although I don't have anywhere to go and no one to see, still, it's the weekend and I have that weekend feeling. It's the feeling I could do anything I want, though nothing comes to mind.

I pull alongside the chain link and shut down the Cummins, pop the air brakes, and watch dust puff up in clouds. I let myself in through the locked gate and when I get to the trailer, I see a note on my screen door. "Tomorrow," it says. "7:00 A.M. in the morning." There's no signature, but then who else could it be?

I start a pile of briquettes in the red Weber barbecue grill (a gift from Mrs. G—or possibly a direct donation from St. Vincent's), then take a shower in the little stall. When I'm done, I empty the holding tank onto the vegetables. By now the charcoal is white ash and radiating enough heat that I can barely get close. I bring a couple of kielbasa from the fridge and roll them onto the grate, and then I open a Corona. I just spear the sausages onto a plate when the phone rings.

"You weren't going to call me back?" the woman says.

I look at the answering machine Conrad has made me purchase, and see the light is blinking.

"I just got home," I tell her. This seems an appropriately neutral response, especially because I don't know who's calling.

"You should have one of those machines where you can call in and check from the road. Messages might be time sensitive," she says. "Don't make me report back that you aren't conducting yourself in a businesslike manner."

And then I know who it is. Niki. From the bank. What in the world? I think. I've made my payments. In fact, I'm always early. For heaven's sake, I *carry* in the check because I don't want to take a chance on the mail. What do they want from me? Cash? Bullion?

"What's up?" I say.

"Well," she answers. "It's Friday night."

Again, I feel I've missed something. An anniversary, maybe. Some sort of fiscal nuance.

"It is Friday," I agree. And then I say, because I can't think of anything else, "Did you have a good day?"

"I did have a good day," she says. "But I'm not having such a good evening. I don't have anyone to hang with. All my friends are out of town, and I'm stuck here. Alone."

Well, I think. How about them apples? I am neither especially bright, nor am I a Casanova. At the same time I do have a pulse, and as my mother had some months earlier observed, young people have certain *desires*. The question now is whether to be suave, aloof, or naïve. And the answer is, as Tootsy once said, whichever will get me the job.

"I could come over," I tell her.

"Or I could come over there."

I think about Mrs. Garcia and for some reason I'm embarrassed, though why I don't know. It isn't like she's my mother. And what difference would it make if she were? I'm an adult. I'm single. Sure, I'm more or less in love with someone else, or if I don't love her, I think about her constantly. But she's there and I'm here, and she's made it clear she doesn't want to be with me, which, of course, completely turns the truth on its head and I instantly hate myself for entertaining the thought. But it's been a long time since I've *been* with someone, as we say.

My next thought is that maybe there's something admirable in my concern about what people think, because it means this is still a special thing, this being with someone. Which means maybe I am not completely without either morality or responsibility, and so, in my mind, I leap five hours ahead and relish what has just happened, what we've done together, the intimacy, the warmth, and I'm thinking where do we go from here? Is this the start of something lasting?

All of this cogitation takes a nanosecond. I answer, almost instantly, "That would be great." And give her directions to my place.

I PREPARE.

I've already showered, so I look around for things to clean. There is nothing, because I have nothing. The bed is made. The dish is washed and put away. I brush my teeth. I wait. I listen to music. "That's the Way Love is," "I Guess I'll Have to Change My

Plans," "Don't Dream of Anybody But Me." Melancholy Bobby Darin, but it's like an appetizer that gets me ready for the big meal.

At eight there's a knock on the door, although I haven't heard a car pull up.

"Hey, Bass. You ain' in bed or nothin' are you?"

I let Mrs. Garcia in and think if Niki shows up now there will be no way to politely or even obscurely justify her presence. I can't say she's my cousin. I can't say we're only friends. Least believable of all would be the truth: she's the assistant to the guy who approved the loan for my truck. Yeah. Right.

"So you ready for tomorrow?" Mrs. G says.

"Sure," I say, not sure at all. "I don't know. What are we doing?"

Her expression is overly exasperated. She's having fun putting me on. "The vegetable stan? We gonna build it? You said you'd help."

I'm still thinking of Niki and the evening ahead of us, so it's hard to focus on rutabagas. "Uhhh. Are we ready? I mean, do we have materials, and tools, and plans?"

"We got everything," she says with certainty. "Anyway, we got the plans for sure, 'cause I drawed 'em. The materials we need to buy. And the tools? I figured maybe you had some."

It's true I do own one universal tool for working on the tractor. It's called a quarter. I drop it in a phone and call for help.

"Nope," I say. "No tools."

"Then how we gonna build this?" she says, thoroughly put out.

I take a deep breath and let it out slowly. I think a minute. If we rent tools, it's more money, and I suspect this project is the very definition of a shoestring operation. On the other hand, what could we need? A hammer? A saw? I don't know. I'm not a builder.

But I know someone who is. "Let me make a call," I tell Mrs. Garcia.

I go through an old notebook and find Owen Youniacutt's number from back in the SWT days. If he didn't know my name when we worked together, I doubt things have improved in the last ten months, but I can't think of who else to call.

A woman picks up and I ask for Owen. He must be standing next to her, because in one second, without a word from her, he's on the line.

"This is Jim, Jim Bass," I say and wait a beat.

"Whadja do? Turn the greasy side up? You in jail? How many people'd'ya kill?"

He does remember me, and he's laughing. For some reason I'm flustered with his response, as if I actually have to explain I wasn't in an accident nor have I been arrested. I tell him about tomorrow's project and ask if I can borrow some tools.

"Nope, never, no how. I don't loan out my tools to nobody," he says. And then he adds, "Do you even know what the hell you're doing?"

"Not really," I tell him truthfully.

"Does anybody who'll be there know what they're doing?"

I look at Mrs. Garcia. "I wouldn't bet the farm."

"Well, shit," he says. "Where is this place?"

I ask Mrs. G and relay the directions.

"Materials on site?"

I tell him, no, I have to pick them up. I say I'll have to use my big flat bed, because I don't have anything else.

"Well, shit," he says again. "Be at my house at six. Drive your car, not your truck. We'll use my pickup. Wait a minute. Changed my mind. Drive the tractor. I want to see that fancy horse of yours. You say you've got plans?"

"So I've heard."

"How about a B.O.M.?"

"I don't know what that is," I tell him.

"Christ on a crutch. This is going to be fun. B.O.M. Bill Of Materials. Just bring the friggin' drawings with you and we'll figure it out as we go."

I tell him thanks. Thanks very much. I'll see him in the morning. Then before I can say goodbye, he cuts in. "Hey college boy, you gettin' any lately?"

I think about Allison and I think about Niki. I've lost the one and by now it seems I've been stood up by the other. "Nope," I tell him. "Not even a little."

AFTER MRS. G LEAVES, the phone rings. It's Niki. My heart jumps at the sound of her voice. She says she's sorry, but can she have a rain check? Something's come up and she can't make it. Fine, I tell her. No problem. I say I have to get up early tomorrow anyway. And then very, very gently, I set the phone back in its cradle. Sometimes I hate it when I'm right.

THE NEXT MORNING WHEN I pull up, Owen has his truck loaded. He's got more boxes and tool bags and *stuff* than I've ever known any one person to own. I recognize a compressor and a generator that's also a welding machine. There are coils of air hose, red and blue, and extension cords in orange and yellow. There are plastic cases, which I assume hold tools, and on a rack above the bed are two ladders.

"You look like a contractor," I say.

"I've built a thing or two."

Behind his pickup is a small flatbed trailer, maybe sixteen feet in length. It's got low side rails and dual axles, but the bed itself is empty. When he catches me looking at it he says, "For the material."

Before we leave, he checks out the KW and seems mightily impressed. I know it's a good tractor, but even so I'm thrilled that he approves. I fire it up and together we stand and listen to the slow rumble. He climbs in and checks the instruments, pokes his head into the sleeper. He shuts down the Cummins and, once he's out front by the grill, heaves open the cowl. When he sees the engine he whistles.

"Well la-de-da. Generally my preference is a Pete, but this here is a fine horse. Just one thing, though. What's with *Buttercups?*"

"I've been busy," I tell him. "But I'm getting that changed."

On the way to Lowe's I ask about all his tools and where he learned to build things, and in fact what *has* he built?

"Once upon a time, chicken coops, fences, barns, corrals. My folks owned a spread. Mom still does. Now it's mostly repairs on my place, but you know how it is. Gotta buy a tool a month or I get the heebie-jeebies."

"Sounds like you lived on a farm," I say.

"Oh, no," he says. "Never a farm. A ranch. There's a difference, you know. A big difference. Don't confuse the two, or you just might get poked in the nose."

I suppose there is a difference, though I've never given it a lot of thought. Where I came from, they say *farm* even when the people raise livestock. I remember Mr. Jeffers being called a pig farmer, not pig rancher, but this isn't the kind of hair-splitting I feel like pursuing with Owen Youniacutt, when the sun is barely up and I haven't yet had a cup of Joe.

We don't say much during the twenty-minute ride to the store, but he asks to see the plans. I'm embarrassed to hand over the paper Mrs. Garcia gave me. It's a single, lined sheet torn from a notebook, and contains nothing more than a child's drawing of a box. There are no dimensions listed or any scale indicated. You would only know what it represented if someone first told you, and then they would have to point to the various features so that you'd know which was a door and which were the flaps covering the windows. Owen looks at the paper, chuckles, balls it, and tosses it in the first trash can we pass. I feel bad because I could have made her a great set of drawings given some time and a clear picture of what she wanted.

"She give you money?" he asks.

I shake my head. "I figured she'd repay me when I give her the bill."

"Tell you what, Chief. You figure in one hand and shit in the other, and I'll give you a side bet on which fills up first."

I want to say, You don't know Mrs. Garcia, but then I wonder if I know her either.

We walk down the lumber aisles, me pushing a flat cart and him designing in his head. We pick up pressure-treated four-by-fours and plywood, then regular two-by-fours and construction-grade plywood. We get hinges and handles and galvanized nails. We get a roll of number 30 felt paper and three squares of asphalt roof shingles.

"How many people coming to this shindig?" Owen asks.

"Dunno," I say. "Maybe five or six, counting us." For all I know, it's two counting us, but I don't want to make what seems to me a bad situation worse.

With this information we go to the paint department and get some rollers and trays, some brushes, some primer.

"You got any mis-mixed paint?" Owen asks the woman behind the counter. "Any rejects or come-backs?" She points us to two five-gallon pails of some god-awful grayish purple abomination.

"Ten bucks," she says.

"For both?"

She shrugs. "Sure. Why not?"

We add the paint to the load.

We're walking toward the checkout and Owen looks at the ceiling for inspiration. "What else? What else?"

I know he isn't talking to me. He's building this thing in his head. He snaps his fingers.

"Hold up there, Scout," he says.

I watch our order while he runs to the commercial sales section, and then outside. Five minutes later he's back with a nice exterior door.

"Special order return," he says. "They wanted half off, which is bullshit. I told him half of half off, and he went for it. But now we gotta buy a big hasp and some carriage bolts, and a *really* big padlock."

We get all of that, and even with Owen's negotiating the bill comes to nearly five hundred dollars on my credit card, about the same as filling the tractor with diesel. My knees are a little weak at the thought. I know Mrs. Garcia will pay me back. I mean I really do know it. I can't imagine she'd forget, but still...five hundred dollars.

It's a short drive to the location Mrs. G told me about. I only recognize the spot because I see her car beside the road. There is no address as such, because there are no structures on this side of the road. Across the street, on the north side and to the west, I can see what is maybe a liquor store, though it's too far away to read the sign. We did pass a few homes to the east, but they appeared abandoned. Except that she has use of the land for free, I can't imagine why she'd want to locate here.

"Good spot, huh?" Mrs. G says when we exit Owen's truck. "People go that way in the morning," she points west, "and that way at night. We're on the going-home side, so they'll stop in here an get food for supper."

Maybe so, I think. But I'm not holding my breath.

The limits of the property are defined by stakes in the ground, with red ribbons tied to the top of each. I assume this handiwork is thanks to Mr. Pennybaker. In terms of a plot for a vegetable stand, it's a substantial piece of land. My guess is half an acre. Aside from the fact that I can't imagine anyone stopping, there will be plenty of room to park if they ever do. The specific area Mrs. Garcia has picked for the shack is relatively smooth, and as flat as you could hope for. Using her foot, she's drawn a rough rectangle in the dirt to show us where to build. Across the street the land slopes up through scrub to the foothills, and then into the mountains. We're just west of Cajon Pass and I fear the day the wind comes howling through there from the desert. Our stand—her stand—will tumble roof over foundation all the way to Chino.

I introduce Owen to Mrs. Garcia. They shake hands, but I sense wariness on both sides, as if he's a salesman and she's a customer looking for a discount. As they're eyeing each other Big Lupe pulls up in his Chevy. All four doors spring open, disgorging a small group onto the property.

"Hi everybody," I say. "This is Owen Youniacutt. Owen, this is Big Lupe, Hector, Angela, Little Lupe and Vanessa."

The baby is wrapped in blankets, lying in Angela's arms. Owen jerks his chin by way of greeting, and the others look slightly off to the side, or down at their feet.

Of Mrs. G's children, only Maria Elena is missing. I doubt she'll show today. From snips of conversation with my neighbor, it sounds like the oldest daughter is moving emotionally further from her mother and her siblings. Everyone is uncomfortable with the situation, but no one seems able to bring her back into the fold.

Owen starts toward his trailer. "We ain't making nothing but shadows here. You three want to help me unload?"

In turn he nods at Big Lupe, Hector, and me. We haul the material to the spot Mrs. G has picked, a location well back from the road, which I'm glad to see. I'd rather have a potential customer drive by so that Angela misses a sale, than have a car veer slightly off the road and kill someone.

Owen directs us to lay the greenish four by fours on the ground, then puts the pressure-treated plywood on top. We use the sheets to square the frame, and I have the notion this project is the grownup equivalent of Lincoln Logs. Behind us the generator is running the compressor, and the compressor is running the nail gun.

"Bro," Hector says to no one in particular and without indicating a specific piece of equipment. "I could use me one a those, you know?"

As fast as he can walk from one location to the next, Owen uses the gun to fasten the various pieces we've put in place. I'm surprised Vanessa doesn't wake and cry with the blasts of noise, but she remains asleep in Angela's arms. Mrs. G has told me Angela is still paying back the money I'd given her, at five or ten dollars a week. I think it's more painful for the mother to accept the money than it is for the daughter to pay it.

"What about me?" Mrs. Garcia shouts over the percussions. "I wanna do sumthin' on account a this was my idea."

Owen takes a breath. He isn't the management type. He doesn't want to supervise. He'd rather do all the work himself than try to explain to someone else what needs to be done. Nevertheless, he drops the nail gun to his side, holding it just above ground by the blue hose, and thinks. He sets the gun on the plywood floor and sweeps his arm in a come here gesture.

"Give me a hand setting up this saw," he says

Together, they arrange a couple of saw horses and lay the door we just purchased over the top. This forms a table, where he places a slide miter saw. He makes her a cutting list and hands her a tape measure.

"You know how to read one of these?" he says.

"Whadaya think, that I got no sense? A course I can read it. Half is the little line between the two big lines, right?"

Owen had taken a step, but stopped mid-stride. He turns back to her and she gives him a smile.

"Una broma," she says. "You ain' the only one can joke, you know. Get on back an help those boys."

I am astounded by how quickly the shack goes up. In half an hour the floor is done and we begin building the walls in the dirt. We all work quickly because Owen never stops to think what's next. It's as though he's on to the next phase before the current one is completed. He points, says a word or two to one of us, and is off, lifting, hammering, pulling tools from his belt the way I've seen a secretary type or guitarist pluck the strings. He never looks, but has absolute confidence his fingers will find what he wants.

The front of the shack is framed for two large windows, but we sheet the entire wall, covering the openings. We tilt this up onto the floor and Owen fires a few nails to hold it in place. He gives Big Lupe and Hector each a hammer and has them attach a two-by-four as a brace to either end. Next we build the side wall with the man door.

I am pleased to recognize the components of the frame, things that I learned in school but had never seen in real life.

"King stud, jack stud, header," I say, pointing.

Owen smiles and gives me a thumbs-up. "Whaddya know? You did learn something."

At noon we break for lunch in the shade of the shack. Mrs. G has made tamales, and she serves iced tea from a large jug. But she doesn't eat with us. She plays with her grandchildren, first Vanessa, and then Little Lupe, whom she scoops up and seems to fly with, whirling him along the perimeter of the property, dipping over the pucker bushes like a crop duster.

I keep my eye on everyone, but especially on Angela. She is different today than when I last saw her. Happier. Lighter. She eats and talks and laughs. Somehow, though I doubt she has gained weight, she appears less gaunt. Her smile transforms her face.

Hector is different as well. He's subdued now and has been mostly silent except for comments about the generator or compressor. It's as if he and his wife have a limited happiness between them, and now that she has stolen a bit of his, he has less for himself.

I know the reality is somewhat different. Months ago Mrs. G told me Hector took one of his customer's cars to the beach. On the way there he bought beer and liquor, and on the way back crashed the car. He spent a night in jail, and I can only imagine the tension between him and Angela.

Thankfully, Big Lupe is just himself. He is willing to tackle any job regardless of how unpleasant, and he proves himself to be quite handy. When we're finished eating, Owen gets him started on the shed roof, which slopes from high in front to low in back. This allows two good-sized openings from which to conduct business, and when I stand back to look, is not as unattractive as I expected. Owen gets Lupe started by nailing down the first course of shingles, which is on the low side, so that subsequent rows will properly overlap and rain won't penetrate. After that, Lupe takes over, setting a steady pace for himself.

Owen takes me inside the building and hands me a reciprocal saw.

"Follow along the framing and cut out the window. We'll use the scrap as the awnings. They can close 'em up tight after hours, and haul 'em open for business."

I look at the saw, and then at the plywood, and then at Owen. I wonder whether he expects me to punch through with the tip of the blade. He shakes his head and takes back the tool.

"Plunge cut," he says. "Start at a steep angle, like so." He starts the cut, then hands me the saw. "Don't fuck it up. I don't want to buy more wood, even if it is your money." He leaves me with that thought.

By the time I have the two big squares cut out, Owen is back with hardware. We attach hinges, and then he rigs ropes and pulleys. To the outside we fix hasps for padlocks. I haven't had this much fun since…well, maybe basketball. But maybe not even then.

"Pancho," Owen calls to Hector when he sees him standing by the generator.

My skin prickles when he says it. I want to tell the group Owen never uses anyone's correct name. He calls me all sorts of things, too. I want them to know he is not being demeaning or racist. But Hector trots over as if everyone calls him as Pancho and he's only been waiting for his next assignment.

"No sense standing around playing pocket pool," Owen tells him. "Take that pail of primer there and pour yourself a tray-full. We got rollers in the bag. Start around the back side and by the time you're done we'll get to painting. Get your mother-in-law to help. That should keep her out of trouble."

Eventually we all have rollers or brushes in our hands and paint on our clothes. The details take longer than the main structure, but by late afternoon we step back to admire a functioning, painted, asphalt-shingled, locked-door vegetable stand. I can't believe it, and I don't think Mrs. G can either.

"Just like I drawed it," she says in wonder. "Now, only one thin missin."

Even though I'm twenty feet from Owen, I feel him bristle.

"You tell me what I forgot and I'll kiss a duck."

"The sign," she says. "It's gotta say *Angela's*."

And the last piece of puzzle clicks into place, at least for me. I know what has changed Angela's demeanor.

"You got a duck?" Mrs. G continues, smiling. "Or you wan me bring my own?"

"Save it," Owen says. "I didn't forget. The sign's in my garage. Angela, right? Big black and red letters?"

"Nooo," Mrs. Garcia says. "Angela's. Yellow and blue."

"Good," Owen says, "'Cause that's the way I did it. Yellow and blue. It was too wet to haul, but we'll put 'er on next week."

He walks off then to start loading his gear. When he's out of earshot, Mrs. Garcia turns to me.

"He's hokay, that friend of yours," she says. "I thin we gonna keep him."

CHAPTER SEVEN

TWO MONTHS RUNNING I haven't seen Niki when I've come in to make my truck payment. Maybe she's been out sick, or at lunch, or in a back room. For all I know she's been let go. Maybe that's what she meant when she said something came up. I wouldn't know, because she hasn't called since the evening our "date" didn't happen. She's the one who cancelled, so I figure if she hasn't felt it was important enough to let me know what happened, why should I check on her?

But today when I come in, she's there behind her desk, scribbling away at something as usual. She looks up then and crooks her finger to call me over. I feel like doing to her what she did to me, which is to say ignore her. But of course I don't because another part of me, the stronger part, wants some company.

When I came through the door, I'd angled toward a teller, but now I alter my direction and stand before Niki at her desk like a patron in a gallery asking for directions to the Wyeth paintings.

She says, "Sorry about, you know, the other night."

The other night? The other night means two days ago. It means last weekend, not last season. I shrug as if I can barely remember the incident myself. "Things happen."

"They do," she agrees. "They did. Can we try again?"

I don't know if we can or not, because I'm not certain what it is we're trying. Watching her now, the odds seem fifty-fifty I misunderstood earlier, substituting what I wanted for what she was actually offering. For sure she is more nonchalant, tapping the eraser of her pencil on the desk and smiling innocently up at me, than I would be in her position if I'd asked what I thought (all right, hoped) she asked. Given her current demeanor, she might only be checking tomorrow's weather forecast. If that was the case I could answer *chili today and hot tamale* and maybe get a laugh.

"What do you have in mind?"

"I know this will sound crazy since you drive so much."

"Sock it to me," I say.

"Okay. I need to see my aunt. I really owe her a visit, but I don't want to go by myself. I thought maybe you could ride along and then we'd have dinner or something."

I think about my schedule for the next few days. If Niki wants to make the trip this coming weekend, I could start my run this evening and be back late Friday.

"Where is she, your aunt?"

"Isla Vista. You know where that is?"

I laugh. "I was there two weeks ago. Or actually Goleta, but you could throw a rock from one to the other."

"Do you hate going back so soon?" She wrinkles her nose a little and bites her bottom lip, as if she's preparing for the discomfort of pulling off a bandage.

I shake my head. "Given a magic wand or a bigger bank account, that's where I'd live. If you like, after we see your aunt we could go on up to Solvang and check out the Danish town. May-be take a windmill ride."

"You can do that?" she says.

I suppose I was trying to be clever, but a windmill ride imme-diately sounds stupid, or at least it does to me. And now she be-lieves it, unless she's putting me on, and if she is, she's convincing. Worse of all, a windmill ride sounds vaguely off-color, though I imagine that's only in my head and not at all in hers.

"No," I say. "Just kidding. What time should I pick you up?"

She hands me a slip of paper with her name, address, phone number, Saturday's date, and the time to meet her. Some guys wouldn't like being seen as predictable as she apparently sees me. Seen as a sure thing. Guys want to be dangerous, mysterious. Se-cret agents. Spies. But I'm flattered by the premeditation her note implies. It feels good knowing she cares enough to keep track of when I'll be in and what I'll likely say. In my mind I check off Saturday as definitely busy, and for Sunday—Sunday I count as a maybe.

MY RUN GOES ACCORDING to plan and I'm at Niki's house by sev-en Saturday morning. It turns out she lives not far from me. We aren't neighbors exactly, but the drive between us isn't more than fifteen minutes. She lives on Jefferson, south of the freeway. It's an older neighborhood, probably from the twenties. The houses are small and uniform, painted the color of dinner mints: yellow and pink and green. Driving along her street is like driving on a game board.

I knock at the door and when she lets me in, I see rounded archways and rounded corners where the walls meet the ceilings. The floors are a light-toned hardwood and the one in the front room has a decorative border of a darker color.

"Cool floor," I tell her.

"From the twenties," she says, then adds, "I'm ready if you are."

On a wingback chair near the door is a large, canvas courier's bag, and on the floor next to the chair is her purse. I wonder if in the bag is something for her aunt, or if it holds a change of clothes, a toothbrush, and something frilly. I resist the urge to look too closely, but my heart beats a little faster.

"We can take my car if you'd like," she says. "It might be more fun."

And it is. Beside the house I see a rag-top Volkswagen Beetle, dark green body and tan roof. I don't want to leave my car in the street all day, and possibly overnight, so I pull it around hers and in front of the detached garage. As I'm locking the car door, she throws me her keys. "You drive."

It is early May, which means we can expect weather anywhere from damp overcast to scorching heat. Or both. We pull away from her house in the former, and therefore leave the car's top up. Through San Dimas and up over Kellogg Hill, the sky is gray as dove's feathers. But by the time we hit the outskirts of L.A., the sun has burned away the low haze and the sky is too glaring to view without sunglasses. And then, marvelously, as we climb out of Simi Valley and toward Castaic Lake, the clouds dissipate and the foothills pop up like paper cutouts from a child's book.

We are going to the coast, but instead of driving directly west I take the inland route, up 5 and across 126, just for some different scenery. We pass the gully where episodes of "Combat" were filmed and where one of the actors died in a helicopter crash. We travel on through Piru and then Santa Paula.

Santa Paula, I think. Saint Paula. My mom. I wonder how she's doing. I haven't talked with her since Christmas. I know I should call, but I'm afraid all we'll talk about is Allison and the baby, and I don't want to do that. I want to think of them in my own way so I can control the vision. If I don't know any better, I can believe they miss me like I miss them. But Mom could spoil that. She could say they're doing just fine, which is of course just what I want on one level. Except on another I want it to be the opposite.

"Penny for your thoughts," Niki says.

"You'd be wasting your money."

"And why is that?"

"Because I'm not thinking anything. Just enjoying the day."

Just before Ventura we pull into a gas station to lower the convertible top. As soon as we're back on the freeway, we turn north and run beside the Pacific. Though the water is undoubtedly cold, wetsuited surfers bob like seals beyond the breakers. To our right are the deeply furrowed cliffs from which hang gliders leap. That is a sport I might enjoy after the fact, but every second in the air would be spent knowing I was about to fall from the sky and smash like a ripe pumpkin against the ground.

As we drive we listen to the radio and I admit to Niki I'm not up on current songs. She laughs and bends forward, tuning in an oldies station, thinking this is what I mean. But the songs we hear are not old enough by two decades for my taste. I tell her to listen to whatever she likes, and she changes stations again.

All this time, and it's been an hour now, we don't hold hands or touch in any way. Someone watching might think we are just friends, or even a notch down from there. We might only be acquaintances. And their guess would be as good as mine, because I don't know what we are either. One problem is that I'm working too hard to figure everything out, instead of just enjoying the experience.

I am thinking, of course, about Allison, which makes even riding in the car with Niki feel like cheating. Simultaneously, I wonder how can you cheat on a person you haven't seen in almost a year, because you left her, and she left you even more, and took with her your child, the child you had together, because that's exactly what you wanted her to do, only not really, or not so completely, or at least not so permanently. Immediately this leads me to wish I had a second chance with Allison, knowing that if I did I would make the same decisions as before, and therefore what's the point?

That's the Allison part of what's going through my head.

The Niki part is that she seems to like me, though I haven't worked out how much, or in what way. It's either in *that* way, or in the way of a friend, meaning someone to talk to, someone to drive her to see her aunt. Someone to kill a day with. The truth is I don't know a thing about her other than she's attractive, that she has a job, and that she lives in a house. (Rented or purchased, I'm not sure.) For all I know she has strange predilections, wacky friends, or no friends. She might torture small animals or volunteer at the homeless shelter. She is a mystery, and I'm embarrassed to admit that is part of her appeal. It's the finding out that attracts me.

We decide to exit in Montecito and go to the Biltmore for a bite to eat. Niki said she was hungry, but then orders only orange juice. I just have coffee and a sweet roll. The bill is a breathtaking twenty-two dollars, and I thank God she didn't want the buffet.

Even with the stops we arrive at the aunt's home by midmorning. Or rather, we arrive at the aunt's apartment. She lives on the second floor of a sea green, sixties vintage, motel-style building. The handrails are wrought iron, and the window frames are aluminum. The complex is altogether unattractive, but it is clean and functional. The aunt's unit faces the water, and I imagine the view is beautiful most of the year.

For security we put up the car's top, and as I lock the doors I notice Niki has left her purse and taken the big canvas bag.

From this I conclude the bigger bag holds a gift for her aunt. The knowledge makes me both happy and sad. Happy, because the pressure is off now, but so is the anticipation. The ride home, for me at least, will be different from the ride here. I think of the aphorism, *Abstinence without opportunity is no virtue*. Only now it doesn't seem as funny as I once thought.

Niki walks ahead of me up the stairs and knocks on the door. A woman, neither so old or so bent as I'd imagined, answers.

"Sweetheart!" she says, and throws her arms wide to accept her niece.

When they are done hugging, Niki says, "Aunt Julia, this is my friend Jim. Jim, this is my Aunt Julia."

We both smile and say hello. I offer my hand but she looks askance, pulls me to her, and hugs me as well. Even though the perpetrator is an older woman, the feeling is pleasant, and I realize I've not been hugged in quite a while.

We follow Julia inside and it is unclear to me whether Niki has prepared her for our visit. When she opened the door, she looked mildly surprised, but minutes after we're seated Julia produces a tray of snack crackers and cheese. She places the tray on a coffee table convenient to the three of us. Niki and I sit side by side on a couch, Aunt Julia sits across from us in an upholstered chair. Luckily, Niki is on the side closest to her aunt. She reaches into her bag and does, indeed, pull out some cookies. She reaches in again and this time gives Julia a little wrapped gift. "Just a book," she says. "I hope you like it."

Julia says she's thrilled, sets the wrapped gift aside without opening it, and they immediately fall into conversation about relatives, mostly Niki's mother, who is Julia's sister. They ignore me completely, which is fine because it allows me to tune out at once.

Instead of talking or listening, I check the room and find the decorating uninspired, but then who am I to talk? The only thing on my walls at home is a calendar from Continental Brokers, each month showing a different tractor-trailer against some picturesque scenery. January is the red hills of Sedona, March the stark beauty of Death Valley sand dunes. The one exception, and the picture I like best, is August. (I looked ahead.) The picture shows a group of fellows playing basketball in a parking lot. One guy has pulled up and is shooting toward a real hoop and painted backboard affixed to the side of a forty-foot van. A mural of bleachers with cheering fans spreads to the front and rear. A notation below the picture says the hoop collapses flat against the side of the van for traveling. That's the trailer I want someday.

There is one thing unusual about Julia's place, and that is a sheet covering something very large and oddly shaped in one corner. I don't say anything, of course, but suddenly the talking stops because they have caught me staring.

"You like my Christmas tree?" Julia says.

It's almost summer. How do I answer her? I gesture neutrally.

"I got tired of buying a fresh tree every year, putting it up, taking it down, packing the ornaments and lights. So I got one of those nice plastic jobbies and now I just leave it up all the time. I take the sheet off after Thanksgiving and put it back up after New Year's. The rest of the year I don't fool with it."

At most, I realize, Aunt Julia is eccentric. She does not appear crazy or ill or destitute, and again I wonder at Niki's motivation to see her *urgently*.

The two of them visit some more while I daydream, and then our visit ends abruptly but pleasantly. Soon we are once again at the open door, where Julia is hugging us and wishing us well.

"Come see me again. Both of you."

She waves, and before we reach the stairs, I hear the click of the latch.

I look at my watch. It's noon. "What do you want to do now?"

With my new understanding of our situation, I have forgotten about Solvang, but Niki reminds me. When she does, I find to my discredit that I'd just as soon head back home. Solvang is west and somewhat north of where we are now, farther rather than closer to home. In other circumstances I'd welcome this or any of ten other fun or romantic spots within a few hours' drive—Cambria or Morro Bay or Pismo. But I realize this is not romance and Niki is not Allison. In more ways than one I feel like a punctured balloon.

Nevertheless, we put the top down once more and head out, and despite myself the beautiful day has a positive effect. At this point along the coast, 101 runs due west. We follow it to Gaviota, and just before the highway turns us inland, Niki spots two whales in the surf, both blowing water and slapping their enormous tails. She is so delighted that I am delighted for her. I look at her with the sun coming from straight overhead, lighting her hair and shoulders, and I think she is really quite lovely.

In Solvang we park on a side street, then walk along Mission, veering occasionally to see a windmill or the Little Mermaid water fountain. In front of a conically shaped phone booth, Niki stops to make a call, just so she can say she did it, but then she can't think of anyone to phone so we go on. We have a late lunch in a little coffee shop and there learn Solvang means Sunny Fields in Danish. I tell Niki that Sunny Fields was W.C. Fields' illegitimate daughter, that she had a successful career as a stripper, and that *her* daughter now makes the chocolate chip cookies. Without blinking an eye, Niki says that's all true but I forgot to mention that Sunny's grandfather, Marshall, started the department store.

"Oh. Right," I say. "I did forget that."

On the walk back to the car I'm thinking this has turned out to be a pleasant day after all. The sun is shining, we had a nice meal, and the conversation was agreeable. The experience wasn't everything I'd hoped for, it wasn't *complete* in that certain way, but it was fine. I wanted companionship, and that's what I got. Nothing happened that would later have to be excused, or would make either of us uncomfortable. I can go into the bank and pay my bill, smile and wave at her, and be on my way. Niki won't have any explaining to do to Mr. Foote.

We stroll up Copenhagen Drive, the last street before her car, and pass the King Frederik Inn. There are hanging baskets of flowers bracketing the entrance, and Niki stops to look. I believe she is admiring the color, but now, for the first time, she takes my hand.

"This okay?" she says.

And that's that.

We fetch her bag from the car, come back to the hotel and get a room, and we don't come out until Sunday.

CHAPTER EIGHT

J UNE FIFTEENTH. AMANDA'S BIRTHDAY.

At the toy store I consider getting her a wooden pull train with two connected cars and a round-headed engineer, but reject the idea in favor of a doll. I don't know what kids can do at one year old, but I suspect it doesn't include operating a train. The doll has no moving parts, is too big to swallow, and looks sort of like a mushed pillow, but I decide I don't like it. I replace the doll with a book, and the book with a mechanical device that pops plastic balls out of a spout, then rolls them along a trough back into a clear holding container. The balls are in primary colors, which I guess is a good thing for kids. It seems their stuff is always gaudy. And the balls are contained in the clear plastic tube, which also seems like a good idea because that way they won't get lost. But I don't really care for this either.

I return the gadget to the shelf and instead unfold a small pink and white blanket with alphabet blocks and baby giraffes and kangaroos. This is nice. Nothing to break. Nothing to go wrong. Soft and inviting. But aren't these for babies? And are you still a baby at one?

I refold the blanket and plink out a tune on a tiny xylophone, though I suspect Allison would consider the choice of a musical instrument as a deliberate act of aggression. A sort of insult-to-injury thing.

I leave the store, skipping the notion of a toy completely. I realize I'm probably only getting something to impress Allison anyway, because Amanda won't know that whatever it is came from me, and in fact she doesn't know who I am anymore than I know who she is. So I decide on a card instead, which now seems more appropriate as it will convey all the sentiment a toy would, and will get there quicker, although that may not be especially important because unless it arrives in the next hour anything I select will be late.

But next door at the card shop I realize I don't have a clue what the sentiment is that I hope to suggest. So I buy nothing there either and go home empty-handed, telling myself that this is the way things are, and whatever happens in life is exactly what should happen, though I don't believe that for a second and curse myself for not planning better.

In this way I miss my daughter's first birthday.

CHAPTER NINE

THE GOOD NEWS COMING from my weekend with Niki is that I'm finally and truly and forever over Allison. She, Niki, is beautiful and smart and funny. She has a good job, and maybe most importantly she's here in the flesh. So to speak.

The further good news is that there is no offsetting bad news. I am happy, and have been for such a long stretch that I must revise my world view, developed, I have to say, as a direct result of my parents. Their view is this: Karma or God or fate extracts a toll for happiness. Or if not a toll exactly, it seeks equilibrium. The same way nature abhors a vacuum, karma or God or fate abhors an imbalance of emotions. Certainly my father believes that, and until recently I'd have bet my mother did as well. My grandmother, my father's mother (of course) actually said as much. If Kitty and I were having too good a time in her presence, she would scold us and warn, "Laugh before dinner, cry before bedtime."

Her philosophy, and my father's, is that lives are weighed on a balance-beam scale, and you must therefore spend as much time in negative territory as positive. A stretch of events equaling a plus four (winning a game, having pizza at lunch, making all the green lights) earns you an equivalent minus (breaking a shoe lace, missing a lay-up, getting celery in your lunch instead of malt balls). In their world, sadness must balance happiness to keep everything spinning joyfully (and mournfully) along.

I used to think the same way, but no longer. And even if it were true, I now have a hedge. Before I met Niki, I'd endured such a long period of sadness that I'm due an extensive run in the opposite direction. And in fact she and I spend the summer in pure delight. When our schedules match up, we take day or week-end trips, and the bigger the block of time we have the farther we travel. We drive up the coast to Big Sur and San Francisco and out to Napa for the balloon rides. We camp and hike in Arrowhead, and a few times travel to Las Vegas. On one such outing we visit Hoover Dam in the morning and later have lunch at Boulder Marina. After we eat, I kneel down on the edge of the dock, and even before I start throwing popcorn, the carp begin to boil in front of me. They are a wriggling mass, climbing over one another's backs so that the ones on top are actually out of the water. Their toothless mouths gape and smack audibly. They are disgustingly funny and Niki, who has never seen such a thing, says, "Ewww." When I do throw handfuls of popcorn, the fish curl and dive and wrap in such a tangle that if they were thinner, like eels, I believe they'd tie themselves into one inextricable knot.

When I'm out of popcorn, they line up again like hungry dogs waiting for a treat. And then for some reason, maybe just to see whether I can, I stab my hands into the water and pull out one golden, giant, sucking carp. I lift it toward Niki, holding it close to her face and say in my best fish accent, "Give us a kiss."

She shoves me, and I nearly tip backward so that I have to drop the fish or fall into the lake. The carp flops and shudders on the deck, and then he's into the water and swimming away. Niki laughs, then I laugh. We hug and kiss and the sun bounces off the water. Some of the diners cheer us on. We are the ideal couple. The center of attention. This, I figure, is what life's all about.

But it isn't just my love life that's going well. My little business is also humming along. There is plenty of work and no break-downs, so that money comes in more or less steadily. My bills get paid and there's cash in the bank. For four months it seems things couldn't be better.

It's true I don't see Mrs. G like I used to, but whenever our paths cross I do get updates about the children. I learn Guadalupe now makes occasional trips to his company's facility in Oregon and that he has a larger crew under his direction. I find out Maria Elena is also doing well at her work, though the rift between her and her mother is a wound time has not healed. Mrs. G tells me her daughter has recently changed her name from Garcia to Grassley.

"She toles me it will help her move up in the company. But then I toles her right back, *caca*, whas a matter with you? You ashamed to be Mexican or somethin'? So then she cries an hollers an toles me I should unnerstan', but if I doan, I can mine my own business."

While I'm hearing this, nodding and sympathizing, I decide never to let Mrs. G know about my own name change. She wouldn't appreciate mine was for a different reason. Mine wasn't about shame. Not heritage shame anyway.

But the first thing I hear about whenever I see Mrs. G is Angela and the vegetable stand. She tells me things got off to a slow start because "our" vegetables weren't ready to harvest by the time the stand was opened, so they had to go out and buy produce from other farmers. I wonder aloud how she could make any money doing that, but Mrs. G says making money wasn't so much the point. She says the idea was to give Angela something to do so she'd feel better about herself. So she'd have something else to think about besides Hector and the kids. Also, Mrs. G had figured Hector would never neglect the babies, so if Angela wasn't home to take care of them, he would have to be.

"Prolem is," she says, "I fine out sometimes he drops the kids at the neighbor's an goes off drinkin'. At lease he always comes home again."

I tell her I'm proud of Angela, but I'm even more proud of her. After all, it was Mrs. G who got things rolling.

When I say these things, I am being magnanimous but also sincere. Sincere because both women deserve recognition for what they've accomplished, and I honestly do admire them. And magnanimous because—why not? Things are going great for me.

Or they are until September, when my mother calls.

"Jimmy?"

"Hey, Mom. What's up?"

"Oh, Jimmy. Mrs. Trindle phoned. First she called nine-one-one and then she called me and apologized right off the bat. She said she didn't mean to bother me, and she knew there was trouble between us, your father and me, not Mrs. Trindle and me, and…"

"Whoa, Mom," I say. "Take a breath and tell me what happened."

"Your father has had a stroke."

She says this clearly and matter-of-factly, so differently from her first comments it takes me a second to shift gears.

"He's alive?" I ask.

"Thank God."

And then she's back rambling. She tells me how the neighbor, Mrs. Trindle, noticed Dad's sprinklers had been running for quite some time. At first she let it go because Dad's car was in the drive, so she figured he was home and would take care of it himself. But then she saw the water was washing dirt into the street, and even though it wasn't *her* water, she knew Emil wouldn't allow such a thing. She came over looking for the shut-off, but when she couldn't find it, she went to the door and knocked and knocked, but no one answered. Then she looked in the window and saw him lying on the floor, his legs and arms all catawampus, bent back and spread out. The door was unlocked and she went inside, but he looked dead so she didn't want to touch him. But she did phone nine-one-one and they came right away.

"Now he's at Mercy," Mom says. "He needs someone with him. But Jimmy, I can't go back there. Not right now. Not yet."

It's clear what she's asking, but I don't volunteer. She's living her life now, and I want to live mine. Besides, I don't see that he deserves a sacrifice from either of us. I think of a lifetime of slights and disappointments Mom and I have endured, and interestingly in my column it isn't that he wouldn't help me buy the truck. No, the first thought in my head is a particular ballgame.

It wasn't a playoff or anything, just a game, but in all my years of Little League and the first three years of high school, this was the first one he'd been to. The first time he didn't have someplace more important to be. I was so happy. I wanted to show him how those tough games of catch with him had paid off. How I was proud that I'd stood up to his fast pitches and taken the pain time after time. Proud that even though I was afraid of him, I kept going.

We'd already started when he came to the field, and from centerfield I watched him climb the bleacher steps and sit next to Lew Daniels, a friend of Dad's from the foundry. Lew's son Chris was on the team with me. Lew and my dad were talking, but once when I was going up to bat I called out, "Hey, Dad" and he watched me strike out. Of course I wished I'd gotten a hit, but everyone strikes out sometime. I figured he must know that. And anyway there was lots of game left. I'd do something later that he'd get a kick out of. It would be something we'd relive at dinner, and he'd go on and on to Mom about this hit or that catch.

Nothing exciting happened until the top of the ninth. We were the home team, so I was out in the field, back in center. I was bent over, hands on my knees, then up and punching my glove, then walking back and forth to stay loose. There were two outs and we were up by a run. I watched the hitter and the runner on first, gauging what they had in mind and weighing that against our fielder's positions and Mike, our pitcher, and Brian behind the plate. But while I was doing this, I was also watching my dad and Mr. Daniels. They were talking and laughing.

Mike looked down and got the signal, nodded, gathered himself. He checked the runner, lifted his left leg, swiveled it across his body, and let fly a fast one.

Crack.

The runner took off, sprinting for all he was worth. I could tell the ball was well hit, and that it was coming between me and right. As it arced up, I took off running, keeping the ball in sight, watching for Eddy charging toward me from right field, gauging how far the ball would fly. I figured I had the advantage, because Eddy would have to backhand a catch and I could reach straight out, the direction I was running. I called it, and called it, and called it.

Now I watched the ball and the fence. The ball and the fence. Six feet high, chain link. The shot was going to be a homer, and with a man on and not much time left, it would be hard for us to come back. But I could stop them, right here, right now.

I watched Eddy slow up. Good, I thought. I want this catch. I *need* this catch. I timed my jump, climbed the chain link with my cleats, caught the ball, and won the game.

But I'd had to reach far over the wire barbs atop the fence to do it. My gloved hand was outside the field, so that when I came down the spikes dug into the skin. I was pierced from ribs to armpit, hanging there like a hooked fish.

"Jesus," Eddy hollered, and tried to lift me off. But he could only ease the pressure.

Bert Larson ran from left and George Fallon up from second. Together the three of them got me up, and clear, and down again. I was embarrassed to be hurt, so I stood as straight as I could, though I was holding my arm tight to my side. Blood soaked my jersey. I tried to smile, but my face just wrinkled up. The stands broke into a roaring cheer. I looked for Dad and saw he was still bending Mr. Daniels' ear. I realized then, he'd only come to the game to talk with his friend. He'd never seen a thing I'd done.

"Jimmy?"

"Uh-huh."

"So you'll go see your father? You'll let me know how he's doing?"

"Yeah, sure," I tell her. "I'll go see him."

Omission, commission. Seemingly opposite, but sometimes not.

Not guilty, innocent. Seemingly equal, but sometimes not.

I CALL NIKI, TELLING her about Dad and that I have to go back to see him. She's encouraging, even sweet, and wishes him, and me, all the best. Of course she says she will miss me terribly, and I tell her the same. What I don't tell her is that if I can manage the time off, I intend popping across the ole Mississipp to Illinois and seeing Allison as well. Now that I'm completely over her, I see no harm in a visit. And while my mother might be satisfied with a phoned-in report, I figure as long as I'm traveling I might as well kill that bird too. My life will then be free of social obligations insofar as the ones outside of those I enjoy with Niki.

My problem is the business. For several months I have used Continental Brokers to our mutual benefit, but that doesn't mean we're joined at the hip. Conrad has at least two dozen truckers he can call on, and I'm aware that commerce is sometimes a matter of habit. If I'm gone for any length of time I fear he may forget me, so before I tell him my plans I consider alternatives.

I phone Terry at SWT and after a bit of BS I tell him my predicament. I'm not above playing on his sympathy regarding my dad, and it has an impact.

"I lost my old man," Terry says. "There isn't a thing in the world I wouldn't give to see him again. You're lucky you have this chance."

Until now I haven't felt lucky, but maybe he has a point.

"Have you thought about getting someone to cover for you?" Terry asks.

I tell him that's actually why I've called. Anyone I trust, and there aren't many, is already working for him. But since Terry is plugged into the industry, I wonder if he could recommend an unemployed driver. For a moment he's silent and I know he's giving my question serious consideration.

"If you had to pick someone from here," he says, "who would it be?"

Without hesitation I tell him Youniacutt. Owen.

Terry laughs. "He'd get the job done, all right. But he'll talk your ear off while he's at it. Of course you won't be there to talk to, so it might work out."

His suggestion isn't registering. How can Owen work for me if he's working for Southwest?

"The truth?" Terry says. "We're slower than hell. I'm finding maintenance jobs for the guys so I can stay out of trouble with the union, but it kills my cost/revenue ratio. This would give me a chance to furlough someone, especially if the someone wouldn't go complaining to the shop steward. I could talk to our boy if you'd like."

I tell him that would be great. Terry has my home number and says he'll have Owen call if it looks like everyone is in agreement. An hour later my phone rings.

"Hello?"

"Heard you got your tail in a crack."

I have to smile. "I do need to be gone awhile. Maybe four or five days."

"I could help you out that long," Owen says. "Besides, I've been wanting to drive that shiny red horse. You ever get the name changed on the door?"

"Not yet," I tell him. "But I'm going to do that."

"Can you have 'er changed by the time you take off?"

"I'd like to leave tomorrow," I say. "I doubt I could do it that quickly."

"Guess I'll have to tape over it then. I don't need no light-loafered truck-stop princess calling me Buttercups."

"I doubt that would happen."

"You never know," he says. "How'd your neighbor's vegetable business work out?"

I tell him it was rough going at first, but once the vegetables came in here at my place, Angela's costs went down. More than that, Mrs. G had the idea of parking friends' cars at the stand to make it look busier. When she did that, people began stopping on their own, and now there's a regular clientele. And one more thing: Mrs. G had a friend who owns a lunch truck stop by every afternoon. He sells the people hot food while Angela does the vegetables. The place is practically a roadside diner now.

"Crafty old broad," Owen says.

I tell him I have a load scheduled for tomorrow, so I'll postpone my trip another day if he needs time to make any adjustment.

"What adjustment?" he says. "Give me the damn keys and get out of the way."

With my replacement lined up, I feel I can call Conrad and tell him what's going on. When I say who's stepping in he laughs and says, "That knucklehead?" But I can tell he approves. I give him Owen's number so he can reach him at home if need be.

The next day I give Owen a brief tour of the rig. When we get to the trailer I tell him the left brake actuator rod sometimes sticks.

"Could have some dirt on it," he says. "Can you kick it free?"

I tell him I do. All the time. Then I give him Conrad's number so he can check in while he's on the road.

"That knucklehead," he says, and it occurs to me that despite the vast area covered, this is a small community.

I'VE MADE AIRLINE RESERVATIONS and Mrs. G says she'll take me to Ontario. I'd like Niki to do it, but of course she's working. I'm stuffing the last of my things into a backpack when there's a knock at the door.

Before I can answer Mrs. G steps in. "I figured you wasn't naked or nothin'," she says by way of a greeting.

The last item into my backpack is a teddy bear. I've neglected to wrap it, and naturally she sees it right off.

"Doan tell me thas for your papa."

"Who else?" I say.

She wags her head, but leaves it at that.

September's weather can be balmy or rainy or asphalt-meltingly hot, which is how this day is turning out. The sun is cooking Mrs. G's Gremlin, so that my skin prickles when I sit inside. Beads of sweat pop out on my forehead and drip from under my arms. I feel like I've sprung a leak.

We head up to Mission, and then east to the airport. I'm thinking about the days ahead and it seems Mrs. Garcia is thinking about something too, because neither of us speaks for a mile.

Finally she says, "Only my Guadalupe doan give me no problems."

This must be the end of a calculation she has made. I visualize a contest where her children stand on a stage and she passes them one by one, holding a hand over each head, and then reading the applause meter to determine a winner.

"Maria Elena," she continues. "Ay-way. I'd be better off with a dog. An my Angela, she blames me for sending her an Hector to the church tha time for counselin'. She says for him, bein in jail those couple a days did more good than talkin with the priest, only tha din lass long either. She says Hector thins if he doan do nothin bad, then thas good. Trouble is, he doan do nothin at all. Angela is feelin' so bad, yesterday she says the D word to me."

"Damn?" I suggest.

"Divorce. Then she gets mad at me when I say she should keep tryin'. She says what do I know? I only din need no divorce 'cause my husband save me the trouble by leavin'."

Apparently I've missed several episodes of this ongoing drama. I don't know if this jail incident is the same as the other, and I don't know anything at all about counseling. But if I get into it with her now, I'll miss my flight sure as anything.

We pass a drive-in theater on the left, and then long stretches of strawberry fields, fallow now, on the right. Mrs. G gives the fields a nod and says, "We ain't doin' that," as if I've suggested we should.

Four hours later I land at O'Hare and take a puddle jumper back to Muscatine. There I rent a Taurus, driving it north along 61 toward Davenport and then beyond to Benton Junction. It's nearly seven by the time I reach the hospital, but I'd bet the temperature has not cooled one degree. I'd forgotten that here in the Midwest night brings darkness but little other change, whereas in California we live for the relief of evening. I suppose it's the heartland's humidity that holds the heat. As proof I'm right, I'm dripping wet by the time I cross the parking lot and enter through the hospital's automatic glass doors.

"Hi," I say to the lady at the information desk. I imagine she's a volunteer. She's small and thin and gray-haired. Her eyes are a startling cornflower blue. "Can you tell me the room number for Emil Bassovich?"

She looks at the clock, as if the current time will determine where he's located. "Visiting hours are until nine. Family?"

"I'm his son," I tell her, and can't remember ever saying those words before.

She tells me four-thirty-four, bed A. When I ask how to get there, she says, "Hold on a minute, young man."

The woman writes the room and bed numbers on a large adhesive-backed tag. The label has a red, scalloped border and is the type that might say, **Hi, My Name Is** at a school reunion where everyone has changed too much to be remembered by sight. The woman tells me to put the sticker on my shirt and then points me to the elevator. She says to check in at the nurse's station before I go to his room. "Cee Cee," she says cryptically, which makes me think of Mrs. G.

I exit the elevator on the fourth floor. When the doors slide open, I'm looking at a sign that says Critical Care. Below it another sign says No Children, and below that No Cell Phones. I have neither. With me.

There's a dark-skinned nurse sitting behind a partition. Her white tag says Bujji, but I don't know if that is a first name or a last.

"Okay to see Emil Bassovich?" I ask. My shirt is too damp for my paper tag to stick, but I have it my hand. I show it to her like a cop flashing a badge.

"Mr. Bassovich is gedding an MRI. Id will be dwenty minutes or so."

Her voice is mid-eastern, rising and falling so lyrically it is nearly birdsong.

"You may waid here if you like. Or, you may come back lader. If thad is whad you choose, dell the woman downstairs do call me and I will have her send you up."

I'm tired and it feels late, though I realize seven o'clock here is only five at home. I don't have a room yet, so I figure I'll find a motel close by and turn in. I thank the nurse, saying I'll be back tomorrow.

On the way back to the elevator I see a large erasable board I missed earlier. The patients' names come first on the horizontal lines, and after them the gender, the attending doctor, the charge nurse, and any special instructions. I find my father's name and follow it across. There is the male symbol; circle and arrow. R. Smalley is the doctor. B. Singh the charge nurse. The cautions say *Choking Danger. No Liquids.*

Full circle, I think. Roger Smalley did my tonsillectomy when I was ten. He confined Kitty to bed for measles and made her miss a school picnic. He signed her death certificate.

I take the elevator down and I'm turning for the exit when I feel a hand on my shoulder. "Glad I caught you," the voice says. "I saw your name on the visitors' sign-in. I was about to have you paged."

It's Dr. Smalley. I don't have anything against him; none of his interactions with our family have been his fault. But even knowing that, he gives me the creeps. I associate him with all sorts of unpleasantness. He is shorter than I remember, and the skin on his neck is loose. His eyes are hooded. He's wearing a bowling shirt.

"Let's grab a bite," he says, still holding me. "We can chat a little. How's your mom?"

I stammer, "She's, you know, fine."

He turns me with his hand as if I were eight years old and needed steering. I want to resist. I want to say, Hey, Buddy, I'm all grown up now. I own my own business and have a girlfriend and we have *sex*. Except I don't say any of those things because I *am* eight years old as long as his hand is on me. Suddenly I do need steering.

We follow a yellow line on the floor and end up at the cafeteria, where he marches me in front of the food selections. I look at the deviled eggs and tuna sandwiches, the orange Jell-O, the carrot cake, and I never want to eat again. Nevertheless, we both pick a few items and I follow him through checkout. For the cashier's benefit he waves his hand over his tray and mine, then pays for both of us. I try to say thanks, but I'm still eight, so nothing comes out.

At the table we pull out plastic chairs, leaving one on either side unmoved so that we don't sit beside each other. Dr. Smalley pinches together two packages of Sweet'N Low, shakes them like an old thermometer, and tears the tops from both. He stirs the contents into his iced tea and fixes me with a stare.

"When I asked about your mother, I guess what I was really doing was acknowledging the rift between her and your father. To be truthful, I was hoping she would come herself."

I mumble something meant to excuse her, something about wanting to see a different part of the country, but even to me it makes no sense. Dr. Smalley seems not to notice. It's clear he has a speech prepared and means to deliver it regardless of which family member is on the receiving end.

"Sometimes a death in the family, especially the death of a young person, is like rot," he says. "In the dark that rot eats away at everything and everyone. But out in the sun it dries up and blows away. I believe perhaps that's what your mother was looking for, a little sun."

He doesn't know anything.

"Could be," I tell him.

"Could be, indeed. And could be for you as well. You left out of here pretty darn sudden yourself. Would I be off the mark speculating you went looking for a little sunshine?" Dr. Smalley pushes around the beef stroganoff on his plate as if he wishes he'd picked something else. He scoops a chunk of meat onto a fork but then sets the fork on the plate. "I guess California would be the place for that, huh? Lots of sun out there."

I want to tell him he's veered from the metaphorical to the literal, and thereby lost the meaning of both. I push away my untouched plate and look at my watch.

"I'm going to get a room," I tell him. "I'll be back tomorrow."

Though he hasn't had a bite either, Dr. Smalley dabs at his mouth with a paper napkin. "No need for a room," he says. He cocks a cheek up from the chair and fishes something from his pants pocket. "I took the liberty of gathering your father's personal things. Not strictly protocol, I know, but we're all friends here." He hands me a key. "Stay at your folks' place. It's close and it's free. There might even be something in the fridge. Get a good night's sleep and we'll talk again in the morning."

The last place in the world I want to be is my old home. I've left behind that part of my life, with all the old mistakes. I only accept the key from him as the path of least resistance. I stand, pushing my chair away with the backs of my legs, and pick up the tray. But before I can leave I have to say something.

"Just because Mom left doesn't mean she doesn't care."

Dr. Smalley raises his eyebrows as if this shocks him. "Of course not," he says, innocent as can be. "I never meant to indicate otherwise. For either of you."

I FIND A MOTEL on Tremont and settle in, meaning I lie on the bed and kick off my shoes and turn on the television. The picture comes in grainy, as if someone is shaking salt and pepper onto the dancers. I change channels, but the picture quality is the same and the programs don't improve either. There's a woman selling some sort of complex apparatus that, along with diet and other exercise, is supposed to help you lose weight while it flattens your stomach.

No shit, I think. Diet and exercise to lose weight. Now there's some original thinking. I hurl my pillow at the screen. "There were no fat prisoners at Auschwitz," I shout. "You want to lose weight? Don't eat. It's that simple."

I turn the channel to someone training dolphins, and then to a telethon raising money for a Public Broadcast station. Peter Noone is on a stage, singing to an audience of mostly older women. They've got tightly permed hair, and he got his teeth fixed.

There's nothing worth watching, and I grow angrier with each performer and each program, not because they're lousy, but because somehow they are all Dr. Smalley hinting I'm not a good son. Even so, I don't turn off the television. If I did, I would still hear the doctor in my head, but without any distraction he would be louder, so I settle for watching the dolphins as the least offensive of the bunch.

At eleven I shower and then turn in. The sheets are clean and cool; the faint odor of a pine cleaner is not altogether unpleasant. Nevertheless, I lie awake for hours, thinking of more things than my brain can handle. Maybe I do sleep a little, because all those thoughts mash up into one stew, where Kitty becomes Amanda, and I'm kissing Allison, who is Niki.

But later still when I dream of Dad, he is just Dad. I wonder who he'll be when I see him tomorrow.

SEVERE BUT NOT LETHAL is how Dr. Smalley described Dad's stroke. "Severe but not lethal," I repeat over and over on the way to his hospital room. I have not seen my father in six years, and in that time I've spoken less than a hundred words to him. We are not close. We aren't pals, as I've heard other sons describe their fathers. But neither is he a stranger. I am so frightened he will die. I am so frightened that I am angry with him beyond description. How could you do this? I want to ask him. After all we've been through already, how could you?

At the nurse's station I say good morning to a different nurse, this one also dark skinned but small as a child. I can't imagine she weighs a hundred pounds. When I ask to see my father she simply smiles and nods.

Until now I have been walking with a crisp, purposeful stride to show anyone watching how matter-of-factly I'm handling the situation. But once I pass the nurse's station my pace slows as if I'm coming to the limit of an elastic tether, or walking through air that has suddenly thickened to the consistency of water. That's it, I think, like trying to walk under water.

I enter the room, and though it is a double, there is only one occupant. He's near the window, with the drape surrounding his bed pulled back. The head of the bed is tilted slightly upward, and I wonder if that is to help his breathing, though I don't know whether or not respiration is compromised by a stroke. In the breast pocket of his gown is a small box, with wires running to his chest. From under a wide swatch of tape on his left wrist I see the end of a needle, to which a rubber tube is attached. The tube splits in a Y, one side ending in a stoppered vial and the other going to an IV bag. The man lying in bed is hollow cheeked and yellow-white. His beard stubble is gray. His skin has the dimpled texture of fruit. I don't know this person.

"Dad?"

His eyelids pull back. His eyes are small and lusterless, open but registering nothing. I wonder whether he is blind on top of everything else.

"Emil? Someone has come a long way to see you."

Without me hearing, Dr. Smalley has slipped in behind me. Dad makes a guttural sound, but I'm not certain it's in response to either of his visitors. I think maybe now he's having a heart attack. But then his lips part on the right side and pull into Elvis Presley's sneer. He is smiling.

Doctor Smalley goes around to the opposite side of the bed, speaking slowly, enunciating precisely, as if he's giving instructions to a child trapped behind a door. "Emil, we're going to show Jimmy how you're doing, all right? I want you to move your right hand for me."

On command, Dad's right hand does float toward the ceiling, levitated, it seems, by a force outside himself.

"Good," Smalley says when Dad puts his hand down. "Now can you move your right leg?"

The sheet at the foot of the bed bumps upward like a magic trick.

"All right. That's very good. Now let's do the other side. Can you wiggle the fingers on your left hand?"

The fingers of Dad's right hand stir.

"And how about the *left* hand?" the doctor emphasizes. "Can you move those?"

There is nothing.

"Let's try your left leg. Can you raise that?"

Nothing.

Dr. Smalley goes to the foot of the bed and peels back the sheet. He runs a fingernail up the instep of Dad's left foot, causing the big toe to pull back and the others to spread.

"Babinski's reflex," the doctor says to me, replacing the sheet. "You had the same response until you were about two. All normal children do. But the presence of the reflex in adults indicates damage to the nerve paths connecting the spinal cord and the brain. It tells us, in other words, that the wires are not properly connected. Emil," he says to Dad, "I'll be back to see you tonight, but I want you to do some work while I'm away."

He puts Dad's left hand on his stomach and his right hand on top of the left. "Use your good hand to make a fist of the other, all right? Roll the fingers up, and then straighten them out. Use your right arm to raise your left. Move it back and forth across your body, up and down toward your head and feet. All right, Emil?" No response. "Work on that. Think about moving your hands and feet. I'll be back later." On his way to the door he pats Dad's toes, then signals me to follow. "I'm going to borrow Jimmy for just a minute, and then he'll come back to visit."

We go out into the hall and head toward the elevator. As we walk, Dr. Smalley lifts his chin and purses his lips. He's assembling his words just so.

"As I told you earlier, this episode should not prove fatal. But I can't say to what extent your father will recover function, or how long rehabilitation will take. I wanted you to know those things and to see him perform my little tests, so you'll have a better understanding of what we're facing."

What we are facing. What WE are facing? *We* doesn't sound like the doc and my mom. It doesn't sound like the hospital staff. Thanks for the offer, but include me out. I'm here because Mom asked me to come. I didn't volunteer; I was conscripted. I'm happy enough to file my report and retire as Private Second Class Bass. I'm not looking for a promotion to Sergeant Saint. I just want to go home.

At the elevator Dr. Smalley pushes the down arrow. When the doors shudder apart, he steps inside but holds his thumb to the *open* button so the doors won't close.

"Full recovery is never foregone for anyone," he says, "regardless of how routine the illness seems. Kids still die of chicken pox. Sometimes a simple broken arm doesn't mend properly and the person lives with the pain for the rest of his or her life. Or the injury becomes infected, the infection spreads, there's organ dysfunction, and the patient succumbs. Jimmy, your father doesn't only need pills and physical therapy. He needs someone to care about him. We might be able to make his muscles work again, but he won't ever be whole without someone in his life. I don't blame your mother for leaving. I don't blame you either. You folks have had a real tragedy, and I know as well as anyone that Emil can be a difficult man under the best circumstances. But now you're going to have to weigh those things against...I don't know what." The doc sighs. "Against family, I guess. Obligation, maybe. Whatever you call it, you're going to have to figure out what your father is worth to you."

He lets go of the button, and just before the doors close he winks at me.

I SPEND THE DAY with Dad, though I doubt it does either of us any good. I talk to him about Niki, but only because it makes me feel closer to her. I tell him about my work and how much I like it. I lift his arm and his leg, both of which have surprising weight given how thin he is. Just once I go to the end of the bed and run my nail up his instep the way Dr. Smalley did. I get the same reaction, which makes me feel like a kid who has to pull a random lever or push an obscure button just to see what will happen, and just because there's a sign telling you not to.

I stay hours past lunch, but I can't bear going to the cafeteria just to come back to the room. Finally, I leave around four, feeling more adrift than I've been in years. It's as if my father is sawing away at the last string tethering my old life to me. Soon he will cut through, and the balloon encapsulating my childhood will float away. For a long time I thought that's what I wanted. Now that it's so near, I'm not sure.

I'M ON MY WAY back to the motel when I remember I've got the key to my parents' house. There is nothing there I want to see, and yet I'm again under the influence of some odd, compelling force. It's a force I don't understand, and yet it makes me talk myself into what should be easily avoidable.

I tell myself maybe I should see that the lawn is watered or that no food was left out to spoil. Maybe I should buy Mrs. Trindle some flowers as a thank-you. Lucky died last year, but nevertheless I want to run by to check his water and food dishes.

These ideas come to me in a straightforward manner, without mystical components. It's only a house, I remind myself. Just a space defined by walls. Nothing there can hurt me. Yet even while I know it's true, I have the feeling I'm whistling past a graveyard.

In no time I pull into the drive.

Unlike my father, the house has changed not a bit. On the living room wall there are the two plaster-cast images of calypso dancers. The man is wearing ruffled sleeves and is playing bongos; a similarly dressed woman shakes maracas. Over the white brick fireplace there is a sunburst clock. Around the corner, in the kitchen, another clock. This one a cat wagging its tail in opposition to the moving eyes.

I go to my bedroom and find everything as it was when I left: basketball trophies and ribbons, a school pennant, a racecar lamp. In Kitty's room, I lie on the bed, hoping to pick up some aura she's left behind, some scent or trace, but of course there is nothing after so many years. I wander down the hall to my parents' room, my father's room alone now, and see that it's the shabbiest of all because it has been occupied, worn down, without maintenance. There is a threadbare path in the carpet from the door to his bed. The room smells of unwashed clothes. In his closet there are the familiar work shirts, with his name in an oval patch, the dark blue Dickies pants, the Red Wing boots. I shove the clothes along the wooden rod, looking for what, I don't know. And then, tucked against the wall at the end, I come upon his heavy leather jacket.

It's a pilot's coat from World War II, though Dad was never in the military. To the best of my knowledge he's never even flown in a commercial plane. The jacket was given to him by his Uncle Alex when Dad was married. The coat has fur cuffs and a big fur collar. The leather is dark brown and cracked. It smells like a ball glove or a saddle, and squeaks when it moves. It's the jacket Dad wore when I shot him.

I was fourteen. I owned a Daisy Spittin' Image BB gun, and I'd shot a .22 at paper targets at camp. I knew to hold the stock of the rifle tight to my shoulder. I figured I knew how to handle a weapon. Our first hunting trip would be my chance to show Dad.

He'd borrowed a little single-shot 410 shotgun for me from a work buddy. We left before daybreak and got to Carsten's farm as the sun was coming up. It was late November, cold as the dickens. As we left the car I pulled on gloves, but then kept my hands in my pockets anyway. And even though my hat had ear flaps, I wrapped a scarf around my neck. Two other men were already there, waiting for us. Dad called out "Hey," and introduced me, but I was shrunk down into my clothes and never caught their names. We went to the back of the car and he handed me the 410 out of the trunk, plus one green, ribbed shell. For himself he slid three red three-inch magnums into his Winchester, producing a satisfyingly mechanical *snick*.

When everyone was ready, the four of us took off across a stubbled cornfield, grass and broken cornstalks crackling under our feet. Any standing water was frozen into a cloudy mirror reflecting the sky. I was on the far right, with Dad next and the others staying in line. There was no conversation, just all of us breathing clouds, and me wiping my nose on my sleeve.

We'd come to hunt pheasant but didn't see a bird or any other creature for more than an hour. Occasionally one of the men would throw a corn cob or small pumpkin at a likely looking blowdown or slash pile, but they scared up nothing. I figured we'd do this until someone called it a day, then we'd go home. I was disappointed, because I really wanted to get a bird. Then suddenly, Dad stopped dead.

"Bernie," he hissed, pointing.

What he saw was a line of quail scooting across the field and down the far side of a rise.

"Quail are better than nothing," he said in whisper. "But if we go straight for 'em, they'll stay low in the brush. We'll never get 'em to flush."

"We could throw something," one of the men said.

Dad shook his head. "Never get close enough. I'm going way wide around through the trees. I'll come up behind and drive 'em this way. When they come over the rise and see you, they'll take flight. Jimmy, you stay here with the fellas."

He took off, holding the shotgun mid-barrel in one hand, crouching low, giving the birds a wide swath until he got to the line of trees. I lost him then. I waited, tensed and ready, but he was gone such a long time that I eased up after a while. The other men didn't talk to me, but eventually they sank down to a knee or sat, so I sat too. I laid the gun down so I could put my hands in my armpits. Fifteen minutes passed. Maybe twenty. The sun was higher but held no warmth. But at least here, lower to the ground, I was out of the breeze, more protected than before. I grew drowsy, lost inside my clothes.

I went into a little daydream, pretty much forgetting about shooting birds. I was thinking about pancakes for breakfast and being home when we heard their *bob-white* call. The men stirred, and I felt kicked awake. We all grabbed our guns. Together the three of us watched a couple dozen quail come scurrying over the rise, waddling as fast as their legs would go.

"Too far," one of the men said. "Wait 'til they fly,"

My heart pounded. I wanted to take a bird to show Dad something. Maybe that I was as good as anybody. Maybe that I was a man. I wanted to be first to shoot. I lifted the gun to my shoulder, aiming at the covey, though not at any one bird. I waited as long as I felt I could, but the quail never took flight.

I'd started to squeeze the trigger when something in the scene changed. It was my father coming over the rise behind the birds. He filled my vision. I couldn't take my eyes off him, and I couldn't stop pulling the trigger.

By God's grace he saw me at that exact instant. He hollered, "NO" but also took the collar of that big leather coat and pulled it up over his head. I never felt the kick or heard the explosion of the gun. The next sound, the only sound for me, was that of sand thrown against a canvas tent. Just that.

Before I could even breathe, I saw my father fling back the coat as if merely dusting himself. I thought, in no order, because everything came at once: I shot my father. He is dead. He is not dead. How can a person be shot and still live? I am so frightened. I am so happy.

As he walked toward us, I let the gun slip to the ground. I expected, I hoped for, a beating. Kitty was still alive at that point, and so I thought a beating was the worst thing in the world that could happen. It's what I wanted. It's what I deserved. I knew I would survive a beating, just as he had survived being shot.

My father came to me as if the other men weren't there. He snatched the gun from my hand and without a word continued to the car. He didn't look back to see that I was following. I sometimes think if I'd been tardy he would have left me standing there. On the drive home he didn't acknowledge me in any way. As far as I know he never mentioned the incident to anyone. Days and weeks and years passed like that, like as long as he held this thing inside him he could use it against me. He made sure this sliver, this foreign body, would never come out, so it would never heal. And it never has.

I take the jacket from the hanger, folding the coat over my arm. On the way out of the house I see that the grass is browning and that Mom's azaleas, the ones she fussed over so much, are more than dormant, they're dead. I open the rental car's door and toss the jacket on top of my backpack, and head for the quarry.

OUTSIDE OF TOWN THE road climbs a gentle rise through a stand of pine, then dips down again as it comes into open countryside. There are two colors in this world, blue and tan. The sky and the land. The fields go on like gentle rollers in the ocean, and I want to show Mrs. G, *this* is how you grow corn. Acres and miles and seas of corn. I pass Tillmans produce stand, angled across one corner of the intersection so they can catch the traffic from both streets. I see they've doubled the shack's size and given it a new coat of paint. But now that the growing season is over, the building is locked up tight. Next month they'll reopen, selling pumpkins and knobby squash, and then they'll close again at Thanksgiving and stay that way until spring.

A few miles farther on I pull onto the abandoned quarry road and stop at the entrance. Someone has put a new chain between the old steel posts, and now there are three warning signs; red-barred circles with graphics instead of words to show the dangers of entering: slip and fall, drowning, coyotes. They've forgotten one other consequence, but maybe there's no picture for ruined families.

I lock the car and slip around one post. When my legs brush through the tall grass, cicadas broadcast static like radios unable to tune in a station. I see the tire ruts are overgrown, obscured now and partially washed away. Technology seems to have accomplished what barrier chains and mothers could not; the kids are home carrying out video death instead of playing here, flirting with the real thing.

I walk a quarter mile along the ridge before the water comes into sight. I turn and start down the embankment, sliding on the loose earth but stopping well above the water's edge. I want to remain higher for a better view. I don't know what it is I'm looking for except that being here is something I have to do.

A series of rocks juts out from the side of the hill and I sit on one of these, bending forward, my knees up, my arms resting along my legs. The cicadas have stopped humming and there is no breeze to carry sound in from somewhere else. It is still as a church.

And then I see it. Or rather I see *them*, the two scenes. I look out over the water and pick the exact spot Kitty dove into a rock. I picture where I was, how in three or four strokes I might have reached her and kept her above water. Or how, instead of looking the other way to splash fight with Gary Epperson, I could have yelled STOP! and prevented her jumping at all.

Next, I look a hundred yards off shore and calculate the center of the quarry, the deepest part, where two weeks after Kitty's funeral I tried to set things right. I didn't leave a note. My aim wasn't to have anyone miss me or to feel sorry. I just wanted to be gone. It wasn't right that I was alive and Kitty dead.

I'd ridden my bike and remember thinking the colors that afternoon were clearer and brighter than they'd been in weeks. The little corn stalks were emerald green, as if they'd been cleaned and waxed, and the sky as blue and soft as a baby's blanket. When I'd left the house there was still plenty of daylight because we were so near summer, but by the time I got to the quarry the sky had darkened in the east. I walked the bike past the gate and down the gravel road. I sat on a smooth piece of shale, maybe the one I'm sitting on now, and looked out over the water. On the sides of the pit I could see where roads had been cut, spiraling down to the bottom. I saw the scrape marks in the dirt where giant shovels dug out the earth.

I walked downhill to the shoreline, put on the big jacket I'd brought along, and dove in. As I swam I could feel the jacket filling with water. I felt my jeans and my shoes weighing me down.

Because I was below the surface of the land, I couldn't see the real horizon, just the sky at the edge of the quarry rim. I supposed it was still light to the west, but for me the world was only the deep blue-black above, the crescent moon coming over the border of the quarry, the stars beginning to appear.

I treaded water, waiting to get so tired I'd give up and sink. I figured it could take a while because I was a strong swimmer; a life guard the year before, and scheduled to be one again after graduation. But if death was slow coming, that was all right with me as long as I was with Kitty and away from the world. I paddled and kicked easily, moving my arms in big figure eights, plowing back and forth with my shoes.

At first it was peaceful, the warm night and warm water. I imagined it was like being in a womb. It was pleasant to think I was only slipping back to where I came from.

But that was my belief when paddling was easy. After a while I had to work harder to keep my head up. In ten or fifteen minutes I was truly growing tired. My muscles burned. I began not to see the sky, which had been so beautiful. I began not to see anything. All I could focus on was staying afloat. I worked my arms harder and kicked with purpose. My chin went under and I drank in water. I started to choke and thrash. I went under again, deeper, then fought back to the surface. I stopped thinking of why I was there, or thinking at all. Without meaning to, I wriggled out of the jacket and pried off my shoes, and I swam. There were no sounds but my splashing. I told myself to slow down, to stroke like I'd been taught. But I couldn't do what my mind told me. I churned and beat and flailed, a mile it seemed, instead of a hundred yards, until suddenly I was at the shore again and onto the rocks. I sat with my knees to my chin and my arms around my legs, rocking back and forth, and finally, finally crying, not for Kitty, whom I'd cried over for days, but for myself for being such a pathetic coward who couldn't do anything right, not even this.

Now as I sit here on this warm afternoon, it occurs to me I was mistaken; what happened was a good thing. Kitty's essence was completely and irretrievably lost when she died. But Amanda, my daughter, MY DAUGHTER, has value all her own and deserves the chance to blossom into whatever it is she can be. I've messed up, badly and more than once, but I didn't add to the failure by swimming back to shore that evening. Because if I wasn't here, or rather if I wasn't *there* with Allison, Amanda wouldn't be. She'd simply not exist and therefore have no chance at all.

As I think about this, a feeling of well-being washes over me. It's like narrowly escaping a horrible accident but understanding that as bad as the outcome could have been, it has passed and has no power over me now. I feel the quiet calm of having made a correct decision and seeing it through. I assure myself once more that Allison will be all right without me, and I have put myself in a position where I can do Amanda no harm.

I sit on the hillside until the light fades. Finally I get up, dust the seat of my pants, and head back to the car.

BUJJI IS AGAIN THE charge nurse. "Nice do see you, Mr. Basso-vich," she says. "Your fadder is much improved dooday. Would you like do see him?"

I follow her into his room and notice the other bed is now occupied. The curtain is partially pulled, but as I pass I see a decaying man with eyes sunken and shut, and his mouth hanging open. He is skeletal and reminds me of a concentration camp victim, so that I immediately regret my comment to the television pitch-woman last night.

The head of my father's bed is elevated a little in order for him to sit more upright than yesterday. His eyes are open, though the left one droops a little. His lips move in recognition when he sees me.

"immy," he says, expelling the word in a puff, as if he were exhausted from running. "Ood a eee ooo."

"You're better today," I tell him.

I stand on his right side, while Bujji is across the bed on the left. "In da fudure, Mr. Bassovich, we will wand you do stand on this side do dalk wid your fadder. Id will force him do durn his head and use his good eye. Id will be pard of his derapy, learning do compensade. But dere is dime enough for Dad. For now, enjoy your visid." To my father she says, a little louder, as if he's out in the corridor, "Your son is here do dake care of you, Mr. Basso-vich. You are a lucky man. Some people have no one." She smiles at me as she leaves the room and I wonder if she's had a talk with Ole Doc Smalley.

I don't cross to the other side as the nurse suggested, but pull up a chair and sit beside the bed. My father closes his eyes, done in by the few words he's spoken. Yesterday he looked like the man in the next bed, which is to say he looked near death. Now, though he appears twenty years older than his true age, he seems merely ill, so there is hope. I watch his chest rise and fall as he breathes through his mouth. I see how wattled his neck has become. His face is flushed and his whiskers look like pin feathers. He snores faintly.

"You awake, Dad?"

No answer.

I pull the thin cover to his chin. Over on the IV monitor I watch twin red LED lines descend a scale. Seventy-five, the numbers say. What does that mean? Rate of flow is my guess, but what are the units? Seventy-five what per what? Is that good or bad? Should I worry or be relieved?

For several minutes I occupy myself with the mechanics of my father's health because numbers and calculations are controllable. And if they are not, they are at least understandable. And if not that, then quantifiable. I tell myself I want a problem I can get my hands on, not some vaporous, rank chill.

But then Bujji Singh's words come back to me, and I realize she's making promises I can't keep. I can't care for my father. Taking care of people is exactly what I'm not good at.

I take Dad's hand in both of mine as I trace the wires fixed to his chest. From there I glance to the tiny television on its articulated stalk like a dentist's drill. I look at Dad again.

This dried-up man here, weak, his hair swept up like wild grass, his cheeks sandy with stubble, is my father. I take comfort in the warmth I feel from his hand. "I can't stay," I tell him. "I have to go."

I say this, but still I don't leave. I sit, holding his hand, touching him, watching his chest rise and fall.

It's an hour before I stand and take a last look, drinking in his image enough to last for a long time. "Goddammit," I utter aloud, and turn to leave.

I FIGURE IT'S FASTER and cheaper to pay the drop charge on the rental than it is to go back to Muscatine, fly to Chicago, get *another* car, and then return it to O'Hare. So even though it's late by the time I hit the highway, that's fine with me. The drive from Benton Junction to Mundelein is only four hours, and besides, the workday traffic is now gone and the road is clear. Before I leave Davenport to cross into Illinois, I pull off to use a pay phone.

"Mom," I say when she picks up. "I've got a surprise for you."

I tell her I'm coming to visit, and I can almost see her clap her hands. I've debated how much to say about my intervening stop to see Allison, but in the end I figure it won't make things worse, and might even help. Though she hasn't said it in so many words, I know my mother is disappointed with me. She doesn't understand I had to do what I did, precisely because I *did* love Allison and I *do* love Amanda, even if it isn't in the diaper-changing father sort of way.

I give Mom the flight information, and she says she'll pick me up tomorrow at RKD, the Knox County regional airport in Rockland. I tell her I'll fill her in about Dad when I see her, so the conversation winds down pretty quickly. I'm about to sign off when she says "I'm glad you're stopping to see the girls. Be sure to give them my love."

This simple phrase conjures up pictures of a future that will never be. I know this, but I can't stop the images. In the first, I come home from work to find Allison at the stove fixing dinner. Then I'm sitting at the table when Amanda comes in from school and tells us about her day. She's excited and says she's tried out for cheerleader but doesn't yet know the decision. She grabs a cookie from a ceramic bunny and heads to her room. Next, the phone rings. It's Mom calling to say she's coming over later tonight. She wants Allison's advice on new curtains for her condo.

But before I get to see what décor the two of them come up with, a robotic operator on the real phone says if I want to keep talking I need to put in more money.

"Sorry about that," I tell my mother. "Anyway, I gotta go. See you tomorrow."

Back in the car, I head down West River Drive, and just past the Bix Beiderbecke Memorial make a left on 67. The Rock Island Bridge is straight ahead, and as I start up the entrance I can't believe how excited I am to see Allison and the baby. A hundred feet above the Mississippi, I start tapping a beat on the steering wheel and singing "You're Nobody 'Til Somebody Loves You." I'm clear to Aurora before I realize I haven't thought of Niki all day.

CHAPTER TEN

MUNDELEIN ISN'T EVEN A town; it's a village. I learn this and other information when I stop at the visitors' center the next day to get a map. I figure the best thing is to drop in on Allison unannounced because I don't want to hear she doesn't want to see me. If I just show up, there isn't much she can do.

I pass the seminary and turn left over the railroad tracks, then wind through a section of established homes bordering Lock Lomond. Two minutes later, I see Allison's car in the drive of the last house on the street. Ten minutes after that, I see Allison herself. She has come outside to learn who is parked in her parents' drive, not leaving but also not coming in. Of course she doesn't recognize the rental, and for a minute she doesn't know the driver. But I can tell the instant she identifies me: her smile fades and her features harden. She steps closer to my door but stops short and folds her arms across her chest.

"Well, whaddya know?"

"It's me, all right,"

Here I expect a fight, starting with a barrage of stored up, thought out, even rehearsed, invectives. But if I don't get out of the car it can't escalate into anything physical, so I stay put.

"What are you doing here?" she wants to know.

Truthfully, I'd like to know the same thing. Am I here because I think my mother expects it? Do I honestly believe Allison and I could get back together? And if it were possible, do I want to? No. I don't. I'm doing the right thing leaving Amanda alone with her mother.

But that doesn't answer the original question, does it?

"Don't tell me you were just in the neighborhood."

Thank you, Lord, I think. She's pitched me a soft one and I'll hit it out of the park. "That's exactly it," I tell her. "I'm on my way to see Mom. I had a stopover in Chicago, so I figured I'd check on how you're doing."

"Ever thoughtful," she says. "So like you."

No one says anything for a long time, and I think this is the end of it. I'll back out of the drive and pull away, look in the rearview mirror, and that will be my last glimpse of her. In my head I'm running through taking the car back, checking on an earlier flight, calling my mother—when Allison uncrosses her arms and steps back from the car.

"I suppose you might as well come in as long as you're here."

But I don't want to go in. Not yet. Seeing her twists my heart. She has cut her hair short, and if I used such words, I'd describe the style as "darling" or "cute." As it is, I don't say anything. I just stare at her white blouse tucked tightly into the waistband of her shorts. I'm amazed how she's gotten her shape back. Better than her shape, actually. Right now, with the sun on her shoulders and her hands on her hips, Allison looks like an ad for energy bars or for the joys of hiking Alaska's wilderness. She has spent some time in the sun and has acquired the color of a toffee confection. I wonder if she's gotten this shade at a local plunge, and if that's the case I wonder if she's attracted much attention. I don't see how she wouldn't.

"How about we walk a little first?" I say.

She gives me a wrinkled-mouthed look that seems unrelated to my request, as if I've put something sour on her tongue. Then she looks down at her sandals and says, "Give me a minute. I need to change my shoes."

She goes in the house, and I exit the car. Minutes later she's back wearing new yellow tennies and white ankle socks. "Let's go," she says.

We head off across a greenbelt, and as we walk I fight the temptation to take her hand. Why can't we just stroll all day, I wonder, under this canopy of trees, this warm, clear sun? What harm would there be in that? We aren't enemies.

We round a corner and I get my first glimpse of Lock Lomond, the little manmade lake. Near the shore, mallards paddle unhurriedly, green helmeted, metallic. They look like shiny little wind-up toys.

We both stop at the same instant to look, then Allison turns to me.

"The thing I can't understand..." she begins to say.

I wish she would finish the sentence, because if she'd tell me what she doesn't understand, I could explain it to her. I could clear things up and everyone would feel better. But I need a place to start talking, because now that I'm with her, my ideas aren't so clear. Alone, I'm brilliant and logical. I know why I had to leave this beautiful woman and our baby. But now that she's by my side, my thoughts don't hang together so well.

To get the ball rolling I say, "How's the baby?"

It does roll, but it's the wrong ball.

"She has a name. It's Amanda."

"Yeah," I say. "Mom told me. How's Amanda?"

Allison looks at me with such intensity, I try to figure out whether she's going to laugh hysterically or break into a scream.

"Perfect is how she is."

She says this with some bitterness, which I don't understand. I've always figured if she loved me back then like she said she did, it meant she knew me through and through. And if she knew me, she must know I'm not the kind of person who would do something just to be cruel. She ought to appreciate that I had a good reason for what happened.

We walk another twenty feet and I lean against the back of a bench. Allison stands before me, spreading the fingers of her left hand while she gathers Amanda's attributes with her right.

"Five teeth. She's been walking since May. She's smart and inquisitive. Laughs at anything, a funny face or a tickle, or if you hold her feet to your nose and say they smell. She almost never fusses. My mom would snuggle her all day if I didn't insist on my turn. And of course Dad is crazy about her."

There, you see? I want to tell her. Everything is fine, just like I knew it would be.

She starts walking again, down to the shore and then away from the house. I take this as a sign she's not in a hurry to get back, which means not in a hurry to get rid of me. We walk along silently for a time, each of us with our hands behind our back, for my part to ensure we don't touch. I'm enjoying the wonderful day and being with Allison and letting my mind go blank. But she is preparing a statement she has no doubt considered for nearly a year and a half.

"I'd like to know what your plans are regarding our situation."

I don't answer immediately but eventually say, "Well…" I draw out the word to gain a little time, but it doesn't help. I can't come up with anything. Then I remember Mom talking about obligations, and I certainly want to fulfill any responsibilities I have.

I'm not a flake. "I sent you money," I tell her. "A year ago. But the check came back." To me this is vindicating, but Allison shakes her head. I did bring the bear with me, but now I realize I should have thought to write a check besides. "I can go to a bank here in town," I tell her. "We can go now. I can get you some cash."

She looks at me curiously. It's as if I'm new in town, and Swiss. She doesn't understand German, and I don't speak English. We'd like to converse, but we're confined to expressions and gestures. She shakes her head. "Jesus, I really don't know about you," she says. "I really don't."

Without another word, she turns and heads toward the house. I'm several steps back, sorting through the possible list of things she doesn't know, and I have to jog to catch up. Coming up behind her, I see Allison's legs disappear into her shorts and I can't stop myself thinking I know where they end. I know right where those legs go. I've been there, and it's a place I'd like to be again.

Then we're side by side and she doesn't look at me, but she says, "Would you like to see your daughter?"

ALLISON WAS RIGHT; AMANDA is perfect.

She jostles around as if her legs are solid from her heels to her hips, and then she softly crumbles into a pile like there isn't a bone in her body. She doesn't come to me or ignore me. To my child I am a piece of furniture, something to navigate around.

On the other hand, while Allison and I visit in the living room, Mrs. Stovall hovers at her daughter's elbow like a brewing storm. First she stands behind the chair Allison occupies, then comes around to sit on its upholstered arm. She doesn't say anything, but glares at me as if I'm a salesperson of gimmicky kitchen gizmos. When finally she says, "I'll make some lunch," I interpret this as a variation of "Here's your hat. What's your hurry?"

Nevertheless, with Mrs. Stovall out of the room I relax a little. I give Allison a quick recounting of Jim Bass Trucking, hoping she'll see the business as a worthy accomplishment. I tell her about Mrs. G and about Owen helping out while I'm gone. I don't mention Niki. I tell myself since nothing is going to change regarding either woman, there's no point bringing it up.

While I go on and on, Allison puckers her lips and nods. She's taking it all in, but I don't know how to interpret her reaction. What I want is for her to smile, to say she's missed me. I'm thinking how to steer the conversation that direction when we're called into the kitchen. Mrs. Stovall has prepared a salad using vegetables from her garden. There is also bread she baked earlier. The food is so appealing I momentarily question whether she really wants me gone.

Allison puts Amanda in a highchair and cracks open a jar of something orange. She feeds the baby with a spoon the size of my little finger. There is little conversation as I eat. Occasionally Allison stabs a cucumber or tomato with her fork, but mostly she pushes her salad around the plate. All this time, Mrs. Stovall moves silently around the room, rinsing a plate or glass, putting them on the drain board. I wish someone would say something.

"You're like a pioneer," I finally tell Mrs. Stovall, "growing and fixing everything yourself."

I say this to break the silence, but also I mean it as a compliment. I'm trying to say she is self-sufficient and displays all the good qualities that implies. But as with my other attempts at conversation with her, she doesn't respond, as if I'm simply not there.

It occurs to me then that maybe I'm not there, at least for them, or for them in a way that matters. They have dealt with my absence and moved on. The hole I left has filled in as surely as pulling a rock from a stream; the water closes in and removes all evidence of the disappearance. The rock may have never existed. *I* may have never existed.

Ah! I think. But wait just a minute! There's the baby. MY baby. You can't ignore me, because you can't ignore her. She is only here because I am here. *Concubito ergo sum.* I mate, therefore I am. I feel strangely satisfied with this notion, though I've said it only in my head, and only to the lettuce.

Allison takes Amanda from the highchair, and immediately the baby toddles up to me as if she's only been waiting for the opportunity. She stretches out her arms in an unmistakable gesture. I don't move.

"Pick her up," Allison says.

Then, before I can stop myself, I reach down and lift Amanda under her arms.

What happens next is hard to explain, because although I don't know what I expected, it certainly doesn't happen. There is no jolt, no electric shock. I experience no revelation, no lightning bolt of understanding. I haven't been saved. Instead, the result of holding my child is more like sipping some exotic liqueur that seeps down my gullet to my toes, hits bottom, pools there awhile, then spreads warmly upward so slowly and subtly that I don't realize I'm completely and irredeemably drunk.

"Hi there," I say to her. "What's new with you?"

In answer she bats my face with random, flailing motions. She drools constantly from lips so red they look like berries about to burst open. She stands on my leg, bouncing, saying, "yahhh, yahhh, yahhh, yahhh" over and over.

"She's teething," Allison tells me. "Are your hands clean? Stick a finger in her mouth and let her chew on it."

I do.

I feel sharp little nubs punching through the gum, which itself is hard enough to make me wince. She grinds and chomps and sucks my finger. I smell milk on her breath. As she works on my pinkie, I search her face for traces of me or Allison or Kitty. Anyone from either side. I find nothing there and yet I know, somehow, that she is mine. I made her. I'm responsible, though I am wholly incapable of fulfilling the duty. I also know if I don't leave soon, something irreversible will happen. Something that won't be good for my child.

"Here," I say to Allison, handing over the baby. "I have to catch a plane." I stand to leave but then remember the bear. "Wait a second."

I run out to the car, fetch the teddy bear from my backpack and run back in. I hold the toy out to Allison.

"Don't give it to me," she says, fixing me with a look that dares me to ask the question.

I hand the bear to Amanda, who takes it and gnaws the ear. In twenty seconds the head is soaked in slobber.

I WISH I'D BROUGHT a book, because even after I return the car I have to wait in the terminal for hours, not the short time I led Allison to believe by my quick exit. I check out the magazines at Hudson's, use the restroom and buy some coffee. I wander up and down, riding the moving sidewalk back and forth past my gate, while watching thunderheads build in the distance. Finally it's close to time for my flight. I take a seat near the gate as the area around me fills with the people who will be my fellow passengers.

Mostly they're businessmen wearing lightweight suits and carrying briefcases, but there are folks of all ages and persuasions. Two women dressed in matching jogging suits look anxious and keep touching each other's arm. A young mother is trying to manage two rolling suitcases and a baby carrier. A skeletal man with wispy hair and a Roman collar sits with his hands folded in his lap, staring ahead, watching nothing at all.

But the fellow who grabs my attention is a black kid about my age. There's a green duffel in the seat beside him, and he's wearing a sharp-looking Marine uniform. He's so crisp and handsome he's like a movie star. I've never considered joining the military, but now I decide that if I ever signed up, Marines is the branch I'd choose. He sits very straight in his seat, almost on the edge. He's wearing earphones, and his eyes are closed. One hand can't stop tapping a beat on his knee.

The way he looks and the way he moves make me think of Smokey Robinson, so I start thinking of Smokey Robinson songs. After "I Heard It Through The Grapevine," I think of "I Second That Emotion," which has the line "And a taste of honey is worse than none at all." So of course my next thought is of Allison and Amanda, which makes me get up immediately and look for a phone. I drop in a fist-full of quarters and punch the numbers. After two rings Niki answers.

"Hello?"

"Hey, Hotstuff."

"Mmmm," she says. "Miss you."

"Miss you, too. I'll be home day after tomorrow. You want to pick me up?"

"Now there's a line I haven't heard before. Is that some sort of reverse psychology?" Then she adds, "I can't wait."

"Me too," I tell her.

The phone is probably fifty yards from my gate, but I hear over the PA the announcement we're boarding. The folks I was sitting with rise in unison and crush toward the gate, even though it's assigned seating and I suspect no one will actually be left behind.

"Did you see your dad?" Niki asks.

I tell her how I saw him the first day, and then how he'd improved by the next visit. I'm not specific about the elapsed time, what happened when, so it sounds like seeing Dad is all I've done until I came to the airport. I see no sense in complicating things with a conversation about A and A. I'll get back to my regular life, and things will go forward like I'm truly past Allison and don't have a child at all. Which is the truth in any practical way. I just need to keep reminding myself.

"We're boarding," I tell Niki. "I'll call you tomorrow with the time I'll be home."

"I'll be there," she says.

It's DARK BY THE time I deplane at RKD. I walk down the ramp and almost into Mom. She's standing so near the door there's hardly enough room to squeeze past. I recognize her, of course, but only in the way that she registers as someone familiar. It's as if for all my father has aged, she's grown younger.

"Wow," I say.

"The new me," she answers, arms out, twirling around.

"Yeah. I guess so."

Her outfit is a bit much. With the bib and straps, it reminds me of *lederhosen*. She has knee socks and penny loafers and a blouse with red and green stitching. In fairness, she is not as out of place as this may sound. The people streaming by don't actually stop and stare. I wouldn't either, except this is my mother.

"You look...really good," I tell her.

She grabs me and kisses me on the forehead. She'd kiss the top of my head except I'm taller than she is.

"And you," she says, pushing me away, "look mahvelous..."

I wonder if she's been drinking.

I sling the backpack over my shoulder and we head for the car. On the drive to her apartment she talks a mile a minute about all the things she's been up to, the adventures she's had. Day trips, she calls these outings, though to me it sounds mostly like scouting yard sales. She speaks about her work at the gas station as if she's the marketing director for Proctor and Gamble. She says she's never seen anything like the East Coast, so ruggedly beautiful she can't believe she lives in such a place.

"And Jimmy," she adds, nearly breathless. "I know I'm not on the easternmost point. That would be someplace like West Quoddy Head."

I shrug an okay, which means I accept the information as accurate though I have no personal knowledge.

"But even so," she continues. "Even so. I get up early every morning and I get my coffee, and go out on the deck and look east. The sky is black, of course—always darkest before the dawn—but then it gets a sort of purple, then dark blue, light blue, then pink, then orange." I'm afraid she's going to take her hands off the wheel and start gesturing. "Every day I watch old Mr. Sun come up and I think, even though it may not be true and probably isn't, still, I think to myself—but then who else could I think to *but* myself?—I think, I'm the very first person in America to see this new day. Isn't that something!"

I once was blind, I think to *my*self, and now I see.

For the rest of the trip she's slightly more subdued, and I say nothing at all. When we arrive at the apartment, she parks in a graded area cut into an embankment just off the road. There seems to be no designated parking for the complex, just random patches of asphalt. In front of us is the back end of her building, which is as she described; wood-sided, board and batten, weathered. I wonder why the designers didn't think to put the entrances at street level. Instead we have to walk down a steep asphalt drive toward the beach, and I can't help worrying about Mom trying to negotiate this slope in the winter.

The condo she shares with Susan Martin is upstairs, the middle unit of five. The stairs and walkway appear to be the same weathered wood as the siding, except that they are under an over-hanging roof, which gives some protection and keeps them from being as faded. In the dark I can't see the ocean, but I can taste the salt in the air and I hear the low rumble of waves in the distance. The sound immediately makes me sleepy.

"I think I'll turn in, Mom," I tell her as we push through the door.

"Oh, no you don't, mister" she says. "We're going to visit. I've waited too long for this. I'll make us some tea."

While she puts on the water, I use the bathroom, mostly to stay out of her way. When I come out again I sit on the couch, spreading my arms across the top in either direction.

"Where's Ms. Martin?"

"Susan had a meeting tonight."

"Work?"

Mom shakes her head. "She's in a club. Poetry. She asked if I'd like to join, but I said, no thanks. Moon, June, spoon. That sort of thing isn't for me."

"Croon," I say. "Prune, balloon, raccoon."

It's a game we played when I was kid.

She laughs, remembering, and takes down two cups hanging from hooks under a shelf. "Pontoon, platoon, monsoon."

"Macaroon, Saskatoon, honeymoon."

She's really laughing now. "Lampoon, Brigadoon."

"Cartoon."

"Baboon."

We're down to one word at a time, running out of ideas. She pours tea, adds honey to mine.

"Doubloon," I try.

"Dragoon," she says.

I can think of more: buffoon and cocoon. Or I could do Kowloon and Cameroon, though my guess is Mom doesn't know these places. Anyway, I'm getting tired of this.

"I give up," I tell her. "You win."

She catches her breath from laughing, and then she's serious. "Oh, Jimmy. It's so good to see you."

Into what they probably consider their living room, though it's more like a big nook attached to the kitchen, Mom brings the two cups of tea. She sets the cups on coasters on the low table, then plops onto the couch herself.

"All right," she says. "Tell me about your father."

At first I don't know what to say, but once I start, things just come out. I tell her how nice Bujji, the charge nurse, was. I say how Dad seemed to improve in the short time I was there, but how stroking his instep produced the reflex action. Whenever I slow down, she asks questions to rev me up again. What's he look like? How much does he weigh? What does Dr. Smalley think? What do *I* think? Will Dad be able to live on his own? Should we get him a nurse?

Some things I can answer, but many I cannot. I'm straight with her and don't withhold any facts, though emotions are something else. For instance, I don't tell her I know Dad never approved of me. That somehow I've always fallen short no matter what I did.

Actually, not somehow. If I'm honest—and why not be honest, since this is just to myself?—even lying semi-conscious in a hospital bed he saw me as weak or flighty or undependable. I know he did. I could feel it. Dad made a living in the toughest occupation, operating a drop hammer. Standing all day in front of a forge furnace, manipulating metal, pounding it into shape, making it conform to his will. He's a man's man, and if he isn't pleasant all the time, or even most of the time, at least you know where you stand with him. At any rate, that's how I believe he sees himself.

In contrast he thinks whatever I have was unearned. But that isn't even the important part. In these last years, I know he thinks if he had been there that day at the quarry, Kitty would still be alive. Dad wouldn't have let it happen. He would have found some way to prevent her drowning. He's never said those words, but then he never said one thing about my shooting him either, and don't tell me he hasn't recalled that day a thousand times.

But I don't say any of this to Mom. What good would it do? The best thing for me is to not care. Not care about Dad or Allison or Amanda. Not care about Kitty. You should only worry about things you can fix, and I can't fix any of those. So from now on I'm just going to worry about me.

"And how's my little Amanda?" Mom asks. "Cute as a button, I'll bet."

I don't want to picture my daughter, but it's like when someone says don't think of bananas, that's all you can see. The more I try to blur her image, the more I remember holding her just hours ago. I feel her bouncing on my lap, her new teeth chewing on my finger. I can smell her baby powder scent.

I smile at Mom before answering, trying for something noncommittal like, "Oh she's fine," or "Growing like a weed." But these sentiments stick in my throat. Literally. I cough to clear the blockage, but when I try to speak I feel like I've swallowed a golf ball. I hold up a finger to say, just a sec, and cough again. The pain in my throat makes my eyes water. I wipe my face.

"Honey, are you all right?"

It doesn't help that she asks. By now I can hardly breathe. I stand and go to the door, walk outside and down the stairs. The ocean is louder now, and I wonder whether the tide is coming in until I realize the sound is my heart pounding in my ears. I wipe my eyes again, which are now streaming. Mom calls from the balcony, "Honey? Honey?" But I don't turn around or even try to answer. With luck she'll think I didn't hear. Without luck—without luck I'd be exactly where I am.

I find the asphalt drive we came in on, but instead of walking uphill to the road, I turn toward the beach. Soon enough the pavement ends and I'm on the sand. In a dozen steps I'm at the water. I turn again and parallel the waves, walking fast. My walk becomes a trot and then a run. I can't see more than a few feet in front of me, but I sprint on, as fast as I can, as far as I can, trying to catch one thing or outrun another. A half mile down the beach my lungs burn and my legs ache. I pull up, face the ocean, rest my hands on my knees. I breathe through my mouth and spit and gasp.

Across the water, a quarter moon is laying down a shimmering ribbon from the horizon to me. As I watch the reflection break apart and coalesce, a thousand moons then one, I shout to the waves, "What the fuck is wrong with me?"

CHAPTER ELEVEN

"I LIKE THAT HORSE," OWEN says by way of greeting He's come to return the tractor, which he's parked alongside the fence in front of my trailer. I can tell he's glad to see me, and not in the relieved way a babysitter is glad to see the parents come home. He's had a good time. I was gone only long enough for him to take a run to New Mexico, but still he got to see some new country.

Like me when I worked for SWT, Owen is utility in the local area, which gives you about as much variety as you're going to get without being a long-haul driver. But even then, if you work for a common carrier, you go to the same one or two terminals trip after trip. For Southwest it's either up 5 to Oakland and San Francisco, or 99 to Stockton and Sacramento. Drivers can go south to San Diego, but then it's two turnarounds a night. Not much fun.

A couple of the line guys use the distance between terminals to their advantage, if you can call it that, by having a wife and family at each end. I don't see how they handle it. Or why. It seems to me you set yourself up for missing twice as many birthdays, twice as many dance recitals, twice as many anniversaries. Making excuses for one of each would be bad enough. And imagine keeping track of what you told who, or paying double mortgages and car insurance. Life is adequately complicated for me, and I only have a girlfriend. And, of course, the other stuff.

"Do you want cash?" I ask Owen, remembering we never actually discussed his rate or method of pay. A driver's compensation can be figured by time or miles or a combination of both. And I can give him folding money or a check. I don't care what he chooses, I'm just grateful for the help.

"Let's play it straight," he says. "How about a check for what I would have made at Southwest?"

"I know you worked more hours," I tell him. "And you had traveling expenses besides. Meals and a room."

He shrugs. "Whatever you think is fair."

Inside my trailer I make out a check for the whole delivery receipt, less the fuel and Continental's fee. This is twice what he would have gotten at SWT. When I turn to go out again, I see he's standing at the door.

"I'd bet you don't get a lot of company."

I'm not sure what he means. Is he saying I'm not well liked? That I don't have friends? That I'm messy?

"Not a lot," I agree.

"'Cause you'd have to take turns breathing in there."

"It is small. That's for sure."

I look around and smile, thinking of Niki and me lying in the little bunk last night. You have to plan each move and then let your partner know what you're thinking, or you're liable to get stuck or maimed. If privacy weren't an issue, we'd be better off in the back seat of my car.

I hand Owen the check, which he folds into his shirt pocket without reading. That's okay. When he goes to cash it, it will be a nice surprise.

"I'll run you home," I tell him.

"How about stopping along the way for a drink?"

Sure, I figure. Why not? It's afternoon, and I don't have a run for two days. Besides, I'm still trying to get settled from my journey east. I covered six thousand miles there and back, though the real distance was traveling from twenty-three to eight years old, and from being a not-very-good son to a not-very-good father to being a pretty-good son, and back to being whatever I am now. A regular guy, maybe. That's my goal anyhow.

Owen lives south of the 60, but we go north to Holt in order to stop at La Casita, a little whitewashed block building between a commercial glass shop and a muffler place. I've passed it a hundred times with no thought of stopping, but the way Owen talks it's like a Kasbah, so I can't wait to get inside.

Until I am inside.

La Casita turns out to be less than nothing special. The building is L-shaped, with the small leg of the L defined by the actual bar. The longer leg stretches from the street entrance to the parking lot out back. There are two pool tables in the back section, a few upholstered booths along the wall, and four tables spaced across the floor. At the bar is a line of stools leg to leg. Above the bar, glasses are hung upside down in slots, and on the wall behind is an animated Hamm's sign that shows fish swimming up a short waterfall and the Hamm's bear swiping at them over and over.

Beer is a commodity, I think. A given brand is the same from one location to the next, so the only hope an establishment has to set itself apart is its ambience. Here they've selected the dive motif.

We pick a small round table between the bar and a booth.

"Nice, huh?" Owen says

"You bet."

"How about some lunch?"

Owen raises his hand, and from the gloom a waitress appears.

"Well, Sugar Plum," he says to her, "if you don't look good enough to eat."

She smiles but doesn't answer. She makes a show of holding her pencil over the order pad while she cocks a hip and bounces impatiently. We order enchiladas because that's the only thing left beside some albondigas, which she says is nearly out and in any case has been on the stove for hours.

"Ya shudda come earlier," she says in a not very Mexican accent.

"You wouldn't want me coming *too* early, would you?" There's a wink in Owen's voice if not in his eye.

The waitress just looks at him, then saunters off.

"Nice girl," Owen says. "Great tits. I love the peasant blouse. Can't remember her name though."

"Maria," I tell him. "I saw her tag."

Without a hint of irony he shakes his head. "That's just since the place became the La Casita. She's been Lily and Gretchen and Sue. I can't remember the others. In the last five years the bar has been the Shanghai, the Shangri-La, the Roundup, the Hof Brau and the Boom Boom Room. Depends on how much money the new owner wants to spend on décor. The people pretty much stay the same though, the waitresses and bartenders. They just change costumes and fix a different sort of food. Now it's the La Casita. The little house."

"If it's *the* La Casita," I ask, "doesn't that make it 'the the' little house?"

"So now you're a professor?" Owen asks.

We talk about the load he handled for me and about our mutual friends at Southwest. Maria brings our food, which is surprisingly tasty. I decide maybe the-the little house is worth a second visit after all. When we finish our pitcher of beer, I order coffee and Owen gets a shot of Wild Turkey.

"Just in case, Honey Bunch," he tells our waitress, though I suspect she has no idea in case of what. I know I don't. When our drinks come a few minutes later, he lifts his glass in a toast. "Never up, never in," he says, and throws the drink to the back of his throat.

He doesn't shudder, so I shudder for him.

It's NICE TO BE home. As much as I claim to like variety, I also like routine. This seems contradictory and may in fact be part of my problem, if I have a problem, and I believe I do. I've not yet identified the problem, exactly, but I think it has to do, in part, with thinking. And as I look back on that thought, I see that's precisely the case. I think about things too much. I analyze and weigh and compare. I balance and measure and match. I should, probably, just *do*, but I don't.

In any case, it's good to be home. And the reason is routine. A nice routine. Some work, some love, some conversation.

The Friday after I'm back, Niki and I go to Glendale to see *Ryans Daughter*. It's playing at the Alex, where I've gone by myself to see *Sunset Boulevard* and *On the Waterfront*. *Sunset Boulevard* is where I fell in love with Nancy Olson. I'm also in love with Sarah Miles, which is one reason I want to see *Ryans Daughter* again. This will make my fourth time.

"What is it with you and old stuff?" Niki asks me after we park and are walking to the box office.

"What do you mean?" I think I know, but I'm going to make her say it.

"What do you mean, what do I mean? The old songs, the old movies. Are you like reincarnated or something? Were you born a hundred years ago?"

"*Ryan's Daughter* isn't that old," I tell her. "Nineteen seventy."

"That's exactly what I'm talking about. You weren't even born yet."

"Almost," I tell her, which I believe is a pretty good defense. "Besides, I don't like old, I like good. And how can you do better than David Lean?"

"Who's he?"

"The director."

"Never heard of him."

I sigh. "*Bridge on the River Kwai, Lawrence of Arabia, Doctor Zhivago.*"

"That last one I've heard of," she says.

I figure it's a start. "What an eye he has," I tell Niki, waving my arms around. "Wait 'til you see the panorama shots in this movie. They'll take your breath away."

"You're kidding. You've seen this already?"

I don't say anything. I know what's coming, and answering would be like stepping in front of a punch.

She shakes her head, takes my arm, and says, "Boy, can I pick 'em."

I buy our tickets out front and we walk through the open courtyard to the theater proper. Though it's only minutes to show time, the place is nearly empty, which I can't understand, but which gives us our choice of seats. I take Niki right to the center, just under the mezzanine. There are a few PSAs and a short, and then the movie starts. As I sit with Niki's arm through mine, I think how great this is. The theater is fabulous, and the movie is fabulous. I like that this is such a different role for Robert Mitchum; he's not cool and understated like in *Out of the Past*, or the tough-but-actually-nice guy like in *Heaven Knows Mr. Allison*. Here he's just thoroughly human and humane. These actors are so believable.

Niki and I settle in and watch Rosy give herself, resulting in disappointment, to Charles. We learn about Doryan's injury. I'm taken by Father Collins' crustiness and by the sweep and scope of the countryside. I nearly forget I'm in a theater until Niki whispers to me, "Doesn't he have a son?"

She says this is just as the villagers, including Trevor Howard as the priest, who reminds me of Father Watters back home, are collecting the shipwrecked German guns from the beach. It's what you might call a high point.

"What? Who?"

"The main guy. Doesn't he have a son?"

The main guy? "Robert Mitchum?"

"I guess," she says. "Doesn't he have a son?"

"In the movie?"

"No. In real life."

This is such a beautiful scene. There's the rocky, windswept Irish coast. The villagers pulling together in common cause. Rugged, rebellious Tim O'Leary leading the way. Even Michael, the village idiot, is helping. Like Lean's other epic movies, this one was meant to be seen on the big screen, and I want to take advantage of the opportunity.

"Yeah. I think so," I whisper.

"He's an actor?"

"Who?"

"The son. He's an actor?"

"I think so."

"What's his name?"

If there were people around us they'd dump popcorn on her head, but there is no one close enough to do it. I can't do it myself because I don't have any.

"I don't know," I tell Niki.

"That's how I keep them straight," she goes on. I don't respond, hoping this will be the end, hoping to withhold fuel from the fire, but it doesn't help. "Him and the other old guy. I get them confused." She thinks a minute then says aloud, although I believe this is still part of her internal rumination, "Maybe they both have sons. And maybe both the sons are actors."

O'Leary is caught by Doryan, who is outnumbered but armed, where the villagers are not. I know O'Leary is about to get shot, so I don't want to look at Niki right this second, but I have to because there's so much exaggerated movement next to me. I turn to see her poking herself in the chin, over and over.

"The one with the dimple. I get him and this one confused. Are they still alive?"

I want to tell her, yes, Tim O'Leary has just been shot but he's alive. He is also about to deliver one of the great lines of the movie, which I will miss because I'm talking to you. And yes, Robert Mitchum is alive, and so is Kirk Douglas, and Kirk's son, Michael. Everyone's alive. No one is dead. But I don't say that, or anything. I'm so taken out of the moment, I stand and move to the aisle. By the time I reach the exit, Niki is there at my side.

"Come back," she says. "Don't be like this. If you think the movie is that great, we'll watch it. I promise I'll be quiet."

I know I'm being unreasonable. I know the movie isn't that important, and I understand Niki isn't interested in the things I am. But I wanted the whole evening—the drive together, the movie, dinner afterward—to stand for more than what they actually are. I wanted them to stand for my normal life. The life I want and the life I'd have if she'd just cooperate. A life free of sick fathers and changing mothers, of ex-girlfriends and a child who doesn't know me. But Niki won't do her part.

I keep walking, so she puts her arm through mine and follows along. "Mad at me?" she says.

I look at her pixie face, her smooth skin. I turn and kiss her forehead.

"Not mad," I tell her. "It's just that—like you said—I've seen it before. I was getting bored. Ready to eat?"

It's fall, the best time of the year. At least I think so. The temperature is warm but not hot, the air is dry, the sky is clear. And if that isn't enough, today is Saturday and I'm not working.

I sleep until eight, get up, use the john, and sit in my underwear on the edge of the breakfast-nook bench to tape up. Before someone thought of pre-wrap, I had to shave my legs about half way up my calf, but now I use pre-wrap instead. I start behind my toes, almost to my arch, and spiral the foam to mid-calf. Next I flex back my foot to ninety degrees and take a couple wraps of sport's tape just below the top of the pre-wrap. I do the figure eight from outside to inside, over my arch and under my heel, back to where I started, and then the heel lock, which is sort of like the figure eight but longer, back to the end of my Achilles and down again. Then I go the opposite way; lower Achilles, down under my foot and up the other side. When I do the three stirrups I roll my foot out, because I figure if I twist my ankle, the most common thing would be to roll it the other way, so I want a little pre-tension in the other direction. Next I do three horseshoes, starting at the inside above my ankle bump and overlapping as I go down. I do one more heel lock up, and one more down. Finally I do individual circles all the way up my shin.

Once the right side is done, I do it all again on the left.

When I stand, it's like my feet are in casts. When I walk, it's like I'm walking in ski boots. And I haven't even laced up my high tops yet. I feel like a gladiator. Like a race horse.

I pull off my underwear, slip on a jock, replace the underwear, and pull on shorts. From the back of the trailer I grab my shoes, a sweatshirt with the sleeves cut off, and my basketball.

The next order of business is food, so I take myself to breakfast at McDonald's. Two egg McMuffins, hash browns, coffee. When I finish I'm still hungry, so I get pancakes and eggs.

I head back in the direction of home but stay on Towne Avenue and go to the park.

I'd rather play in a gym, but none are open that I know of, and anyway it's great to be outside. I park in the lot beside the tennis courts and cut across the grass to a block of six asphalt basketball courts, three wide and two deep. I choose the northwest corner so the sun won't be in my eyes when I'm shooting, and also because there's grass on two sides, which slows the ball if I miss.

For the next hour I shoot alone, working an area, top of the key or baseline, mostly jumpers, but sometimes I fake and drive for variation. Once in a while I'll post up like a big man, swing and hook. Sometimes I just goof around. By ten I'm wringing wet, loose, wishing I had somewhere to use the energy I feel. I look behind me to the tennis courts and see two young kids batting a ball back and forth across the net. They aren't actually playing a game, but I'm glad to see they're outside having fun. Two courts east of me, three older kids walk onto the asphalt and start shooting hoop. I figure they're high school and probably on the team. They're pretty good. There's a lot of shake-n-bake. Behind the back stuff, between the legs. A lot of name calling. Yo mama this and that.

"*Yo mama so ugly, when you was born the doctor slap her.*"

"*Yo mama so fat she eat Wheat Thicks.*"

I know they're going to ask me to join them. Guys who play at that level aren't satisfied with Horse or Around the World, and you can't do much else with an odd number of players.

Soon enough one of them calls out, "Hey, wanna play? Two on two?"

I'm smiling to myself. "Okay. Sure."

As I walk toward them, the kid who called me fires the ball. I have to drop mine to catch his. He's the biggest of the bunch and looks the oldest. I figure him to date the head cheerleader, not because he likes her but because he thinks that's the way the world should work.

"Ten by ones," he says. "Win by two. Winner's outs."

The ancient rules.

They pair me with the kid least likely to succeed. He's small and unsure, probably younger than the other two by a year, which, at that age means something. He's not bad, but he hasn't grown into himself. I want to ask him, "Are you ready for your close-up, my friend? 'Cause I'm gonna make you a star."

With only two to a team there's no need for shirts and skins, so we all strip to the waist. We shoot for outs, but the big kid hits his jumper right off, which starts my side on defense. Naturally I guard the showoff. I learn his name is Duchon. My partner is Teddy, and the other kid is Bret. Duchon doesn't want to give up the ball, so although I suspect Bret is open most of the time, he doesn't get much opportunity to score.

We run around the court, sweating gallons. Our skin gleams in the sun like various colored woods under marine varnish. I hang back, learning about my opponent: Can he go to his left? Does he head fake before every shot? I'm making notes, trying to give nothing back that he can use. I don't let him score at will, but I don't press that hard to stop him, either. I want to watch his rhythm, get in sync with him. I can hear Teddy and Bret pushing each other around under the bucket. They're grunting, and I imagine they're slipping off each other's wet skin.

"Shoot the damn thing if you're not going to pass," Bret tells Duchon.

He does let fly then, but I don't turn to follow the ball. I wait, and wait, watching to see which way he'll break. And anyway, I know where the ball is by watching Duchon's eyes. Finally he cuts left and I pivot to box him out. He climbs my back but can't get around, and the ball falls to me. It's five zip, them. But we've got the ball now and things are about to change.

I go to the top of the key. Stop. Pop. Nothing but bottom. One, five.

Teddy takes it out, hits me at the post. Turn, fall away. Two, five.

Duchon's expression changes. He's less mouth now and more hands in my face. Teddy is smart enough to come up and set a pick, so I start that way, bump Duchon into him, then step back for a jumper.

Three, five.

I keep this up until Duchon gets the point: Leave me alone and I'll hit the shot. Come out on me and I'll go around.

It isn't fair, I know. I've got five years on him, and ten thousand games against guys twice as good as me. Earlier this morning Duchon was the biggest fish in a small pond. Now he's wondering if he's forgotten how to swim. And this is just the first lesson.

Teddy and I win the game, then play another and another and another, until we lose track. We don't win every time, but we win most of them. When we take a break, Teddy and I go off by ourselves. I'm wiping myself dry with my shirt, and he's spinning the ball on the tip of his finger.

"You're good," he says.

"I played some college ball."

"I play at the high school. JV."

"Keep it up," I tell him. "You've got good fundamentals."

He doesn't answer, but I know he's beaming.

I use my sweatshirt to wipe under my arms. I can feel the salt crystals, taste them in my mouth.

At the tennis courts, I drink from the bubbler. I put my toes up on the edge of the concrete curb and lean forward to stretch my hamstrings. Teddy drinks next, and on the way back he says, "So what do you want me to do?"

I shrug. "If you're winning, why change your game?" But then I say, "Duchon is going to start having Bret help him out. They'll double team me, and when they do you'll be open. Do you know a give-and-go?"

"Pick-and-roll?" Teddy says. "That's what we call it."

"No," I tell him. "That's the opposite. Pick-and-roll is, you set the pick, I drive, you roll and screen out your man, I hit you or keep it. Give-and-go is more like posting up. You post, I pass to you, cut by close enough to lose my man, and either you hit me or keep it yourself. Let's do 'em both, not every time, but mix it up."

"Cool," Teddy says.

We get back to the court and start again. We've been at it for hours and everyone is stiffening up. But it's so much fun no one wants to quit. Teddy and I again dominate, winning most of the time but not caring when we lose. I don't have a watch but I figure it must be near three.

We've got the ball and it's game point. Our plan has been working perfectly, me pulling the opponents out, leaving Teddy unguarded under the basket. I'm at the top of the key dribbling, and then for some reason, some feeling I have, I look to the side and behind me. Niki is there, watching.

By now I'm so full of myself, I don't realize she isn't smiling.

I go farther out, three-point range if there was such a thing on this court. Duchon doesn't know what to make of this. There's no sense guarding me that far from the basket, so he lets me go. I imagine he thinks I'm setting Teddy up again. I go to the sideline near half court, almost to where Niki is sitting on a bench, and let go a long, arching shot.

Fall back, Baby, as they used to say.

I turn to her, not even watching, but I hear the ball crash through the chain net.

"Game," I call out. I can be a bit of a showoff when the mood strikes me.

But Niki hardly reacts to my theatrics. She's not thrilled, not disappointed. It's like she's holding herself tight and doesn't want to give up anything. I wonder if something is wrong.

"How did you know I was here?" I ask her.

"I stopped to see you, and your neighbor lady was out in your yard digging up something. She said she saw you leave early this morning with a basketball, so I drove around until I found a court. Actually," she says, pointing to the Duster, "I saw your car before I saw you."

"What a detective," I tell her. "I'd better never try to put something over on you."

"Interesting you should bring that up," she says.

From the pocket of her sundress she takes the two-by-three K-Mart photograph Allison handed me as I left her house. It's A and A from last summer. The two are dressed similarly and are leaning across a table, nose to nose, both with their chins in their hands. It's a good picture. On the back I've written, "To Daddy."

"If you don't want people snooping in your trailer, you should lock your door," Niki says.

She gives me the photo like she's an attorney and I'm a witness who needs my memory refreshed. Except, of course, I don't. I've memorized every curve of their faces, their skin tone, the curls of their hair. Looking at the picture now, I could tell Niki how they smelled, if she really wanted to know.

There's no sense in handing the photo back. After all, it's mine. But I don't have a dry pocket to put it in, so I just hold it cupped in my palm.

"We should probably talk about this," I tell her.

Niki answers, "I can't wait."

CHAPTER TWELVE

WE DRIVE OUR SEPARATE cars back to the trailer, and Niki politely waits while I sit in the open doorway and hang my feet outside, cutting the tape from my ankles. For the five minutes I snip and peel, she doesn't say a word, nor is there so much as an encouraging mumble when I pass by her to clean up. In the shower I don't exactly stall, but I don't hurry either. I run out the hot water, which doesn't mean all that much in terms of time spent, then stand in the bracing cold as long as I can manage. When I finally open the bathroom door it forms a barrier across the hallway so she can't see to the back of the trailer. I go there sans towel to slip into clean clothes, and I'm up front again a minute later.

Niki is sitting on the breakfast nook bench, which is the only actual seat aside from the two lawn chairs outside. But they won't fit in the trailer. For me to sit, she'd have to slide to the wall, but then we'd be side by side and couldn't look at each other. This might or might not be a problem. But without a doubt there is another difficulty—I haven't eaten since morning and it's now midafternoon. Going to a nice restaurant for a sandwich and a beer would be a way to resolve both troubles.

I make the suggestion.

Niki is unreceptive.

"I don't know that I want to go out to eat with you right now," she tells me. "Besides, I can't see this discussion taking much time."

I can't correct her on her opinion of dining out; she feels what she feels. But Niki is dead wrong about the length of our talk.

I prop myself against the refrigerator and start explaining, and don't finish until it's dark outside. I tell her everything, or almost everything. I begin with Kitty's death, but skip over my late-night swim in the quarry. I tell her about me coming west right after high school, and also about my name change, both of which she thinks are adventurous and cool. She listens intently to how I met Allison in school, how I was drawn to her because she was from the Midwest like me, and that I knew she was a transplant by the way she said "warsh" for wash, and "beg" for bag. I tell Niki about the pregnancy and Amanda's birth, how I was there at first but came to believe I wouldn't be the best guy to raise her.

She stops me there. "Maybe I can understand you thinking it then, but how about now? Are you now ashamed of leaving them? Do you think it was a mistake?"

What she's asking is about my past, but also it's about our future—mine and Niki's. Part of what she wants to learn is whether I'll leave her too, when things get tough, so I think a minute before I answer.

"I wish the world was a more perfect place," I tell her. "It would be great if things were purely right or purely wrong. But life isn't a math problem with one correct answer. It seems to me most decisions are shades of better and worse. Back then I did what I felt tipped the scales to the better end. I think the same thing now."

She seems satisfied with that, so I move on to my recent trip. Of course Niki already knows about Dad's stroke, but we talk about what that means for everyone involved, and especially what might be required of me. I tell her that before I visited Dad I wanted to forget about him, to get him out of my life. And now that I'm home I'm angrier than ever because I don't want to love him, but I can't help it.

"I think it's wonderful you want to take care of him," Niki says.

"No, it isn't," I say. "If you're going to help someone you should *want* to do it, but I don't. Which means he's still making me do things I don't want to do."

"Maybe you're doing it for your mother?"

I agree that's a possibility, though the explanation doesn't feel quite right.

Next I tell Niki about Mom's weird transformation I'm not sure I like. My meltdown at Mom's place seems irrelevant, or at least unhelpful, so I slide past that part without a word. To wrap things up I mention in an offhand way that because I was so geographically close to Allison and Amanda, naturally I stopped for a minute or two to say hello. I pass this off as the smallest of no-big-deal. As if I didn't say anything earlier because it hardly registered with me. I say Allison slipped me the picture as I left, and I must have put it in my pocket without thinking.

With that information I feel I'm finished, or at least I've covered all I care to, but it leads Niki to ask the one question I was hoping she wouldn't.

"Are you still in love with her?"

This is not a simple inquiry and can't be met with a simple answer. If I say "no" either too quickly or too slowly, she'll think

I'm lying. If I say "yes," I suspect things are over between us. I need to respond carefully, or I'm going to lose a part of my life I like a lot.

"I want the best for Allison and the baby. If that's love, then I love them both. But do I love her in the way I love you? No."

By now I'm so hungry I'm light-headed, but this reply has the potential of taking us in a new direction because Niki answers, "You love me?"

It occurs to me I've never said the words to her before, as if I'd tucked them in a sock like a rainy-day fund. So although the mood in the trailer has definitely lightened, I dispel any lingering storm clouds with a smile and a "Whadda you think?" I'd like to add, "Can we eat now?" but I wait one more beat.

An hour ago I moved from leaning against the refrigerator to joining her at the table. Now Niki slides across the seat and bumps her hip into mine, getting me to stand. She follows me up, and as we face each other she reaches out and puts her arms around my neck. She lays her head on my chest.

"You should have told me all of this from the beginning," she says softly. "I want us to share everything."

I'm thinking about what food I've got in the trailer. I know there is cereal and probably some milk, and I definitely remember a half stick of summer sausage. If I'd already had supper, I'd ask her my own question about trust: *How come we never go to your place to spend the night?* But I don't dare risk one more diversion.

Niki lets go of my neck and takes a small step back. She slips first one and then the other yellow spaghetti strap from her shoulder, then reaches behind herself and unfastens the row of buttons. When her dress falls to the floor, she looks like a figure atop a cake, smooth and shimmering, standing in a yellow froth confection. For just a moment she turns away from me and undoes the fasteners holding the bunk against the front wall. When she lowers the bed into place, she turns back and takes my wrist, tugging me gently.

"Let's start sharing right now," she says.

I'm not good at this. What I mean is, I'm not good at resisting an invitation to sex, even though it isn't, or wasn't, the first thing on my mind. Allowing it to happen somehow reminds me of caring for my father; maybe what I object to in both cases is that they weren't my idea.

I follow Niki two steps to the bed as if I've had a lobotomy, and of course we make love. As soon as we're finished, she rolls her head onto my chest and shoulder and falls asleep. I haven't turned out the lights, so I brush her hair from my eyes and stare at the ceiling, counting the rivets in the plywood seams. I can see twelve without turning my head. That's my rule, how many can I count moving only my eyes. Niki breathes softly: in, out, in. I feel her ribs move so slightly. I count the rivets maybe ten more times, maybe twenty, until I feel it's okay for me to ease my arm from under her head. I swing my legs to the floor, stand, and pull on my shorts.

Quietly, I take a carton of milk from the refrigerator and a box of Frosted Flakes from the cabinet. Now I shut off the lights so she won't wake. At the breakfast nook I sit in the dark, alternately tipping the box of flakes into my mouth and then the spout from the milk carton. I crunch and swallow.

Earlier in the evening I'd leaned the photo of Allison and Amanda against a coffee cup on the table. In the faint light drifting through the window I see the picture is still there, though now only the white border is visible and not the image itself. I stare at it nevertheless.

I eat the dry flakes, washing them down with the milk, until both are gone and there's nothing to do but go back to bed.

THE HOLIDAYS ARE A good time for many businesses but tough on others, including transportation companies. By late November retailers have most of their Christmas merchandise on the shelves or in the stock room and won't reorder until January. Also, municipalities and businesses have come to the end of their yearly budgets, so they aren't purchasing, and consequently trucks aren't carrying. And then there's the festivities themselves. People are at parties or shopping, or thinking about parties or shopping, and in either case not a lot of work gets done.

But my company is so small, I'm not affected in the way bigger ones are. It doesn't take much to keep me going; a couple of loads a week will pay the bills. Even so, Conrad favors me over his other clients. He gives me as much as I can handle, and sometimes more. I take it all because I'm afraid if I turn down a load it's too easy to forget me next time. Soon there is so much work lined up I call Owen to see if he can give me a hand. He says he'll try to arrange things, then phones back half an hour later to say he'll do it. He's owed vacation time at Southwest and tells me this will give him a chance to blow the carbon out of his old Peterbilt. I don't believe for a minute that's his real motivation; I've seen his rig and I'd bet it's as clean inside as out. My thought is he likes the independence and the variety he gets working as an O/O. He also likes the double dip, getting paid by both Southwest and me. After his two weeks are up, I give him all the revenue from his runs, which makes him, in his words, happy as a dog with two dicks.

Niki and I are doing okay during this time, which is to say from the night of our *big talk* to now. Maybe it's because our visits are mainly by phone. She's as busy at the bank as I am on the road, so she doesn't pressure me to be more available. In fact, she apologizes for not coming around more often.

Days before Christmas I do my holiday shopping, picking up for her Linda Ronstadt's *Lush Life* as a possibly more palatable introduction to the standards. I choose the CD for the playlist: "Skylark," "When Your Lover Has Gone," "My Old Flame," but especially for its title track, and the fact that Billy Strayhorn composed the song when he was just seventeen. I like to keep that sort of information close at hand in case I'm ever under the mis-impression I've done something significant with my life. I also buy Niki a nice blouse and new floor mats for her car.

For my mother I get a book titled *Have You Lived Here All Your Life?* and sub-titled *99 Things To Do On A Weekend in Maine.* For my father, a pocket knife with his name engraved in the handle. I don't know that he'll ever be able to open it, but it's a gift that seems manly and personal at the same time. I do this under no illusion he will get me something in return. He wouldn't have regardless of his health. When I lived at home his idea of a gift was letting me drive him to get smokes.

The last person on my list is Mrs. G. It's easy enough to choose the category from which to select a gift, but more difficult when it comes to specifics. In the end I buy her a fancy garden wagon with removable wooden sides and big balloon tires. I also get her gardening gloves with sticky green polka dots on the fingers and palms, a new hoe, and a big straw hat. I know she'll make a big deal and fuss, but it isn't really that much. It's just the closest I can come to making her a farmer.

On Christmas Eve, Niki and I go out to dinner and then to a movie. Afterward we come back to my place, where Mrs. G has again outlined the trailer in twinkling lights, making it look like a gum drop. I bring my gifts for Niki from the back of the trailer, and she brings mine in from the car in a shopping bag with rope handles. We pile the packages on the table and dig in.

"Cool," I say. "How did you know my basketball was worn out?"

"It seems your neighbor, Mrs. Garcia, knows you better than anyone, so I asked her."

"Well, thank you. She was right, and this is wonderful." I give Niki a kiss.

I also open a package with a beautiful sweater inside. The selection was Niki's, but again the idea came from Mrs. G.

Niki opens the middle-sized box and holds the blouse to her shoulders. It is cream colored with puff sleeves and string tie just below the bodice. "It's lovely," she says, and gives me a kiss back. She opens the other gifts, making the right noises, though she doesn't ask to put the CD on the player I've bought for this very occasion.

When the gifts are done I make hot chocolate, and then we lie in the bunk listening to George Winston, who tonight sounds melancholy instead of beautiful. Niki again has her head on my arm, but this time we are fully dressed and there's no indication we'll make love. I find this sad not for the fact of it, but because everyone concerned (she and I) seems satisfied with the knowledge. Sometime past ten she rouses and says she'd better go home. I don't try to talk her out of it. We kiss, she leaves, and I pull off just my shoes before I climb back into bed. Sometime later I have the worst dream in a long while.

I'M DRIVING MY RIG, but when I look down I see I'm wearing the livery of a chauffeur. When I look up again the truck has changed to a long black car that bobs along like an ocean liner. When I take my hands from the wheel, nothing changes, the car goes where it wants. I look in the rearview mirror and see a casket, but when I actually turn in my seat the casket is gone and Kitty is lying on a pallet of satin pillows.

"I'm sorry," I tell her. Somehow I know she hears me, though she doesn't answer.

I've been leading the funeral procession, and the line of cars with their lights on stretches to the horizon behind me. Then suddenly none of the streets and landmarks are recognizable, and now when I look in the side mirror, I see the other cars have turned and left me alone. I know they are all at the gravesite, waiting for me, but the car is out of my control and I can't get turned around.

Now Kitty is in the seat beside me, looking straight ahead. She wonders what I'm doing, why I won't take her to be buried, but I can't tell her the reason because she won't do her part. When I say I'm sorry, she's supposed to tell me it's all right, that she understands, and then I'll be able to drive correctly again. But she won't forgive me until I cry, which proves I'm sorry. I do my best to make the tears come, but my cheeks remain dry as sand.

THERE IS A SAYING about the cure being worse than the disease, but I know something worse yet, a cure that's horrible and still doesn't fix the problem.

The next day, Christmas morning, I wait as long as I can stand before I call Allison. Luckily eight o'clock my time is ten o'clock her time. I figure they've already exchanged gifts, probably the night before like me, and have had breakfast, unlike me. It's too early for them to be out visiting, so this should be perfect. I haven't spoken to her since my visit, but what better occasion than Christmas for a casual call? Just a, hey-how-are-you? Nothing that you could make more out of than it is.

I assume it's Mr. Stovall who picks up because he's the only male in the house, although he sounds youngish to be Allison's father. He says hello, and when I ask to speak to Allison there's a strange hesitation. A minute later she's on the phone.

"Hello?"

"Guess who?" I say.

There's another pause, and for a minute I wonder whether the distance is responsible for these gaps.

"Jim?"

Of course Jim. Who else would it be?

"Yeah, you know. It's me. Just calling to say Merry Christmas. Just wanted to check up on you and Amanda. That your dad who answered? I meant to tell him Merry Christmas too. Maybe I can do that when we're through talking."

I figure, let's spread around the good cheer. Make everyone feel warm and wonderful. But there's another pause.

"This really isn't a good time," Allison says.

I want to tell her, sure it is. I imagine them all sitting around the tree in pajamas and robes. It's a great scene.

"What's up?" I ask. "Should I call later?"

This time the break is so long I look at the phone to make sure it hasn't come unplugged.

"Jim, I'm married. A week now. That was my husband, Carl, who answered."

I'm trying to process this, so I'm not upset, just confused. The feeling is like being punched in a fight; the punch doesn't hurt yet because you're not really sure what just happened. For some reason all I can think to say is, "Oh. Okay. Well, then. I'll let you go."

"Jim?"

Is she still talking to me? "Yeah."

"There is some good news." I think I hear her put her hand over the receiver, and I picture her looking around to see if anyone is listening. "I mean, it's good news for you, too. We're moving to Carl's place in California. Northern California, so it's not like we'll be neighbors, but you can come visit. Just one thing."

Here I know I'm supposed to say, Oh? And what's that one thing? But I'm still trying to figure where the punch came from, so I don't answer at all.

"We've decide not to tell Amanda who her biological father is. Maybe someday, but for now she's so young, Carl thinks it would be too confusing."

"Right, right," I say in the most agreeable way, though that isn't at all what I'm thinking. I'm thinking, *biological* father? Don't you mean *real* father? And who the fuck is this Carl to say what will confuse *my* daughter.

My mind is starting to clear and I don't feel so foggy. The trouble is that I now realize what's happening is exactly what I hoped would happen, what I made happen, and so it isn't like I can put up a big fuss about it.

I hang up and it isn't until I put on my jacket and walk out the door I realize I never told Allison goodbye.

CHAPTER THIRTEEN

WHAT SAVES ME IS work. From just after the first of the year until late April, I don't have a day off that isn't required by my log. Even then, I do maintenance of one kind or another to keep busy. I switch out the glad hands; remove, clean, and replace the fifth wheel. There's an entire weekend I spend scrubbing and rearranging the sleeper. I strip the bed and wash the sheets, then vacuum the floor and drapes. I clean out the fridge and restock it. While I'm working, the thought occurs to me that the sleeper isn't much smaller than my trailer, and it's more modern. Except that I'd miss Mrs. G, and I'd still need to park the rig somewhere, it might make sense to just move into the truck.

Another chore I finally find time for is changing the name on the door. I have "Buttercups" taken off, replaced with my name in the same gold leaf. Somehow this seems especially significant, a kind of transition. It's the graduation I never had from college.

The exception to this nonstop schedule is the Saturday I phone Owen to ask if he knows how to clean the injectors on the Cummins. He comes over with his tools to show me, but after we pull one and examine it, he says they're fine. It's nearly noon by then, so I say, "You want something to eat? I could grill some hamburgers." He answers, "Great," and we wind up eating and drinking beer the rest of the afternoon. We sit in the lawn chairs outside my front door and dig our toes into the patch of Astroturf I've staked to the ground.

I find I'm more comfortable with him than anyone else I know. I can tell him anything and the worst I'll get back is ridicule, which is okay because that's what he gives everyone, so it's like he doesn't mean it. Because of this, I tell him things I'd never tell Mrs. G. She has unshakable ideas about right and wrong, but as I said to Niki, I believe things are more complex than simply good and bad. Unlike my neighbor, Owen takes in my stories about Allison and Amanda, my mom and dad, even Niki, without much comment. Every once in a while he'll say, "Jesus, you're a knucklehead," but overall he's tolerant of my behavior. And I need that. Every so often, I just need someone to agree with me.

OVER THE NEXT FEW months I see Niki regularly, and when we're together things are fine. On the days we're both off, she stops by and admires how shiny the truck is, then we go out to eat. Sometimes we'll see a production at the Ahmanson or the Mark Taper or the Pasadena Playhouse. She'd never been to a play before I took her, and I'm happy to see she enjoys them. I still haven't won her over on the music, but I keep trying.

Even with all the social activity most of my effort is spent trying not to think about Allison's marriage, which of course makes me think about her and Amanda all the more. Fortunately, with time, the memory has become only a dull ache. Some recollection or a thought about what she's doing this very minute is no worse than poking an old bruise so you can say, yep, still there. I do get one card from her, giving their address and phone number in

Lodi, but I don't call or write her back. My thinking is that not responding is the best way to hurt her and protect me, while I know without a doubt it hurts me and protects her.

So maybe I can't win, but I can avoid. Conrad intuitively tracks my hours, though not precisely. He gives me more loads and more loads, until I really cannot keep up. Even so, I try to handle it. For one thing, the money is coming in, if not in a gusher, then at least as a healthy stream. I make double payments on my rig and bank the rest because I don't have anything to spend it on. In any case, it isn't the money itself that I care for, it's being able to point to something measurable and say, at least I'm worth *that*. Money is a number, and a number is something no one can challenge.

It's June. Amanda's birthday once again, but still I don't phone or write. I don't want to give Carl the satisfaction. Instead, I celebrate in my own way, which is to give Owen a call.

"Hey, Bronco Billy," he says. "What's up?"

"There's something I want to talk with you about. Could I buy you a drink?"

He lets go a burst of air that rattles his lips like a whoopee cushion. "Is a blue bird blue? How about La Casita?"

Twenty minutes later we're sitting at the same round table as last fall. Given what Owen told me back then, I'm surprised to find not much has changed except the staff. It's still La Casita, but a different waitress comes to take our orders.

"What can I getcha?" she asks. She's younger than our last waitress. Her hair is white-blond and looks fried to crisp. Her skin is equally pale, but sprayed with red bumps. She seems unhappy.

"Just a beer," I tell her.

"Glass or pitcher?"

"Glass."

"And you?"

"Beer and a bump," Owen says.

"Jack Daniels okay?"

Owen flicks his hand. "Whatever you got."

She makes the notes and walks away. I expect Owen to comment, but he doesn't say anything. He's strangely mellow today.

There's a ball game on the television attached to the wall, but no one in the place to watch it except us. The Dodgers are getting trounced again, or that's what I gather from the closed-caption text at the bottom of the screen. Normally I'd be interested, but I didn't invite Owen out to see the Boys in Blue lose another one.

We sit in silence until the drinks come and the waitress leaves. I'm on edge, knowing what he's already told me about being an owner/operator. He, on the other hand, is so relaxed I think he might nod off to sleep.

Owen downs the shot and sips the beer, and then says, "All right, Joe College, sock it to me."

I start by giving him some history, how things are going well and the work load is increasing. He must sense where this is going, but he only nods and smiles like, good for you son. He takes another drink. I bring him up to the present, saying how I hate to turn down work because I don't want Conrad to think there's anything I can't handle. Owen also smiles at this but doesn't otherwise respond. Finally I make the proposal I hope he won't be able to turn down.

"What I'm saying is, I need help, and I'd like that help to be you. Understand, I'm not looking for an employee. I'm looking for a partner."

This, I can see, rocks him. If he expected anything, it was a job offer. This is much more.

"Also, I'm not asking you to buy in. At least not for cash. You've got your Pete. If you're willing to put that in the company and accept regular wages for your time, we'll apply your share of the profit to you becoming an equal owner."

I can see he's skeptical, but he hasn't said no.

"So what's my share then? How long would I just get paid?"

I give him the net worth of the company, then divide by two. I don't add blue sky or goodwill of any kind; the number is based only on the revenue history, money in the bank, receivables, and a conservative projection. Except for my forecast, everything on the gozinta side is hard and fast. On the gozouta side, there isn't much to talk about either. My expenses are insurance, maintenance, and truck payments. I want to tell him beyond those two categories, gozinta and gozouta, nobody can guarantee the future. But he already knows it that.

I don't know what I expect, but if he turned me down flat I wouldn't be surprised. If he put me off with a joke about me being a dreamy-eyed college kid, that wouldn't be a shock either. What I don't anticipate is Owen looking serious, sipping his beer, calculating.

"Why would you do this?" he says finally.

I'm not sure what he means, and tell him so.

In answer he expands the thought. "You've got more here than I could put together in all the years I was on my own. Why would you up and give me half?"

In my head I review what I've told him, because to me it isn't giving anything, it's just spreading his payments over a few years. When I can't see how this could be misinterpreted, I say it all again: I make this, spend that, and I need help if I'm going to do more.

"So that's it?" he says. "Fifty-fifty, and I earn my way over time?"

I try to think of anything I've missed, but can't come up with a problem. "Is that fair?" I ask him. "Would you rather structure it some other way?"

He holds his glass in both hands and looks to see it's empty. Just a little foam around the rim. He pushes his lips out like a monkey, then sucks them back in. He does this several times, like he's trying to work something off his teeth.

"Pistol packin' mama," he says, apropos of nothing, though the reference gives me a warm feeling. "You know we're missing somebody here at the table. If I knew you were going to lay this on me, I'd've asked Iris to join us." He rubs his ear between his thumb and finger. "I gotta think on this, Sport. Right now I've got it good with Southwest. Home every night, union protection, paycheck at the end of the week. I'd be trading that for something neither of us can guarantee." He stands and pushes his chair back, then looks at me with a goofy grin. "Besides, I don't know that I want a partner who isn't smart enough to bargain any harder than you do."

I'm still sitting, but I raise my half-full glass to him. "Never up, never in," I say.

THE NEXT DAY OWEN phones me and we're off to the races. From what I can gather, his wife says he can do what he wants and apparently he wants to be his own boss again. Even so, it takes two more weeks for things to actually settle in. That is, for him to turn in his notice at SWT and for me to advise Conrad that I—we—can now take on twice as much work as before. As a hedge, I figure if Continental doesn't give us all we can handle I'm not under an exclusive contract with him, so I can get work from another broker as well.

The day after Owen starts, I get a call from Terry. I figure he's going to chew my ass for taking one of his best guys, and he does, but not in a serious I-hate-you-and-any-children-you-might-have way. He does call me a bum and a lowlife, but then he says if I ever need a good dispatcher to keep him in mind. It's clearly a compliment, and also sets me to thinking about actually owning a terminal someday and dropping a broker altogether. I start to daydream about our own salesmen and secretaries, dock foreman, maintenance mechanics. I make myself dizzy with the details.

Over the next couple of months, things aren't much different for me except that there is slightly more paperwork and the unanticipated benefit of receiving a discount on parts because we're no longer a one-man operation. We also get an insurance break for multiple vehicles. Harder to quantify is my feeling of assurance, knowing we can keep one truck on the road if something happens to the other, so that there'll be at least some money coming in. One additional pleasure is that I talk with Owen constantly, though we rarely see each other face to face. I've been working alone for a long time, but now it's like having an office mate, even though our cubicles are sometimes a thousand miles apart.

All in all, things are good. I see Niki enough to keep us together, and though I hate to say it, that's enough for me. It seems the less I'm involved with females the better my life is. Sometimes I think if I could just drive and play basketball, I could forget the sporadic heaven of being with a woman and be quite happy with the here and now.

THE FOLLOWING AUTUMN A little thing happens that goes from inconvenient to terrible. The sequence of events deteriorates something like this: You're late to a job interview and cut through the park to save time, but step in a pile of dog crap and have to choose between being late and being stinky, so you choose stinky hoping the crap falls away by the time you actually see anyone. And most of it does fall away, but all the time your potential boss is talking with you he's wrinkling his nose, and after three weeks of the phone not ringing, you know darn well he picked someone else who was less qualified but smelled better and now is making the money you should be making.

That's the parable version.

The actual incident starts when Conrad gives me a load of concrete castings to pick up in Delano and drop in Grass Valley. I leave home in the small hours and stop in McFarland for breakfast at a diner off East Perkins Avenue, a little place called Connie's. Connie is actually a Greek man named Constantine and not a cute young lady like you'd hope. Connie is the cook, and Frieda, his wife, is the waitress. The whole front of the restaurant is glass, though that doesn't say much since it's about as wide as two people standing with their arms outstretched. Inside are four swivel stools at the counter and four booths along the wall.

Frieda is a big woman with a ruddy face and reddish frizzy hair. She reminds me of an English milkmaid, though I suppose that's only because of her complexion; I've never met an English milkmaid that I know of. She asks me what I want and I tell her eggs. Three.

"And hash browns with onions. And toast."

"White, wheat or sourdough?"

"Sourdough."

"Anything to drink?"

"Coffee," I tell her. "And orange juice."

McFarland is a farming community, and I like stopping here because it reminds me of Iowa. I like the men who sit in the booths. They are different men on different days, but they always look the same and sound the same; seed caps and overalls, and complaining about low crop prices or excessive regulations. Their fingers are as thick as my thumbs.

"The thing I'd like to know," one of the men is saying today, "is how the hell we're supposed to grow their food without water? And what gets me worse, the same environmental crybabies who're so worried about some poor tweedle-dee-dee bird losing its home are the very ones who'll scream to high heaven when the price of their corn flakes goes up."

Three other men give their general agreement in the form of clanking silverware and slurped coffee.

"Here you go, Hon," Frieda says to me. "What else can I get you?"

"That ought to do it," I tell her.

She tears off a check and slides it next to my plate. Then she takes the coffee pot around the counter, chatting with the farmers as if they were neighbors as well as customers, which they probably are.

After breakfast I head north ten miles on 99 and exit at Garces Highway, going east. I pass Driver Road and Zachary Avenue, then head down Wallace toward the lake. Almost to the Famoso Porterville Highway, I duck into the fenced yard and stop at the guard shack.

From the cab I look down and ask, "What all do you make here?" I know some of it, of course, but I'm trying to be friendly.

But the guard doesn't answer. Instead, he makes a show of checking a roster to see that I'm expected. From this angle I can see only the lower part of his face, the rest is blocked by the wall of the shack above his window. With what I have to go on he looks like someone who has been in his share of bar fights and won about half. His fingers are wrapped around the clipboard and I see L-O-V-E tattooed on the knuckles of his right hand and H-A-T-E tattooed on the left. Finally he hangs the clipboard back on a nail and points along the front of the building.

"Door sixteen," he says.

I drive past inventory stacked in the yard and recognize immediately what the products are: parking lot bumpers and concrete highway barriers. The layers are divided with four-by-fours and add to maybe twelve feet high. Bad place to be during an earthquake, I think. I swing in close to the dock at door sixteen, then pull away again, finally cranking the wheel hard left. This gets me angled in the right direction for backing; I can guide myself by looking over my left shoulder and out the side window. Close to the dock I ease up, inching back until I bump.

And there you are. Nice and square.

I hop out of the cab, then climb a metal ladder between two bays, going in search of the shipping manager. Soon enough I find him in the dock office. He's built like a ball, squashed down from too much responsibility and not enough authority to pump him up again. He has no hair and looks like he's about to cry.

"Continental?" he asks.

I nod.

"Hope you aren't in a hurry."

"Why's that?" I ask him.

"Hyster's down." He points out the shipping office window to the dock, where I see a yellow and black forklift with an oily stain spreading from under the counterweight. The sight reminds me of a TV crime show. All that's missing is the outline around the body. "I figure it's the transmission," he says, "but can't say for sure."

"You just have the one lift?"

"You're looking at it."

"How long you figure you'll be out of commission?"

"'Til it's fixed."

"How about a rental?"

"Ordered one. Be here tomorrow."

There's a guy standing beside the lift, scratching his head with one hand and bracing his hip with the other.

"That your mechanic?" I ask, hoping it isn't.

The shipping manager looks from the man to me. "If I was you," he says, "I'd get me a room."

I GO BACK TO my rig and crank down the trailer's landing gear, pop off the glad hands, uncouple the electrical, and reach in to jerk the fifth wheel pin. I drive out from under the trailer, leaving it at the dock and hoping it will be loaded by the time I come back the next day. We're too far apart to raise Conrad on the CB, so I bobtail into town and find a phone booth.

"Better call the consignee," I tell him when he comes to the phone. "I can't say how long this is going to take."

"You want to call it off? Reschedule? I can probably find you something over at the coast."

I do have input regarding my assignments, but I figure this one isn't my call. Conrad wants to protect his reputation with his customers just like I do with him.

"Whatever you think is best," I say. "I don't want to get you in Dutch with anyone."

He hems and haws and then says, "They say they'll have a lift tomorrow. Let's give 'em that long. If that doesn't pan out, we'll reschedule."

I tell Conrad it sounds like a plan and let him go. I call Owen but only leave a message. As I hang up the phone, I wonder what to do with myself for the next twenty-four hours. I've got a basketball and change of clothes in the truck, and all I need for sleep is a place to park. But it's ten-thirty in the morning and I hate to waste the day messing around. I think a minute, then dig my calling card out of my pocket. I dial Allison's number.

"Hey," I say when she picks up. I don't say more, hoping she'll recognize my voice right off.

"Who is this?" she says.

"It's Jim."

"Oh," she says. "Are you in the area?"

In a manner of speaking I am, depending on how you define "the area." I'm a hundred miles from her. Two hours. I could be there before one o'clock.

"Yeah," I tell her. "I'll be near your place around twelve-thirty or one. So I thought, you know, maybe we could get a sandwich or something."

It's only true that I'll be in her town if she agrees to see me. Allison doesn't answer right away and I wonder what's going through her head: Where's Carl? What she has planned for the day? Will it be Amanda's nap time?

"If you want to see Amanda, sure," she says. "Why don't I make us lunch and we can eat in the park? Would that be all right?"

I tell her it would, though I'm somewhat disappointed by the way she answers. Of course I want to see my daughter, but I also want to see Allison. The way she answers doesn't sound like she feels the same. Also, meeting in the park feels less intimate than meeting at her house, but what did I expect?

"Do you have a cell phone?" she says. "You could give me the number, and I can give you mine. We'd be sure not to miss one another."

My laugh comes out like a snort and before I can stop myself I say, "I don't think so." I don't want her to think I can't afford one, but until now I never considered it a worthwhile expense; ninety percent of my talking is on the CB.

Thankfully she doesn't make a big deal of my answer and just gives me directions to the park. When we hang up, I look at my watch, take a deep breath, and I'm off.

I DRIVE A HUNDRED miles and she drives three blocks, and I beat her to the park anyway. When I arrive, I look around but she's nowhere to be seen. So that I don't think about the upcoming visit, I take my basketball and shoot while I wait, though I check my watch every few minutes. It seems like forever, but ten minutes later I hear her voice.

"Hello, Jim," she says from behind me.

I turn to see her pulling a wagon with a child, not a baby, riding inside. I'm transfixed by how big Amanda has grown. She's a different person, and I wonder where the other one went.

"Hey," I answer. "Pretty wild." I'm looking at Amanda when I say this.

"Isn't she something?"

Allison walks on and I follow. We go to an area defined by a concrete border and filled with wood chips. There are swings and a jungle gym, and Allison sets Amanda free to play. We walk to a bench along the perimeter, taking a seat as our daughter runs up a set of blue metal steps to a yellow platform, then dives headlong down a red slide.

"So how've you been?" Allison asks me. She hands me a peanut butter and jelly sandwich wrapped in wax paper.

"Okay. Great. How about you?"

"Not married yet, I wouldn't imagine."

This is a non-sequitur and badly worded at that. For a moment I'm confused, wondering if she's talking about herself. When I finally understand, I smile but don't say anything, as if verifying her suspicion that I'm still single would be an admission of failure.

"I saw your truck." She nods in the direction of the parking lot. "Pretty impressive."

This seems the time for me to act pensive and deep, as if Allison and I have both seen a lot of life and can look back from this vantage with wistful regret. Whatever I say next should include the phrase "if only," but all I can come up with is, "Thanks. I've got a partner, too. Owen Youniacutt? The fellow I told you about?"

She laughs. "I remember. So now you're a shipping magnate."

I check for signs of mockery but find none, though I wish I had. Derision takes effort, which means the person being derided is important enough to warrant the trouble. But Allison is merely relaxed, having a chat with someone she—dare I say it—used to know.

Amanda is running from one piece of equipment to the next, climbing stairs, sliding down chutes, peeking out portholes. She's barely older than two and I wonder if she's developed the sense to stay away from the edges of high places. Watching her makes my stomach tighten, especially because Allison seems so unconcerned. I know I can't eat, so I rewrap my sandwich and set it on the seat beside me.

Allison has stretched her arm along the back of the bench and now turns three quarters toward me. "You never call to check up on her," she says. "You don't send a card on her birthday or at Christmas."

"It isn't that I don't care, Ali," I say, feeling exposed.

"You have an interesting way of showing it."

I suppose I'm riled because she isn't. She acts as if everything is fine, and I realize that for her it's probably true. Since we broke up, whenever we do talk I feel I'm the only one in the world who is incomplete. Everyone else has all their duckies lined up, but mine can't even find the pond.

"You know about Kitty," I say, louder than I intended. I'm surprised to find I'm shaking. "Isn't it obvious why I left? Can't you figure it out?" Sometimes I wonder if she ever actually knew me. She acts like the overriding event of my life is inconsequential.

Allison looks at me with a curious expression, then pushes herself standing. She goes to Amanda, who has grown tired of the other equipment and wants to be lifted into a swing seat. I follow, feeling dismissed. She stands behind Amanda, gently pushing her. I'm in front so that I can see my daughter's face. As she reaches the apex of her arc, I catch her feet and send her back to her mother.

"What happened to your sister and to your family was a trage-dy," Allison begins, and I'm glad to know we agree on something. "But you've fixed on that tragedy to the extent you can't see the bigger world. You think it makes you so different, so special, but you're using her death, Jim, to shield yourself. In some way I rec-ognized that early on, even when we were together. But it took getting away from you to see it clearly."

I'm really angry now. She makes it sound as if I arranged for Kitty to dive into that rock so I'd have an excuse to act badly the rest of my life. I try to control my breathing because I don't want to come off like a lunatic. I talk extra quietly and neutral so I don't scare Amanda.

"You think you know how I feel? Just because you're a shrink, you can get inside my head and crawl around and figure me out? You have no idea what I've gone through."

She looks at me, not smiling, not angry. Professionally cool. I hate it.

"If you mean I haven't experienced the exact same thing as you, of course you're right. But I still understand what I'm seeing. If you were a patient I could take more time and ease you through this. But since I never know when I'm going to see you, I'll be blunt. You aren't special, my friend. You aren't different. You're afraid, all right, but in the same way as everyone else. You're afraid you'll make a mistake. You're afraid you'll commit to something you can't back out of. Afraid something better will come along and you won't be available. You're completely incapable of claim-ing a relationship as your own and seeing it through despite the difficulties. You, Jim Bass, are a coward."

That's not true. It's completely opposite of true. I now know what I want and it's her. It's both of them. I can do this now. I know I can.

I wish I could think more clearly so I could tell her. If Allison knew how I felt, how could she not feel the same toward me? But

I also know if I speak it will come out as splutters and grunts, so we push Amanda a bit more.

A minute later my child says, "Me, Mommy."

Allison smiles at her but says to me, "Independent." She steps to the front of the swing and asks Amanda, "What do you say for the help we've given you?"

"Thank you."

"You're quite welcome," I tell her, glad for this new direction.

We watch as she pumps her legs out, pulling against the chains with her hands, then tucking her legs under and swinging back. She goes from nothing to a respectable back and forth sweep. Allison seems completely absorbed in this accomplishment until she turns to me.

"You see how a swing works, don't you? If you just sit there, it's stable and safe, but it's no fun. You never get anywhere. If you want progress, Jim, you've got to risk being a little out of balance."

CHAPTER FOURTEEN

O NE DAY IN MARCH I get home late on a Wednesday and I'm no sooner in the door than the phone rings. Who-ever it is, is blubbering and sobbing but doesn't speak. "Hello?" I say.

No answer, just ragged breathing. I think the caller is a woman, but I'm not sure. When I last phoned Dad he was back home, on disability from work and going to therapy. Now I wonder if some new disaster has happened to him and this is my mother who can't control herself. Or maybe it's Dad's neighbor, Mrs. Trindle. Or Alli-son. Oh God, I think. Not her. Not Amanda. Oh God.

"HELLO!" I shout. "WHO IS THIS? GODDAMMIT, SAY SOMETHING!"

The caller finally clears her throat and says, "Iss only me."

Mrs. G. "Are you hurt?" I say. "Are you home? I'll be right there."

"No," she says. "I ain' hurt. Only, could you come over? Tha would be good."

I slam down the phone and race next door. I knock but don't wait for an answer. The door is open and I go inside. Mrs. G is sitting at the kitchen table with her face in her hands.

"What's wrong? Are you okay?"

I want to do something. Call 911. Get her in the car and go to the hospital. She says she isn't hurt, but I'm not sure I believe her. Mrs. G picks up her head to look at me. Her eyes are red and swollen, but I see no cuts or blood. Nothing seems broken.

"What happened? The girls? Lupe?"

Mrs. G shakes her head. She takes a deep breath and smiles a sad smile. "Din I tole you drinking would kill Hector someday?"

OVER THE NEXT HOUR she tells me what she knows, though it's only the broad strokes. The car he was driving belonged to a customer. A friend of Hector's was with him. A liquor store owner in the High Desert reported two Hispanics had stolen money and beer just hours before Hector was found at the bottom of a canyon. Cash and empty cans were scattered throughout the car. Hector's friend was found crumpled under the dash, drunk but alive.

"How's Angela?" I ask.

"Ay-way. I jus come from there. She says his homie, Oscar Nunez, come early this morning with a idea about a job. Angela toles Hector, doan do nothin' stupid, 'cause she's makin' money at the vegetable stan. Only he says he's tired of her sayin' how much he can have an what he can buy. He says she'll see the money from her business ain' nothing compared to what he can make."

"And how about her children?"

"The babies pull at her clothes and ask wha's wrong, how come she's cryin'? Angela hold 'em up and say, 'Shhh, shhh. Iss all okay.' She doan know what else to tell 'em."

I think about Kitty's death and how I felt. The memory washes over me like a wave. "Give them some time," I tell Mrs. G. "They'll be all right." I say this wanting it to be true, not believing it. "Can I do anything for you?"

"Hector liked you," Mrs. G says. "Would you go to the funeral?"

I ACCEPT THAT PEOPLE die, but if going to funerals is a stitch in our social fabric, we ought to be allowed to substitute funerals of people we don't know, or at least don't care about, for folks we're close to. Put another way, I don't want to go today but feel I should.

For the occasion I've bought a pair of black dress slacks and a white, long-sleeve shirt. I already have black shoes, which are like new because I never wear them, and I own a tie. The tie I leave knotted around the hook of a hanger so I don't have to fuss with a four-in-hand or Windsor or half-Windsor. If the knot was a bowline or hay-hitch, I could tie it with my eyes closed, but the others I might do once every five years so I get rusty.

I'm nearly ready when I hear the exhaust of a VW, which to me always sounds like snow chains on pavement. A minute later there's a tap on the door and Niki lets herself in.

"Thanks for coming," I tell her.

"I'm glad you asked."

"Not exactly a gondola ride down the Grand Canal."

"For better or for worse," she says, which is the sort of thing she's been saying lately.

She's wearing a black dress that could pass for a party outfit and probably is, except she also has a lacy black shawl around her shoulders to tone things down. All in all, she looks so frilly and floaty I simultaneously think of Stevie Nicks and jellyfish, which you wouldn't imagine could be contained in the same thought, but there you are. I'm so damn comforted to see her, I wrap her in my arms and hold her for an embarrassingly long time.

When we go outside, I see that Mrs. G's car is still in her drive. We're early, and for a minute I consider going next door to see if she wants a ride. But as close as we are, we aren't family, not that kind of family, and anyway I imagine Guadalupe and/or Maria Elena will pick her up.

I hold open the passenger door for Niki and then drive north, staying to the side streets and avoiding the freeway. Somehow it seems more acceptable to spend the time moving rather than sitting and waiting. Neither of us says much as we watch the packed-together cities roll by: Ontario and Upland, Cucamonga and Fontana. With their Targets and Burger Kings, their donut shops, their cleaners, the scene could be painted on a canvas, spinning by again and again. Dreams feel more real to me than this.

When I stop at a red light I say to Niki, "Look at them. They don't even know."

"Who?" she says. "What don't they know?"

"The people there, crossing side to side. They don't know Hector is dead. And they wouldn't care if they did know. Keep your head down, stay busy, so you don't have to think."

Her eyebrows are knitted when she looks at me and says, "You all right?"

I can't imagine what she's talking about. I'm fine. "Did you ever read *Watership Down*? The rabbits are all really cowards, see. So when one of them disappears they don't want to pay attention. They just overlook the death. I mean, there's lots of them, right? So what the hell? A few dead here, a few there. What difference does it make?"

"Jim?"

"Yeah?"

"Would you like me to drive? You look pale."

I don't feel pale. It's just that I'm thinking of lots of things at once. I almost laugh and say, here I go again—thinking. But she wouldn't get it.

One of the things on my mind is heaven, namely, is there such a place? I wonder what Niki believes. It probably doesn't matter, but a positive answer would give me hope, which is something I could use right now.

"You never mention religion," I say to her. "Any thoughts about what comes after this?"

"This what?" she says. "This life, this funeral?"

"Same thing," I tell her. "At least for Hector."

Niki takes a breath and lets it out slowly. "My mom makes fun of people who go to church. She says it's a crutch for the weak. But then she'll feed quarters into a scale that tells her weight and fortune. The fortune she believes because it's always good. The weight she dismisses because it couldn't possibly be accurate."

She's quiet for so long I figure that's the end of the story, but I don't know any more now than when she started.

"So? What are you saying?"

She laces her fingers and stretches toward the windshield. When she's done, her hands flop back into her lap. "People do what they need to get by. They believe what suits them."

To me this is surprisingly cynical, but I find nothing wrong in the logic.

"So how about you?" she asks then. "You never talk about church or God or religion. Are you an atheist?"

I think about my journey, my descent: altar boy considering the priesthood, downgraded to a C and E Catholic in college, to lapsed, to nothing. I shrug my answer.

"So you're agnostic?"

I don't answer. I can't even commit to being uncommitted.

Despite my slow pace, we arrive at Saint Teresa's before most of the others. There's a white hearse parked in a semi-circular drive between the narthex and a fountain. A few cars are parked near the rectory. Other than that, we're alone. I drive to a far corner of the parking lot and swing the VW around to keep an eye on things. I turn off the engine and we sit in the car.

"Kitty asked me once if we were God's dolls." Niki doesn't have a clue what I'm talking about, but I'm still thinking of the religion thing. "When he makes us sick and then he makes us well. Or when we can't understand what Sister Josephine is talking about, do you think God is playing with us like His dolls?"

"Jim? You're sweating."

"It's hot," I tell her.

She touches her hand to my forehead. "You're clammy. Are you coming down with something?"

If I am, it's been coming on for a long time.

I hear a car and look over to see Lupe's Chevy. The car stops behind the hearse and out pile Big Lupe, Mrs. G, and a young woman who can only be Maria Elena. A moment later another car arrives and I see it's Angela and the kids. I work the handle and bump the door with my shoulder.

I tell Niki, "Time to go."

AT THE VESTIBULE SHE takes my arm, and we walk up the center aisle to the open casket. Mrs. G is sitting up front on the end, and all the kids are lined up next to her by age. As we pass, I put my hand on her shoulder and she puts her hand on top of mine. We take two more steps forward and look down at Hector. I'm appalled by what I see. He looks like a generic person, not like himself. A mannequin. I have the thought that he'd have done a better job on his own face than the mortician did. The makeup looks like wood putty. I think of the repair job he did on my car, how you can't even tell it's been fixed. How Hector's work looks better and costs less.

All of this makes me want to laugh, and something does come out, but because I'm trying to hold it in, I choke instead.

Niki squeezes my arm tight and I know she misunderstands. She thinks I'm crying, but I'm not. It's just all so goddamn funny, I wish I could share the joke with her.

We stand a minute, looking down. I don't know whether Niki is saying a prayer, but I know I'm not. I'm so mad at Hector, I'm calling him a stupid son-of-a-bitch in my head. Leaving his wife and those kids.

I hear a sob and turn to see Angela holding Little Lupe's chin in her cupped hand. I can't stand it. A fatherless child. A childless father. I let out a sound that isn't a word and nothing I've thought of or planned. Just a long "Aahhggwww."

I run out the side door and along the arcade of the church, finally stopping and resting my back against the stuccoed wall. I bend forward and put my hands on my knees and something comes up from my stomach, not vomit but bile, and I spit and choke and spit again. I punch my thigh with my fist, then punch again. I bang the stucco until the edge of my hand is raw. I slide down the wall, tearing my shirt and clawing my back against its roughness. I hug my knees and sit alone until the service ends.

WHEN I HEAR THE organist start up with "Be Not Afraid," I know it's time to pull myself together. I stand and walk around the outside of the church to the front. I'm just in time to see them slide the casket into the back of the hearse. Niki comes out of the church, sees me, and takes my arm. She's about to say something when Owen and I spot each other.

"Some shitty deal, huh, Boss?" Owen says. "What happened to your shirt? You look like you fell into a fan."

"I tripped," I tell him. "Niki, this is Owen Youniacutt, my partner. Owen, this is Niki Lynch, from the bank."

Owen looks at her approvingly and says, "Must be a full-service institution."

"We do our best." She slips her arm out from mine and offers her hand. "I've heard a lot about you. Nice to meet face to face."

"You going to the house?" I ask Owen. "There's a reception, or whatever you call it."

"Wake," he says and shakes his head. "Not my cup of tea. I'm going to get back to work. You go ahead, though." To Niki he says, "Nice to meet you. Now I know who to see if I ever get in a jam over money."

"I hope the next time we see each other it's under better circumstances."

Mrs. G comes out of the church then, holding Angela around her shoulders. The baby is in Angela's arms and Lupe is trailing behind. I don't want to intrude, so I take Niki to the car and wait for the procession.

When the cars begin to line up, I tuck in about midway. A funeral guy comes down the row, slapping orange stickers on the windshields. When he gets to me he says, "Lights on, please," and moves on.

With the last sticker in place we move out like a mechanical snake, each car a little metal segment. We drive through a semi-rural area of rundown horse properties, where the homes have porches screened in by mesh made nearly opaque with grime. The houses are sided in weathered clapboard. Everything has the appearance of being incomplete: jalopies with three wheels, tricycles with two.

"Kind of creepy here," Niki says. "It's like the people made an attempt at a life but could never quite accomplish it. It's a Hamburger Helper life. All that's missing is the hamburger."

She means this as a joke and I appreciate the effort, but I'm not in the mood.

"You seem so sad," she says.

"I think you were right about me coming down with something."

She waits a minute, then says, "At the church…I didn't come out after you because, you know, I figured you wanted to be alone."

"Sure," I say. "No problem."

The hearse turns down a narrow lane, stops at the corner, then turns right again. We skirt a wind-blown field where dry grass gives way to scattered live oaks. The motorcade turns once more and slides under a filigreed archway, then meanders to the gravesite. We pull up to the curb and a moment later the only sounds are latches opening and doors slamming closed.

Niki takes my hand and we tromp across the grass toward a mound of earth concealed under Astroturf. There's a chrome contraption framing the hole, and rigging spanning the opening. We sit in metal folding chairs, and though it isn't cold, Niki wraps both her arms around one of mine, holding me close, as if for warmth.

As soon as we're home, I go to the trailer to change my shirt. Niki waits with me inside, then we go next door to the wake. Except for the priest, everyone from the gravesite is already at Mrs. G's. Most of the folks are women, probably friends of Mrs. G, though some are younger. These, I suspect, are neighbors and friends of Angela's. Some have little children clinging to their dresses, or carried in crooked arms. There is one old man wearing a tweed jacket despite the heat. He's bent and uses a cane to help him shuffle along. His hair is white, and so is the grizzled stubble on his face. He talks to no one, just fixes a plate of food and sits by himself. It makes me wonder if he travels from one funeral to the next as a sort of moving soup kitchen.

I'm most intrigued by a group of Hispanic guys who travel about the front room as a unit, like a school of fish. They're late teens or early twenties, beefy, with tattoos showing on necks and backs of hands. They greet Big Lupe solemnly and hug Angela, and I wonder if one of them was the passenger in the truck along with Hector. I suspect not, because they all appear unhurt. I'm surprised that despite their size and appearance, they are gentle and respectful. When Little Lupe wanders by one of them, a big arm scoops up the child. The man says to him, "It's a sad day, heh, *mijo?* Come sit with me."

I go into the kitchen to see Mrs. G. She's stirring a pot of some sort of meat in a red sauce. Pork or beef, I can't tell, but it's enough to feed the neighborhood. On the counter there are two Styrofoam containers of tortillas, corn and flour, and beside them bowls of beans and chopped onions, peppers, and cheese.

"I'm really sorry," I tell her. "I wish there was something I could say."

She shrugs as if lifting buckets of grief with her shoulders. "You're here. Thas all you can do." She holds up a ladle dripping with meat and juice. "You wanna eat?"

My stomach has calmed down by now, but not that much. I shake my head. "Maybe later."

I hug Mrs. G and leave to find Niki, who I discover talking with Angela in the backyard. They've never met before, but to see Niki hunched down in front of Angela's chair you'd think they were longtime friends. I keep my distance to give them privacy. When Niki stands, she leans over and kisses the top of Angela's head. They take each other's hands, left in right, right in left, and exchange words that I can't hear.

She sees me and comes over.

"Do you want to stay?"

"No."

"Angela says her sister left already."

"So I heard."

Niki takes my hand and together we walk around the side of the house and back to my place. She has work to do, so we go to her car instead of the trailer. I lean against the passenger's door and pull Niki to me, feeling the pressure of her body along the length of mine. At first she puts her head against my chest, but soon she arches back to look me in the face.

"Funerals are important," she says.

I don't know how she means this or what motivated the comment, so I only answer, "If you say so."

"They are," she insists. "They remind us not to wait for things to come to us. The thought of life slipping past makes me sort of panicky to get moving, to go out and get what I want."

In general I agree with her, though I suspect not in the specifics she means.

"It's time we talk about our future together," she says.

"Sure," I tell her. "That would be great."

"Not today, though. We've had enough seriousness for now."

"Right. Some other time."

"But soon."

"Definitely soon," I say. "Absolutely."

I walk her to the other side of the car and hand her the keys. I open the door, and she gives me a peck on the cheek before she slides inside. I stand in the street, watching as she drives away. As soon as she's around the corner, I go inside and call Allison.

CHAPTER FIFTEEN

I HAVEN'T SPOKEN WITH HER for months, so I'm sure Allison wonders why I'm calling now. I'd be happy to tell her if I knew myself. It's probably the funeral like Niki said, though I'm not entirely convinced. Nothing has changed for *me* with Hector's death. I keep telling myself that. Nothing has changed for *me*.

"Hello?"

"Hey there," I answer.

A long pause. "Jim?"

My first thought is, Why is it always like this? but my second is, she at least got it right on the first guess, so things are improving.

"Yep. Just checking in. Wanted to see what's new with you guys."

Another pause. Based on our last conversation, especially the part about me being a coward, I'm afraid of what might come next.

"Well," she draws out the word. "Amada has an earache. She's been screaming her head off, poor thing."

Good! I think. Of course I don't mean good that she has an earache, but good that here's a nice, manageable problem we can talk about. Something we can solve. Something where no one dies. Kids have earaches, then they get better.

"Have you tried antibiotics?" I ask in a calm, parental voice, as if it's a Saturday morning and we're having our usual cup of coffee.

"Of course," Allison says. "But we're beyond that now. The doctor wants to put in a shunt to help the infection drain."

Logically, I know this is not a big deal. Actually I don't know it, because I'm not really sure what's involved with a shunt, or for that matter exactly what a shunt is. My consolation is Allison's voice doesn't sound panicked in the I-have-to-go-the-paramedics-are-at-the-door sort of way. So I don't feel terribly concerned. What I do feel is left out, and I wonder what other illnesses and triumphs I've missed. But I'm also starting to figure that, like Scrooge, I can change and the future can be better. In fact, as Allison and I talk, I resolve to be different, to call and write more often, which in turn nourishes the bud of an idea I've been sheltering for a long time.

Here's how I've come to my thought: Number one, it's clear I have never *not* loved Allison. I may have cast the feeling in different lights, tried on different approaches, but I have never not loved her. Number two, she has never been actually hostile toward me, which has to be significant given the circumstance. Number three, and most of all, we have a child together. Could there be a stronger bond than that?

So my bud of an idea, my tickling half-notion is: Might we actually get back together and make things work? Might we realize what a mistake we made (all right, *I* made) but still live happily together from this point forward? Things would be messier on her end, the divorce and all, but she'd get over it. I mean, she'd have me. Not that I'm the greatest thing since, I don't know, Louis Prima, but we obviously have a lot in common. The more I consider the possibility, the more plausible it seems.

As she talks I'm thinking about the type of place we might buy, how big, which school district. I imagine how Mom will react, wanting to make a fuss with wedding gifts and coming to visit. I even consider how I'll tell Allison she was right about me. I'll say, I know I was wrong, but look how I've shaped up! See how I've come around! In thirty years when friends come over, she'll tell the story. Everyone will laugh and say they can't believe there was ever trouble between us because we're obviously so perfect for each other.

"There's some other news, too," Allison says.

Her voice has changed, and I'm hoping she won't tell me Amanda has the flu on top of everything else. It's a concern because I know there's something going around. I've had a bit of a scratchy throat myself. I almost mention it when she rushes on.

"I'm pregnant, Jim. Amanda is going to get a brother."

IN THE TWO WEEKS following Hector's funeral, Niki and I see each other regularly, but she doesn't bring up the topic of OUR FUTURE TOGETHER. In fact when she comes over, we talk very little. Both of us seem to need and are satisfied with physical love, anything else being an unwanted complication. Whenever I'm home, she stops by my trailer after her work, showers, and we hop into the bunk. An hour or two later she leaves. Simple. And nice. I could go on like this forever.

But if sex is therapy, she heals more quickly than me. On the third Monday after Hector's service, she phones to say Mr. Foote has given her permission for a long lunch. She asks if I'm free to join her, and when I say yes she asks me to pick a nice spot. I choose Our Daily Bread in Claremont.

The front of the shop is only about a hundred square feet, with three small tables and a long deli case. At the end of the case is a cash register, and behind that on the wall is a blackboard with the regular menu and daily specials in various colored chalk. There's a door in the bead board paneling leading to a back room, which I imagine is as big as the front. This is where they bake the bread the place is known for. The smells fill the neighborhood.

Niki is standing near one of the bistro tables on the sidewalk as I come up. She looks pretty in a dark skirt and suit jacket. She's wearing a white blouse with a ruffled collar, and is holding her purse by the strap with both hands so that it hangs well below her knees. This makes her look young and tentative. I'm a fool for not giving her more attention. She is here, I say to myself, and Allison is not.

Niki smiles when she sees me, and we go inside to a table by the window. A minute later a fellow comes up to us and pulls a pad from what I know is an apron pocket, but instead reminds me of a codpiece. He squats down beside Niki in a ridiculously intimate way and says, "And what can I get you, Miss?"

He's handsome as a TV star, wearing a dark green shirt and tan shorts. His hair is streaked in sun-bleached colors from blond to coffee, and I expect when he smiles there will be a twinkle off one tooth. If he tries speaking with an Australian accent, I may have to hit him. I really don't like this guy.

"What's good?" Niki says, eating up the attention.

"We're famous for our meatloaf," he answers, making the simple statement sound lewd. "The portions are so big, you can take half home for a second meal."

Really, really don't like him.

"Well, you've sold me," Niki says. "Only don't bring a container just yet. I'm pretty hungry."

He smiles at her appreciatively and then turning, stands to take my order. For this, I am grateful.

"Just a salad. Water to drink."

The waiter never actually looks at me, but smirks as he's writing on his pad. If I were to snatch it from his hands, I know it would read: cannot—achieve—erection.

"Thank you, sir. Your orders will be right up."

When he leaves, Niki reaches across the table and takes my hand in both of hers. "You've been so down lately. Is there something besides the funeral bothering you?"

I shake my head. "I'm aces," I tell her. "Right as rain."

"Good. Because I've got some news I think you'll like. Actually," she adds, "it may not be news to you. I don't know how closely you watch this sort of thing."

"Tell me."

She takes a breath like she's preparing for a speech. "You only have one payment left on your loan. You're a model customer."

I knew that, the part about the loan anyway.

"Does that mean I'm due all the rights and privileges thereby afforded?" I say this trying to be as happy as she is. And if not that, trying to be happy at all. I raise my eyebrow in what I hope she interprets as a lascivious gesture. I know I'm competing with the waiter, and I know I'm the only one who thinks there's a competition. But I feel like a malfunctioning machine that's running down or gotten whacked on the side so that every response is ill timed and inappropriate. There's something wrong with me and I'm unable to make it right.

"Never mind that just now," Niki says, smiling. She still has my hand and she gives it a squeeze. "Think what you can do now with those same payments."

I don't want to think what I could do with them, so I stay quiet. The silence goes on for an uncomfortably long time until finally she offers the suggestion she hoped I'd ask for.

"You could buy a house," she says.

Before I can stop myself I answer, "Why would I want to do that?"

Now she lets go of me to raise her hands. I think of the pope giving a sermon, or a fisherman showing the length of his catch.

"For one thing you'd be more comfortable," she says. "You're so cramped where you are. Also it's a smart financial move; you'll be building equity." She hesitates, then gives me a smile. "If you had a house, I could move in with you."

I knew this was coming, but even so it's an effort to keep the smile on my face. I answer, trying to sound as if I'm teasing, as if we actually want the same thing and my response is a sort of foreplay. "But you already have a house."

Her face softens. She is vulnerable. She's going to tell me something important. Something intimate. Something, I believe, she's been working up to for weeks.

"Actually, the house I live in is my grandmother's. She's been in pretty good health until recently, but…" Niki smiles a sad smile and shrugs. "I can't be with her during the day because I'm working at the bank. And now she can't be alone. She's going to live with her daughter, my Aunt Julia. You met her, remember?"

I tell her I do, and I realize this is why we haven't spent a night at Niki's house. It wouldn't have been private. The knowledge buoys me.

"Anyway," she continues, "the house is up for sale. So I thought, you know, this would be the perfect time for us to get more serious."

Serious.

I think about where I am in life. I'm twenty-five; not old, not a kid. I don't have Allison and never will. With Allison goes Amanda. I do have Niki, if "have" is the right word, which I don't believe it is. You don't *have* someone like you have a pizza or a flashlight. But certainly I do like her. Maybe I more than like her. What would be so bad about living together? I can't come up with a deal breaker.

"Sure. Great," I tell her. "I'll start looking."

EXCEPT I DON'T. I find other things to spend money on. Shirts that I have no room to hang. Cases of fruit drinks that sit outside my trailer. Industrial-sized packages of soap. I buy a master set of wrenches and a roll-around to store them in, and then give it to Owen because I have nowhere to keep it. Probably what I should buy is a new car—now *that* would eat up some cash. But I can't bring myself to do it, which is when I realize I'm not psychologically capable of squandering money. I'm doomed.

I PAY OFF THE truck, and my savings account grows. I consider buying long-term CDs, but Niki says I need to stay liquid because we might find something irresistible and need to come up with a down payment. She steers me to a money market account instead.

Early in June I start thinking of Amanda's birthday and I wonder what's the best thing to do. Should I send a card? Should I try to see her? Or should I once and forever put both Allison and our daughter out of my mind? But that isn't an honest question, is it? I've been here so often before, I have to finally admit it isn't the option I once thought it was. Here's why:

A few years back I smoked a cigar when a friend had a baby, but otherwise I've had no experience with tobacco. Rarely do I drink too much alcohol because I get sick and the bad feeling outweighs the good. I've tried pot twice, but I'm so self-conscious the only feeling I get is stupid, and stupid isn't something I need help with. What I'm saying is, I don't have an addictive personality. I can take or leave almost everything.

Almost.

But not this. Not her. Not them. To quote Cole Porter, I've got them under my skin. And I always will.

I DON'T KNOW WHAT three-year-olds enjoy, or what they can do, or how big they are, so when I go shopping I ask the saleslady in children's wear for help.

"And this is a three-year-old?" she asks.

Yes, I tell her.

"Then probably a 3T." She says this with the slightest twist to her mouth, as if I've asked what time is Midnight Mass or who is buried in Grant's Tomb. "But some children are smaller, so she may take a 2T. What does she weigh?"

I tell her I don't know.

"And this is your daughter?"

I confirm her understanding.

"But you don't know what she weighs?"

I tell her my daughter lives with her mother. I haven't seen them for a while. In return I get a look that puts me in the category of *those* fathers.

"Then how about a gift certificate?" the woman suggests. "That way the mother can pick out what she knows will fit. Perhaps the child doesn't even need a summer outfit. The mother may want to look ahead to winter."

I don't want a gift certificate. I don't want to look ahead to winter. I want something really special for my daughter, and I want it right this minute.

"Thanks anyway," I tell her. "I'll just look around."

I go through the racks of 3T size, figuring it's my best shot. If the clothes do happen to be big, I'll tell Allison I did that so Amanda can grow into them. But I'm hoping everything fits right out of the box. I go a little crazy because it all seems so inexpensive. I get her several pairs of pants, several tops. I get three dresses: yellow, blue, and pink. I get her a floppy hat with big, round flowers. I pick up socks and shoes, but put the shoes back thinking they're too hard to guess the fit. When I finish with the clothes, I go to the toy store in the mall and pick up a watercolor set and a toy camera. And then I get a card. It's a bunny springing in the air and on the front it says "Hopping". Inside the card reads "You Have a Wonderful Birthday." Amanda couldn't possibly get the pun, but maybe she'll like the picture. I haven't had this much fun in a long time.

When I get home, I call Conrad to see what's available around the fifteenth. He starts down the list and tells me on the twelfth there's a shipment of train car wheels to go from Colton to Rancho Cordova, just outside Sacramento. I tell him that's perfect and I'll take it. Finally I call Allison, telling her I'm going to be in the area.

"Wow," she says. "Two calls in less than a year. I'll have to get a restraining order."

She has to be kidding, but even so my heart sinks a little. When I don't answer, she laughs and tells me to lighten up. Not only would it be all right to stop by, she invites me to Amanda's birthday party, which is, of course, what I've been angling for. Before she says goodbye, Allison adds I can finally meet Carl.

Oh boy! Lucky me.

On Monday I drive east toward San Bernardino, but get off the freeway at La Cadena and go south to the Southern Pacific yard. I wait two hours to be loaded, but when the guys finally get to me, they're marvelously efficient. One man runs a specially rigged forklift that grabs the hub of the wheel so he can place the edge on the trailer deck. There, another man rolls the wheel, all six hundred pounds, into position and drops it precisely into place. He wears not gloves to protect his hands but flaps of leather attached to his wrists by a thong. The flaps hang down and cover his palm so that the wheel rim rubs against the leather as it rolls. He does this as easily as a boy coaxing along a hoop with a stick. No one mentions that if the wheel becomes unbalanced and falls toward him, he'll lose a leg.

They finish just before noon and I have forty new, shiny train wheels stacked like overlapping poker chips along the length of my trailer. Twenty-four thousand pounds of solid steel. It takes me half an hour to chain down the load, and when I leave I take the back way up 395 and then across 58 through Mojave and Tehachapi, instead of the more obvious Grapevine route over 5. The back way is slower but not as steep, so although I trust my brakes and the Jake, why take a chance?

This route empties me onto 99, which is also slower than 5, but I figure it doesn't matter. Whatever route I take, I couldn't make it before the customer closes. I wind past the towns of Earlimart and Pixley, then Lindsey, olive capital of the world. At five-thirty I pass Selma, the raisin capital. I think about another California town, Gilroy, the garlic capital, and wonder who determines the status of these places. Is it the sort of thing you can just declare, or is there an international board that sanctions the titles?

When I drive through Chowchilla, a pickup truck passes me. It's an old Chevy with a lumber rack holding ladders. Inside the beat-up bed are tools and hoses and power cords. A magnetic sign on the passenger door says Frank's Plumbing—a great place to take a leak. I laugh out loud, and as he goes by I toot the air horn. The driver sticks his arm out the window and waves.

At quarter to seven I'm at the consignee's location. I pull alongside the fence to park. I shut down the rig, trade my heavy boots for tennis shoes and my jeans for shorts. I climb down from the cab and throw first one leg and then the other up on the bumper. I lean forward to stretch my hamstrings, then lock the doors and go for a run.

When I return an hour later it's still light outside, but just. I crawl into the sleeper and shower, then zap some pizza in the microwave and drink ice tea. I lie in the bunk, which is twice the size of the one in my trailer, and read a Jeff Parker novel. I have the window behind my bed open, and through it comes a warm breeze and a chorus of frogs. I wonder if Amanda knows what a frog is. I wonder if she's seen fireflies. I wonder if her mother and Carl will give her swimming lessons. I wonder if she'll ever call me Daddy.

THE NEXT DAY THE train wheels come off the trailer faster than they went on, and by ten I'm on the road headed south. Conrad has found me a load of crated motorcycles to pick up in Vacaville, so I head down 80 and I'm at the dealership by one. It's Tuesday, and I'm doing fine. If I hustle I can make the delivery and be back in Lodi by Thursday, Amanda's birthday.

But there's a delay. At first I can't find anyone who knows about the shipment, and when we finally find the person who arranged the transfer, there's no one to help me load. I volunteer to run the lift myself, but the warehouse manager won't have it. Liability, he says. Only their employees can handle the equipment. I doubt if that's the case as much as he's gone around peeing on everything in his domain. I mean after all, if just anyone can get the work done, why do they need him? So I wait in the truck, reading until late afternoon, until he finally knocks on my door and says I'll have to come back in the morning.

There goes my easy turn-around. The bikes go to Riverside, which is five hundred miles south, not far from my home. I'd never get there and back in time for the party. I phone Conrad to ask if I can delay a day, and he says he'll call me back. Half an hour later he does, saying the consignee can wait that long but no longer. They need the merchandise for a weekend sale.

I leave the dealership and head north and east on 80 toward Davis, looking for a place to spend the night. As I drive, the sun bobs in my side mirrors, pushing the truck's shadow in front of me. Suddenly I'm very tired, though I've done little actual work.

Just out of town, I pull into a Perko's, find a slot among the rows and rows of trucks, and shut down the engine. It occurs to me I'm a turtle, carrying my house on my back. Wherever I stop, I'm home. I leave the rig and walk through the narrow canyons of trailers, forty- and forty-five footers, thirteen-six high, one-oh-two wide. Some are reefers with their coolers running. Some are silent as stone.

Inside the mini-mart I call Owen. He's home now, back from a milk run to Salton Sea, El Centro, Calexico.

"Hey, Chief," he says. "Hotter than hell here. What's the news with you?"

I tell him about the warehouse manager causing a delay, and how it irritates me to change my schedule. He laughs and answers I need to relax. My biggest worry tonight, he tells me, will be the lot lizards prowling the truck stop, drumming up business.

"Didn't I ever tell you about Peaches and Patches?" he says. "One summer night in Missoula a couple teenage hookers come banging on my door. They're dressed like Catholic school students: knee socks, short plaid skirts, crisp white blouses. I looked at that and said to myself, Oh, Lordy. Here's trouble and nothing but. Let me ask you something, Scout."

"Ask," I tell him.

"What it is about knee socks that get a guy going?"

I say I have no idea.

"Me either, but I'm volunteering to do the research for the good of mankind."

When Owen finishes his story, I walk from the grocery area, through a double door, to a space separating the store from the restaurant. Here, there are racks of real estate fliers, coupons for local attractions, and a row of vending machines: candy, gum, chips. There's also a Plexiglas box filled with stuffed animals. For a buck you can try your hand at snagging a toy and dropping into the delivery chute. I know from watching other people that most attempts fail, and the sensible approach would be to just buy a toy at the store. Nevertheless I give it a try, hoping to add something to Amanda's pile of gifts. I'm out five dollars by the time I give up.

I push through the next set of doors, and a hostess approaches me with a menu curled against her chest.

"One?"

"Just me," I say.

Though I'm alone, she places me in an end booth facing the other patrons. She offers a menu, but this is another one I know by heart.

"Pam is your waitress," the hostess says. "She'll be with you shortly."

A minute later she's at the table and takes my order for chicken fried steak and mashed potatoes. While I wait for dinner to arrive, I watch a family on the other side of the aisle and two booths down. The dad and son face me; the mom and daughter face them. From what I can see of the girl, I'd guess she's five or six. The boy is probably seven or eight. The girl's dark ponytail reminds me of Kitty.

The meal comes and looks good, which is to say it looks like the laminated picture in the menu. But when I finish, the food sits in my stomach like a water balloon, and I wish I'd ordered something else. I leave a couple bucks on the table, pay the ticket at the register, and head back to the truck. I climb into the sleeper through the cab and wash up. It isn't actually late, but I can hardly keep my eyes open. I read a little, turn out the light, and think of the family in the restaurant. I especially think of the little girl, who looks like Kitty, and the boy who doesn't look at all like me.

THE NEXT MORNING I pull to the pumps and put two hundred gallons of number two in the truck. I leave Perko's at seven-thirty and I'm in the dealership's parking lot before they open. This time they're ready, and by ten they've got me loaded. I strap down, and I'm back on 80, heading south. Past Travis and Fairfield, I swing south at Chadbourne to 12, then east. Once I clear Suisun City I roll through delta wetlands, watching egrets and cranes strut the reed beds, snapping up their feet as if they've stepped on hot rocks, then poking their beaks down into the water for some insect or small fish. I cross the river at Rio Vista, where 12 turns into Kettleman Lane. I follow this into Lodi, looking for a market or shopping center, someplace with a large parking lot. I'm not sure where I'll put the rig for the night, but onboard I've got eight Harley Davidsons that run probably twenty grand apiece, and I'd rather not have them walk off. I call Allison to tell her I'm in town but that I'll see them tomorrow.

"Don't be silly," she says. "You can stay the night with us."

I tell her the problem isn't a place to stay, it's security. I don't want to leave the truck.

"You can park it in front of the house," she offers.

I've never been to her house, but I can imagine a quiet residential street with barely enough width for two cars to pass. If that's what the place actually looks like, I won't be welcome. I tell Allison I'll come take a look, but that I don't hold out much hope.

She gives me directions, and it turns out I'm only five minutes from her home. In fact, I'm at the market they regularly use. I pull out of the parking lot, head back the direction I came, make a right, another right, and roll up in front of their place. As a sort of measuring stick, I center the truck on their lot and see that from tip to tail my rig is longer than their house.

I don't even consider shutting down the engine because my vision of the street was fairly accurate. The houses are neat and clean and modest, all the grass is green, all the lawns are mowed. There isn't a car on the narrow street, and since I see no driveways or garages in the front, I assume there's an alley running behind the houses. If so, the alley would be narrow as well, and in any case I don't trust the load to be safe back there. I'm about to climb out of the cab when the front door opens and Allison and a man (who else could it be but Carl?) come out. By the time they're at the curb, so am I.

"Good to see you, Jim." Allison grabs both my arms, which is not so much a hug as a control move. I think she doesn't want me being demonstrative in front of her husband. Or maybe at all. When she releases me, the fellow beside her sticks out his hand.

"Hello, Jim. I'm Carl."

I say he sticks out his hand, and he does, but this is not his first reaction to me. His first reaction is to bury both fists in the pockets of his Bermudas, which is sign language for my-wife-is-making-me-be-pleasant-but-if-I-had-my-way-you'd-be-down-the-road-pal. *Then* he shakes my hand.

I mumble something like, nice to meet you too, which of course I don't mean any more than he did.

I do not want to like this guy, so I look for something specific to criticize. But he doesn't cooperate. His appearance is as bland as pudding, though not really objectionable. He's as tall as me, fifty pounds heavier, soft, losing his reddish blond hair, freckles sprayed across his face like he got splattered with a paint gun, but really, who cares about that stuff. I don't have to sleep with him.

And then I see Allison's belly and it hits home like never before that she *has* slept with him, and even though of course I've known it all along in an abstract way, seeing her like this gives me a kick between the legs. If I think about the particulars I won't be able to talk with them, so I think of something else.

I tell Carl, "I can't leave the rig here. Any ideas where I can go?"

I phrase it this way knowing he'd love to tell me where to go, but can't under the circumstance. He's on a chain and I've put a steak just out of his reach.

"People park in the street all the time," Allison says. "Why can't you just leave it?"

My truck takes up more than half the width of the pavement, and I'm not sure even a small car could squeeze by. I'm considering how to point out the fact without sounding like a smartass, when Carl says, "It'll be fine. Come on in and we'll have something to eat."

Without an answer from me they turn to go back inside, so I climb into the cab to shut down the engine. The low rumble has been like the backbeat to a familiar song, like the lub-dub of a heart. When it's gone, the silence hums a tone in my ear.

Amanda, it seems to me, has grown half again as big as last time I saw her. Her hair is now shoulder length, though it's wispy like mine. She sits in a regular chair with the help of a booster seat. Her movements are no longer random like a baby's, but she eats primarily with her hands and not the spoon Allison has given her.

"Sweetheart," Allison says to her, "do you remember Mommy's friend?"

Amanda is noncommittal, but I feel like an embarrassing social disease that must be explained away. There is nothing for me to do but keep smiling.

Our meal is steak, macaroni and cheese, and broccoli. Carl drinks a glass of wine and Allison has tea. They ask what I'd like and I say, beer if you've got it. I'd like to add, "And keep 'em coming," but I don't.

Minutes after dinner starts we settle into a conversation that fascinates me with its ordinariness. Carl isn't chatty, but neither is he antagonistic as I'd expected. Allison is at ease, dividing her attention among us three. I think, these are just people living their life, trying to get along. They are not evil or superior. I will not read about them in NEWSWEEK.

I learn that Carl is a financial planner. Allison has a family counseling practice in town and two days a week she goes to Stockton for the Juvenile Authority, where she works with kids who have been kicked out of school.

"Who watches Amanda all this time?" I ask, thinking maybe here I have something legitimate to complain about.

"Monday, Tuesday, and Wednesday, she goes to work with me," Allison says.

And then as if they've rehearsed the answer, Carl pipes up, "And I work from home Thursdays and Fridays, so I watch her those days."

During dinner Amanda chats away to herself or to the table at large, including me. I don't know what to talk about with her, but whatever I say seems all right.

"Did you have a good day today?"

She nods her head sharply, staring at her mac and cheese like it might get away should she turn her head.

"What did you do?"

"Play."

"And what did you play?"

"Princess and fairies. We built a fort to hide from the witch."

"Blankets over chairs," Allison says.

Amanda sits next to her mother, who tears her food into small pieces, coaxing her daughter to take one more bite of broccoli, and reminds her not to drink her milk too fast. When we finish eating, Carl takes himself off somewhere, which seems suspiciously calculated, because Allison immediately says to me, "Want to help me get her ready for bed?" I wonder whether this move has been previously suggested by Allison and reluctantly agreed to by Carl, but I don't care. I appreciate the time alone with the two of them.

I don't actually do anything to assist, but I watch as Amanda takes two steps up a portable set of stairs and stands in front of the bathroom sink, staring into the mirror. Allison helps her brush her teeth with a very small, very soft tooth brush.

"We're trying to instill good habits," she says.

When the hygiene ritual is complete, we go to Amanda's bedroom, where Allison tucks her in. My daughter lies with both hands behind her head. She's so cute, my throat aches.

"Okay," her mother says. "What will it be tonight?"

"Frog and Toad," says the little voice with conviction.

"She knows what she wants," I say, unjustifiably proud, since I've done nothing to bring this about.

Allison laughs. "Do you know how old these Frog and Toad stories are? But she loves them. It reminds me of someone else who likes old things."

So Allison *does* think of me! I'm absolutely buoyed.

She reads the story with all the emotion she can muster, and although Amanda seems to know each word before it's spoken, she still squeals when Frog knocks on the door and Toad says, "I'm not here." When the book is finished, Amanda asks for one more story and Allison obliges. It's clear this is a ritual, like a rock star's encore. The second book is finished and Allison kisses our daughter on her forehead, then stands away from the bed. I'm looking at Amanda, but off to the side I see Allison nod, indicating I may also kiss our child goodnight. I do, and it is a heartbreakingly sweet sensation. Oddly, it reminds me of certain chord changes in a song, or a perfectly blue sky, or a pretty girl in a stunning dress: there are things in life almost too beautiful to withstand. I want to scoop up Amanda and nuzzle her neck. I want to rub her back and tickle her sides. I want *time*. I want her to be mine forever. But Allison steps toward the door and turns out the light. She closes the door when we're in the hallway.

"Why are you doing this?" I ask.

"What do you mean?"

I know what I mean, but not sure of the words to explain it. "This. Everything. Inviting me in. Letting me see Amanda. Letting me kiss her goodnight."

"Life is complicated," she says, and to this I agree. It's been my point all along. Allison continues in a voice near a whisper. I wonder if her intention is to keep her words from Amanda, or Carl. "And you're the one who's made it this way. The fact that you hurt me terribly, that you changed my future..."

Oddly, then, she smiles and walks away. I wish she would have slapped me, or kissed me. Something definitive. Something I wouldn't have to interpret.

When we get back to the living room, we find Carl has made coffee and there are squares of Rice Krispie Treats on a dinner plate. My hosts sit together on the sofa, and I sit off to the side in an upholstered chair. Allison toes off her shoes, then pulls her feet onto the cushions. She leans against Carl, who puts his arm around her in what I construe as an I-have-her-and-you-don't way. I am jealous beyond imagination. I want exactly what he has.

We talk for a couple of hours; I catch them up on my mom and dad, and a little about the business. They make the proper noises of sympathy and concern and congratulations. Finally Allison gets a devilish look and says, "And what about a girlfriend? Are you seeing anyone?"

I can go one of two ways with this. I can mention there *is* someone but do it incompletely and coyly to indicate a relationship hotter than an old married couple like them should be exposed to. Or I can say there is nothing going on at all, which means, though I realize it's hopeless and pathetic, I am unattached and therefore available. The second approach cannot possibly bear fruit, but it's the one I choose.

"Nope," I tell them. "Nobody special. I'm too busy for that sort of thing."

Around nine o'clock there is some innocent stretching and yawning on Allison's part, signaling it's time for bed. She offers me the guest room but I decline, not wanting to put them out but most of all not wanting to lie awake listening for noises I don't want to hear: the scrape of crates being pulled off the back of a flatbed, or the sound of pleasure in the bedroom next to mine.

OUT IN THE TRUCK, the idea of sex between Allison and her husband keeps me awake most of the night. The reason it takes so long to work through is that I approach the problem analytically instead of emotionally, and there's a lot of ground to cover. A lot of scenarios to reflect on. A lot of variables. I conclude there are two main categories of sex, with countless shadings and subcategories in between. At one end is the Doctor Zhivago/Lara kind of sex. This is the tender, fluttering stomach, our-souls-are-already-one-so-let's-do-the-same-with-our-bodies type. This is the love in the phrase, "Let's make love." It is the consume in consummate. It's what John Denver meant when he sang, "You fill up my senses."

The second type is what I call Charles Bukowski sex. The rut. It is selfish and aggressive, taking and not giving, though in its less offensive forms can be mutually pleasurable and why-the-hell-not. It is a maple bar but without coffee to wash it down, which is to say not bad, just not completely satisfying either.

To a greater or lesser degree we are all capable of both, even with the same partner, and possibly even within the same session. My fear is that Carl and Allison are mainly, maybe exclusively, the first type, while Niki and I are mainly the second, with the first being the more highly regarded, especially by women, though possibly not, since it's my preference as well.

I churn over these things until the morning hours, and when I do finally fall asleep, it is the result of exhaustion and resignation, not unlike what I've experienced wrestling with the certainty that I will die someday and there isn't a whole lot I can do about it.

THE PARTY STARTS AT three-thirty, so Allison has taken the day off. Since Carl is normally home on Thursday anyway, he is also hanging around. After breakfast, the three of us spend the morning setting up folding tables in the backyard. We fill coolers with ice and soft drinks, twist pink and white crepe paper into streamers, taping them in arcs against the garage and draping them from the pergola. By noon the backyard is a pink-and-white fairyland: paper plates, napkins, tablecloths.

After lunch Carl says he will go to the market to pick up the cake they ordered. I say I'll go with him, but surprisingly he says don't worry about it and heads off alone. I can't imagine he wants me unchaperoned with his family, but maybe I am simply too distasteful to ride with.

So I fix him. For the next twenty minutes I pretend it's me and Allison who are married, that this is my house, and even that the coming baby is my son. It's an embarrassing but nevertheless joyful one third of an hour, and of course it's pathological. The only glimmer of mental health in this behavior is that I know I'm doing it, and I'm even aware of what a pathetic S.O.B. it takes to entertain such fantasies. So I'm not completely gone.

All during my daydream, Amanda is running around, looking into the cooler, jostling her gifts, saying "My birthday. My birthday." When I ask how old she is, she holds up three fingers and says, "This many." For a rather long moment I consider putting her in the truck and driving away.

THE FIRST PEOPLE TO arrive are mothers with their children. They leave gifts on a side table, which already has a small pile because I've put mine there first. I hadn't thought until now that this is somewhat conspicuous, especially because Allison introduces me as a school friend who happened to be in the area. I get some lingering looks, but nothing is said.

Around five, a few of the fathers begin showing up. One of them is Brian Osdorff, husband of Marlene, whom I met earlier in the day. They are an older couple without children of their own, but Marlene is a neighbor of Allison's, and the two like to have coffee together when they can manage the time. Marlene is pleasant enough and outgoing, until we hear Brian holler "Hello." Then she pulls into herself like an anemone touched by a probing finger. As he approaches, she continues to shrink until I fear she'll turn herself inside out. Her reaction makes me to want to escape as well, but before I can move to safety Allison introduces me to Osdorff. He grabs my hand and pumps it, pulling me toward him so he can slap my back. He lacks only the white shoes and noxious cigar to be a perfect asshole.

"So what game are you in, Jimbo?"

By "game" he means we've entered a pissing contest, and I know already whatever I say he will trump. If I say building maintenance, he will say landlord.

Me: Policeman

Him: CIA.

Me: Airline pilot.

Him: Astronaut.

I come up with what I hope is vague but satisfactory wording. "Transportation."

He turns in the general direction of his wife and shouts, though she is twenty feet away and has her back to us. "Hear that, Mars? Transportation!" He gives a haw-haw and continues working my arm. "That must be your rig blocking the street. Made me go down a block and come in the other way. Lucky for you I didn't call the cops." Haw-haw.

I smile at him. Weakly.

"I'm in the transportation business myself, only a little different. Got the GM, Chevy, KIA dealership in town. Make you a helluvadeal." His eyebrows rise expectantly, as if I might actually be considering a purchase.

"Thanks," I tell him and try to slip away.

He grabs my arm to stop me. "How about something to drink? Something with a little more…flavor?"

He sneaks a pint bottle of Old Grand Dad out of his back pocket, like he's a kid in school and we're hiding in the reference section of the library.

"I'm fine, thanks," I tell him.

He slides the bottle back and I wonder whether he's ever opened it, or just carries it around to show he's a regular guy.

"So you and Ally were school friends?"

"We both went to Cal Poly," I say.

"Pomona or SLO?"

"Pomona."

"Good looking girl, if you want my opinion."

Really, I don't. It occurs to me this is how a trout must feel with a lamprey attached. I'm wondering if I fake right and go left, could I get around this guy?

"Yes, she is pretty."

"So what do you think about your old sweetheart getting herself knocked up?"

I wonder which he means—then or now?

"We were just classmates," I tell him.

He grabs me again and pulls me close. His voice is low and breathy, and I can feel him exhale onto my ear.

"Let me just say this. I hope the next one looks more like Carl than the girl. Hell," he says louder now, pushing me back and looking me in the face, "*You* look more like Amanda than he does."

Haw-haw.

I'm not sure how I react. Maybe I suck in my breath. Maybe I frown in protest.

"Jesus, son," he says. "Lighten up. Can't you take a joke?"

CHAPTER SIXTEEN

ONE DAY NEAR THE end of summer, I'm doing paperwork and note that we have covered more miles and hauled more tons than in any other three-month period since I started. This is not exactly useless information, but neither is it immediately applicable. It's just something to tuck away, something that pleases me. Of course one reason for this accomplishment is Owen's participation, but I hardly see that as diminishing the record. The only setback during this time is a ten-day period Owen's Pete is down with a front axle problem. The shop has to order the parts, so he tells them to do the clutch as long as he has to wait. In the meantime we ride together and switch off driving, stretching our hours so we can work more days in a row. It isn't as efficient as two trucks, but it isn't terrible.

Besides, it's nice spending time together. I learn a little about his early life and now understand why he didn't act surprised about mine. His father was killed in a tractor accident when Owen was twelve, and his mother had her hands full running the ranch and raising two boys. He tells me he hasn't been back to South Dakota for sixteen years, though he doesn't say why. By the way his voice changes, I can tell there was trouble, but what and with whom I don't know. He says he hardly speaks to his mother and never to his younger brother, so it's probably the brother. Owen warns me not to let this sort of thing happen in my family.

"You say your old man is a hard ass. Maybe so. But at least he's alive, even if he is stove up. There isn't a day I don't think about Neils and wish I could sit down with him for a drink and a talk. The conversation might end in a fistfight, but I'd still love the opportunity."

It strikes me that although he expresses a forgiving sentiment, he still doesn't talk with his brother who is still alive. Maybe it's a do-as-I-say kind of thing. On the other hand I rarely speak with my father who is alive, but would give anything to visit with Kitty, so who am I to talk? Still, something seems off with his advice. I ask him if family is so important, why doesn't he keep in touch with his own?

All he says is, "That train has left the station."

I do try to call my mother, often in fact, but with no success. She's never home, or at least she doesn't pick up. I leave messages but don't get a call back. Then in late August I get a letter explaining her absence.

The letter has no envelope; the paper is folded onto itself and the edges are gummed shut. The paper is the color and translucence of alabaster, but as delicate as bougainvillea petals. When I open it, I see the writing is not her usual, generous, Palmer Pen, Catholic school indoctrinated script, but a miniature version of the same, as if she is trying to cram as much as possible into the smallest space, which I suspect is exactly the case. She doesn't want to pay postage on a second sheet of paper.

Jimmy,

By sharing this with you I hope to make it real to myself, because so far it seems impossible. I am in the Holy Land with my church group. We walked the stone paths Jesus walked. We broke bread on the shore of Galilee. We climbed Masada. I've seen the hills with their lovely white boulders, and the forbidding desert. I've seen the olive trees, the vineyards, the sheep. The kibbutzim. I breathed the air. I am filled to overflowing. I am new.

I am a different person, Jimmy. I almost don't know who that old Paula was. I don't know this new person very well either, but she is wonderfully exciting and I want to learn all about her. I already know she can do things; she organized this trip, for example. Father Orbach, our pastor and guide, told me, "There was not one thing you overlooked. I thought all your lists were crazy, but they certainly worked out for the best, didn't they?"

That was me, Jimmy. He said that to me.

I am so tired of writing, not to you my sweet boy, but just that my hand is tired. One way I raised money for the trip was to sell the idea of people receiving a postcard from their favorite biblical location. Ten dollars each. (Can you imagine?) I have now written nearly two hundred. Jerusalem was the favorite spot, of course, but we also sent cards from Nazareth and Gaza and Haifa. Don't you just love the names? They come out of your mouth like little songs.

Oh, Jimmy, our bus is leaving and I have to go.

Promise me—if you have a dream pursue it. I suppose people often don't because it seems impossible. But the new Paula knows it is not. She knows anything is obtainable.

All my love,

Mom

NIKI BRINGS ME REAL estate listings. We spend Sundays together, looking through the paper and sometimes driving to visit the homes. There is nothing wrong with any of them. And nothing right, either. I find excuses to turn down each one until, by accident, I see an interesting photo on the same page as a residential listing she has circled. The property in the picture looks ideal for me, not for her, because it isn't a house, it's a freight dock with a yard. Possibly it is the future home of Jim Bass Trucking.

I keep the clipping, and when Niki leaves I arrange to meet the seller's agent. Two days later I collect Owen and together we drive out to see the facility. The Realtor is on site when we pull into the parking area. His new Buick is in one of the slots, and I see him in the distance, strolling the grounds. Though it's only ten in the morning, heat shimmers the view like a funhouse mirror. The Realtor has a dark stripe in the middle of his back. He turns toward us when he hears the car.

"Hey there," he calls, raising his arm as he trots in our direction. He offers his hand first to Owen, who has cleared the door almost before we stop, and then to me. "Norm Jennings," the fellow says. "Nice to meet you."

Norm tells us the location is abandoned now (he uses the word "unoccupied"), but previously it was a depot for filling and distributing industrial gases. He leads the way to the L-shaped building and we follow him up five concrete stairs that run beside one leg. At the landing he unlocks a door to the dock itself, where we turn left onto the raised platform.

He sweeps his hand around the empty space like a Miss America emcee on stage. "Fourteen rollup doors, seven on either side."

"No automatic dock plates," I say.

"Well, no," he answers. "But they could be added."

"At thousands of dollars per door?" I shake my head in disbelief. What I don't mention is that we could buy a couple movable ones for a few hundred each and share them between doors.

"We'd have to buy a forklift," Owen says, unlatching a chain and cranking a bay door open.

"And build a dispatch shack," I add.

One leg of the L is the dock platform. The other leg is a set of small offices. Norm unlocks the connecting door to that space.

"No furniture," I say. "We'd have to buy that, too."

I visualize myself off the road and behind a desk, not right away, but eventually. I'd be the TM of my own place, and Owen could dispatch. Or whatever he'd like.

After we poke into each room, complaining about their inadequacy, we go back outside to roam the grounds. Norm points out a metal outbuilding that had been a maintenance shop and needs extensive repair. He keys a monster padlock and flips open the hasp. Together we roll back the door. Sunshine sifts through a honey-colored and fly-specked window. In the dusky light I can just make out a line of bald tires leaned against the far wall. On a ruined bench under the window are tall oil cans with hinged spouts, coils of cable hung on hooks, boxes of filters. Next to the bench, a ten-ton jack. The floor is asphalt, but so buckled and oil-soaked, someone has put down a layer of straw. There is the reek of bearing grease, diesel, and grime. It's even hotter in here than outside. We roll the door closed.

Owen and I walk the yard while Norm trolls ten steps behind like a chaperone. Owen points to the fence, sagging in some places, torn down in others. The asphalt lot is decaying, with potholes big enough to swallow a small car. Weeds rise up through the blacktop. The lot is probably an acre but strangely shaped like a pulled piece of taffy, one side cut at an odd angle by railroad tracks, the other by the street.

From the far corner of the property, we turn back to get a different view of the dock and office. Both need painting, and the metal shed is rusting through the galvanized coat. We stroll back to the cars.

"So, whaddya think?" Norm says.

"Needs a hell of a lotta work," Owen tells him.

"Well, sure," he says. "That's why it's so aggressively priced. But, heck, make an offer anyway. The owners are motivated. You don't know what they'll accept until you try."

"You got a card?" I ask.

He hands me one and deals Owen another from the bottom of a thick deck. He could be a Las Vegas cardsharp.

As he gets in his car, Norm holds his splayed thumb and pinkie to his face. He mouths, "Call me."

He pulls out, leaving Owen and me on the blacktop, looking at the peeling paint, the rust, the holes.

"Well?" I ask.

My partner's face splits in a grin. He dances like he has to pee. "It is friggin' perfect."

WITHOUT TELLING NIKI, I make an offer on the place. If they turn us down flat, she'll never know. If they accept, it will certainly take all my cash for the down payment, leaving none for a house. In that case I'll tell her this is best for our future. If the owners counter, we'll just have to wait and see.

I wait a week, then call Norm Jennings. He's out, but a secretary says she'll tell him I phoned. The next day I miss his return call to me, but the message on my machine says the brothers who own the facility are out of the country and can't be reached. They'll be unavailable for at least a month, maybe longer.

So much for motivated sellers.

In the meantime, Niki keeps bringing me possibilities for houses, and I keep stalling.

I GET A CALL from my mother and learn she is back home in Maine.

"I'm just pouring a glass of tea," I tell her. "I made sun tea in a glass pickle jar."

I expect her to comment on this, but she doesn't, so I get my drink and settle into the breakfast nook to hear the tale of her fabulous trip. She starts with the take-off from La Guardia and doesn't stop until landing back in the good old US of A. I hear it all—the sights, sounds, and smells. Without a doubt she has been more places, seen and done more things in the last year, than in all the rest of her life. As she talks, I think how proud I am of her, and how happy.

But when she has finished with the details of the trip, she tells me about a detour she took on the way home; Mom stopped in Iowa to see my father. Here her voice changes from highly inflected to nearly monotone.

"I rented a car, Jimmy, the cheapest one because what do I need with an SUV or a big sedan?"

"Right, Mom. You don't need one. A little car is fine."

Perhaps this is where I've gotten my frugality.

"Of course I didn't need a map, I know every street by heart. But the strangest thing happened when I was driving through the old neighborhood; it was all so familiar, what I would normally call home, except I didn't care about it anymore. I mean, I saw which places were fixed up and which were rundown, but neither made me happy or sad. I just put the good in the good column, and the bad in the bad, but I didn't feel anything. The columns didn't add up. I didn't care."

A breeze blows through the trailer's open window and lifts the vanilla colored curtain. The air is shockingly hot and dry, but at least it's moving. I take a sip of tea.

"So," Mom continues, "I got to our house and parked on the street. I didn't even want to pull into the driveway. I walked up and knocked on the door, even though I still have a key, because it seemed like someone else's home. I waited and waited. It took a long time, but I heard all this shuffling and then your father answered. We looked at each other for quite a while before he invited me in."

Over the last couple years, I've occasionally phoned Dad but I haven't seen him since the hospital. I know how he sounds but not how he looks. So I ask.

"He looks just awful," Mom tells me. "Shrunken and old. I probably weigh more than he does. He must not have shaved for days. He still had on his bathrobe, and it was after lunchtime. Your father used to be so strong, even fierce, but it's like he's just given up. When I asked how he felt, he said, as pretty as you please, 'I'm managing.' Such a sourpuss. Poor me. Boo-hoo. After that I couldn't bring myself to tell him how *I* was. I didn't mention the trip or anything. I felt no matter how wonderful my life has become, if I say anything at all he'll make it seem unimportant or distasteful or selfish." She pauses and then says, "I want your father's negativity out of my life, Jimmy."

She's already left him, so I wonder how much more of a separation there can be. Is she talking divorce? Name change? I drink a little tea, hesitating before I ask the question whose answer I'm not sure I want to hear.

"What does that mean, you want him out of your life? Is this it? You're never going to see him again? You'll never talk? Ever?"

My mother has changed more than I thought possible, but even so I can't believe she'd completely abandon her husband. On the other hand, there is a limit to giving. The other person has to try. He has to want to get better or want to be loved. He has to love you back, at least a little. When you hole yourself away and are nasty and arrogant and uncaring, what do you expect will happen?

Finally she answers, "Sometimes I get so mad at your father, I want to spit. But you don't have to worry. I'll call and I'll write. And sometimes—not very often, but sometimes—I'll stop to see him."

I'm tired of people breaking up, so when I hear this I let out a big sigh. "Mom," I say, "I love you."

A WEEK OR SO after Halloween, I need a tool that's in the set I loaned Owen. I call his home, but Iris answers and says he isn't there. I ask when she expects him back, and Iris hesitates a minute, then gives me a different number where I can reach him. Something in her voice prevents me from asking what this is about. I dial the number, and after several rings a young woman picks up.

"Super Eight, Ontario."

"Uhh. Owen Youniacutt, please."

I hear some keys tap and then she says, "I'll connect you."

The phone rings again, but with a different tone this time.

Owen answers. "Yeah?"

"What's up?" I ask.

"Hey, Chief," he says, casual as can be.

"No. I don't mean 'what's up' like 'hello.' I mean what's up? Why are you in a motel?"

"Well, hell," he says. "I can't stay with you in that cracker box."

He says this with conviction, as if he's actually answered my question. I try a different approach.

"Why aren't you at home?"

"Actually," he says, "I've been meaning to talk with you about that."

In about forty-five seconds he explains what should rightly take an hour and a half, and would take my mother until next Tuesday or possibly next month. Basically he says that he and Iris have had an argument. This is an unsatisfactory answer because I've seen arguments, have even been in one or two myself, and none of them ended with either party lugging suitcases to a nearby motel.

But the more important part, for me anyway, is he says he's decided to go home for a while. Not home to Iris but home to South Dakota, to the ranch.

I can't help it. I ask, "Why?"

To which he answers in a three-note sing-song, the verbal equivalent of a shrug. "Uh-uh-uh."

This is not convenient. We aren't swamped, but work is steady, certainly more than I can handle alone. It's true I could find some help, or decline additional work, but I don't want to do either. More than that, we're in the middle of negotiations on the terminal. By now our original offer has been rejected, but we've countered and Norm Jennings says it's under consideration. We've never met the brothers, those mysterious owners of the property, but I hope we do, and I'd want Owen at the meeting.

"How long do you think you'll be gone?"

"Can't really say."

"A week? A month?"

"Yeah. More or less."

More or less?

"What about the terminal?" I ask. "What about work? How can I get hold of you?"

Of course I can't actually hear him shake his head, but I know he's doing it. "Ace, you aren't going to believe this, but folks out where I'm going have indoor toilets and everything. Mom probably still has the old crank-up phone, but if she doesn't, I'll find some way to call. How's that sound?"

I don't know how it sounds. Yes, I do. It sounds tired. Or is that just me? Sometimes, like now, I do get really, really tired.

"Owen?"

"Yeah?"

But I don't know how to answer. I'm probably taking this harder than I should, but I feel let down, betrayed.

"Nothing. Forget it. Just hurry back, okay?"

He doesn't say anything, but I can hear him give the receiver a big, smackingkiss.

OWEN PHONES ME FROM South Dakota. This is the second time in twenty-four hours he's called. It makes me believe whatever the trouble is between him and Iris is serious, and that he wants to hear a friendly voice, not that I've been all that friendly since he left.

I answer, "Jim Bass Trucking."

And he says, "What's the news?"

"In what regard?"

I know I'm needling him, but he's the one who took off, not me. Not this time, anyway.

"In what regard to the dock, fer Chrissake."

"Then there isn't much to tell. The Realtor took in the new offer and they're looking at it. Actually," I tell him, "things are pretty much the same as when you phoned yesterday."

"Excuse me for being interested in our future," he says. I'm trying not to laugh, so I don't answer. Then he adds, "Just let me know if anything happens."

"In what regard?"

"Your ass."

Now I do laugh out loud. I can't help liking him even when he's a pain. "How's things there?"

He tells me it's hard to say. His mother seems to have some disease that makes her dizzy, but the doctors don't yet know what it is. He says his sister-in-law is mainly watching out for her. Then he says, "I called Iris."

"And?"

"And nothing. She hung up on me."

He sounds so down, I say something I hope is mildly uplifting, something that he can't refute. "Well, who knows how things will work out?"

"Not me, that's for damn sure. Hey," he says, brighter now. "I got my nephew with me."

"You have a nephew?"

"Apparently. Seems like a good kid. Not sure about his sister, but I only just met the two of them. Girls, even little girls, seem to give me trouble."

Can I get an *Amen?*

We're both silent for a long moment. Finally he says, "I'll call you," and I know he's through for now.

A FEW DAYS AFTER I talked with Owen, I learn the brothers have declined our second offer. This time, however, along with the rejection is a counter offer. The counter is substantially less than their original asking price, which confirms to me that no one else is bidding. We're still in the game; everyone is still playing. No one has picked up his marbles and gone home.

I don't respond to the Realtor, and eventually Norm Jennings calls me. I tell him it's still too much money and therefore it's probably best if we bow out. I tell him we don't want to insult the brothers, so there's no point in proceeding. He absorbs this information without much comment, but a week later I get another call from him. This time he's laughing as if we're school buddies and both in on some joke.

"Jimmy," he says. "How the heck are you?"

I tell him I'm fine and again apologize for wasting his time.

"Nonsense. I'm here to help. Use me!" I don't answer. After all, he called me. "Well, anyway," he says. "I've talked with the brothers and calmed them down. All they're looking for is for you to come back with something reasonable."

"Calmed them down" strikes me as a self-serving phrase. It makes Norm the hero. We'll see about that.

"I understand what you're saying," I tell him. "The problem is, what's reasonable to me seems unreasonable to them. I know the payments I can handle, so there's no sense in agreeing to something that will sink us in six months or a year or two years."

"No, no. Of course not," he says. "But understand, those boys have a lot tied up in the place. They don't want to get hurt, just like you don't."

I'm home in the trailer, listening to Sarah Vaughan sing of faraway places: "Autumn in New York," "Springtime in Paris," "Moonlight in Vermont." "Moonlight in Vermont" hits me especially hard. The temperature in the trailer has to be in the nineties, but I think of those snow-covered slopes and nearly shiver with the chill.

"Hold on," I tell Norm. I turn down the volume so I can concentrate. Now with the music lower, I can actually hear my heart pounding in my ears, thinking of the possibilities. When I come back to the phone, I try to sound as cool as the song. "I completely agree with the brothers," I tell him. "That's why I said we should call off the negotiation. I stay out of debt, and they keep a valuable property. Everybody's happy."

Actually, as Norm and I both know, nobody's happy. But now we're checking to see who has the higher pain tolerance.

"Jimmy, Jimmy," he says. "Don't be like that. You want it, right? I mean, it would be great for you if you had it."

"Norm," I say. "It just won't work at that price."

We're both quiet until he says, "Listen. I've bought and sold property for these boys before. I know them pretty well, and I know they want to get out from under this place. Understand they'd have to approve this, but what if I could get them to agree to…" He gives me a number.

My suspicion is the brothers agreed to the figure before Norm placed the call. My further suspicion is the number was theirs to begin with. I wouldn't be surprised if they were standing next to him right now, urging him on. Nevertheless, it's a great price and would be irresistible if the place were in better shape. It's still more than I want to pay, but certainly not out of the question.

I take a deep breath and calculate. Our relative positions are like this: Norm Jennings is standing in the lakeside reeds. He's wearing hip waders and his hat is riddled with all manner of lures. But instead of something fancy, he takes a regular hook. From a pouch on his belt he takes a worm, threads it on the hook, and casts it into the water.

I'm a hungry fish, let's say a bass, who sees the hook and knows what it is, knows the danger, but is tempted to nibble the bait anyway, thinking maybe I can get the food and still remain free, all the while understanding if I miscalculate, the result will be highly unpleasant.

Even so, I decide to have a taste.

"Say we went for that price," I tell him. "What are they going to do about the repairs?"

CHAPTER SEVENTEEN

THE SHORT VERSION IS we get the terminal. The longer explanation is it takes two more weeks of negotiation to get there. In the end, the sellers don't make any of the repairs we asked for, but they reduce the price by half the cost of contracting the work. This is acceptable to us because we'll do the fixing ourselves and thereby wind up paying nearly our original offer.

So that's one mark in the plus column.

Another is that Owen has returned and whatever trouble there was between him and Iris seems resolved. This strikes me as odd because the last time I talked with him in South Dakota, his idea to patch things up was to give her flowers. In my mind flowers are for coming home late from work. Flowers are for playing basketball on a Saturday morning instead of going to the rummage sale at church. In my world, problems that require leaving town for three weeks are not solved by giving flowers.

But then maybe I'm not the charmer he is.

One thing that doesn't turn out well is taking Niki to see the terminal. On a bright clear Saturday I call her and say, "Let's go for a ride. I've got a surprise for you." Twenty minutes later I pick her up at her house and as we drive the 10 east I see Mount Baldy standing sharply against the blue sky. I can see the dam at Padua. If I were up there looking west, I bet I could see Catalina. There are no clouds, just two contrails coming in from the desert toward LAX.

All through Upland, then Alta Loma, Niki is smiling out the window. She's still smiling as we roll by Fontana and Rialto, though now she's growing fidgety. "Ooh, I can't wait," she says, bouncing a little in the seat. But when I pull off the freeway and into the terminal parking lot, her smile loses some energy. Her forehead wrinkles and she looks at me a bit confused. "Is the surprise around here?"

"Not *around* here," I tell her. "This is it. This is the surprise."

Her confusion deepens.

I turn in the seat and take her hands, telling her what the place is and why we bought it. I tell her it will be great for our future, meaning not only the future of Jim Bass Trucking but our personal future. I see she wants to ask something so I hurry on, saying how this makes wonderful economic sense, and I remind her that's what she is always encouraging me to think about.

I nod and point to the different areas, laying out the planned changes, but now she slumps back in her seat, folding her arms over her chest. She doesn't say anything. I can see in her face that she's struggling with a problem, and I know what that problem is: I'm not wrong in what I've told her. All the things I've said are true as far as they go. In economic terms, buying the property is a sound move. Financially speaking there's no argument, though of course this isn't about finance. I feel like the captain of a debate team who's won on points but who the audience still thinks is an asshole. This is not a situation that will be put right by a bouquet of roses.

She gets out of the car and walks a few steps. I get out and follow her. She's looking away, but when she hears my footsteps, she turns.

"You lied to me."

"How can you say that? I never said anything."

"LIAR!" she shouts. "You said you were looking for a house. You said that's what you wanted."

I don't remember actually saying that. To me, I acknowledged *she* wanted a house, although I can understand how my comments could be misinterpreted. I start to tell her as much, which in a way is an apology, but she rushes past me back to the car. I hear the car door open, then close with a bang. I'm left standing with my hands in my pockets, looking at the dilapidated building I've purchased, trying to think of the right thing to say, what I will say eventually to smooth things over, until I realize there is no right thing.

A minute later I go back and slide behind the wheel. "I'm sorry. I thought you'd be pleased."

"Really?" she says. "Why is that? Why would I be pleased you didn't do what you said you'd do? What, in my mind at least, you *promised* to do."

It's a good question. I shrug and answer with another question. "I was thinking ahead?"

She pushes herself back in the seat and stares straight ahead. I think this is it. I'll drive her home and we'll never talk again. But then she says, "What am I to you? Someone to share a drink? I'm a date? A FUCK? Tell me. I'd really like to know."

I wince at the harsh words, and I'm shamed by them. I've treated her so badly. And this after treating Allison as horribly as possible. Right now I don't like myself very much.

Since there is nothing to say, I don't speak. I start the car, pull out of the lot, and in three blocks I'm back on the freeway.

We still haven't spoken when I stop at the curb in front of Niki's house. I don't get out of the car, and she doesn't give me a backward glance.

I MISS HER BUT I don't call. Maybe I'm embarrassed. I guess that's it. But I think of her constantly, all the fun we had, which seems even better now than when we were together. It's like looking at photos of a vacation and wishing you were back in that exact spot doing that exact thing, though if you're honest, the sun was actually a little too hot and the air a little too humid.

Still, there is nothing to do but wait out this feeling of loneliness, so, as always, I work. I accept that Niki is lost to me and I'll never have her back.

And then one evening, weeks later, she calls.

"Don't take this the wrong way," she says, "but in the parking lot that day I was thinking of my dad as much as I was thinking of you." She's kind of laughing, so I sort of laugh too, although I'm not sure why or whether I'll like how this might turn out. I fear she'll say her dad was an asshole too. "Not that you look like him or anything. It's just…he used to tell Mom things that weren't true but not exactly a lie either. I couldn't stand how she'd fall for his line, and I guess I thought maybe that's where we were headed. But it isn't, is it?"

I think of how I've missed her the last few weeks. I don't want that to happen again. Ever. "No," I say firmly. "Absolutely not. Just give me another chance, and I'll prove it."

She laughs again, more relaxed this time, it seems to me. "All right, Buster," she says. "Here's the deal. I've made plans. BIG plans."

I swallow hard, ready to take whatever comes. It's like I'm preparing for a medical procedure that someone promises will be good for me, except they aren't the one getting cut on. But her idea is wonderful. She tells me she'd hoped I would want to try again and so she arranged a special weekend. Five days, just before Christmas. We're to leave on a Thursday and not come back until late Monday. Niki doesn't tell me where we're going, just gives me the dates and says to pack warm clothes. My only job is to make sure my schedule will accommodate hers. I tell her I can do that.

When she hangs up, I think about being with her again. And the more I think, the more I look forward to our time together. So I call Owen to tell him I'll be off for a few days. I'm truthful about Niki's plans, so of course he laughs and calls me a pussy hound. Next I clear things with Conrad. I have to keep him happy because we'll continue to use Continental for the next year or so until Jim Bass Trucking can function as a stand-alone company with its own sales force. While we're on the phone he offers a load, which I accept because it's a two-day turnaround that puts me back home on Wednesday afternoon, leaving plenty of time to pack.

TUESDAY MORNING I DEADHEAD north, up through San Fernando Valley, past Newhall and Santa Clarita to Castaic Lake, where I pick up a load of day cruisers and runabouts secured to their own trailers. The boats are sealed in a kind of shrink-wrap protective film, which I appreciate because the forecast is rain. While we load up, I wear a hooded sweatshirt under a heavy canvas jacket. By the time I get the boats and trailers chained down, I'm sweating under all the clothes, and the outside layer is now soaked by the drizzle. I climb into the sleeper, strip to my jeans, and pull on a dry sweatshirt.

The sky is the color of dirty wool, and as I pull onto the freeway I worry that the summit will be closed due to snow. Tejon Pass is 4,160 feet in elevation. When I climb toward the summit through Hungry Valley and Gorman, raindrops hit my windshield with more of a splatter than a drip, meaning they're starting to freeze. I'm afraid I'll have to pull over and chain up, but I make the top without incident and start down the other side. As I do, the rain lightens again to a sprinkle.

My destination is Reno. From Castaic I could have backtracked to 14 and gone up 395, or continued north and cut across at Lancaster Road to the highway. Instead, though it makes for a longer trip, I stay on 5 until just past Wheeler Ridge, then transition to 99. I justify the greater distance because, given this weather, I could easily be stuck in the mountains anywhere from Lone Pine to Mono Lake, which would kill my weekend with Niki. The route I've picked is completely sensible under these conditions and is what most, or at least many, truckers would choose. No one would consider this route out of the ordinary. I've decided on the conservative, responsible, sure-thing path. It's also the one that takes me past Allison's home.

ON AND OFF FOR the next five hours, the rain comes in spits and showers, then the weather clears to partly cloudy, then rains again. In my mirrors, the spray from the tires is a solid curtain blocking my view of the road behind. I make my way through towns that have become so familiar to me, they're all just part of the very large neighborhood I roam. At four in the afternoon the soggy light is already fading. I pull off at Kettleman and wind my way through the commercial and then the residential areas. I stop in front of Allison's house as I did for Amanda's party.

I haven't called ahead, didn't even consider it. I simply assumed it's late enough in the day she'd be home. So when there's no answer to my knock, I am ever so slightly put out, as if she is inconsiderate to be gone when I take the trouble to visit. But more than put out, I am also highly disappointed.

Just to make sure she isn't around back or for some other reason didn't hear the knock, I walk around the side of the house and let myself into the backyard through the gate. As expected, no one is out on this dreary day, but when I turn to look at the house, I'm encouraged to see a light burning in the kitchen. I go to the window and, making parentheses with my hands around my eyes, look inside. Again there is no one, but I do hear water running and take that as an excellent sign.

"Hello?"

No answer.

I rap on the window.

Nothing.

I jiggle the sliding glass door and find it's open. I step inside.

"Allison? Hello?"

The kitchen is to my right, and I look over to see the faucet running full tilt. I shut it off and listen closely. The water was the only sound.

"Hello-oo," I sing out, long and loud. Carl should be at work, and in any case doesn't strike me as the type to shoot first. But still I'm a little anxious about wandering through someone else's home.

I walk through the house, poking my head into each room, finding unmade beds, towels hung on a shower curtain rod, magazines on a coffee table, clothes on an ironing board, until I come to the second bathroom. This is where I watched Amanda brush her teeth. And this is where I find her little two-step staircase overturned, and broken glass on the counter, and splashes of blood on the floor.

"ALLISON!"

I race back through the house, out to the back, to the garage. The main door is unlocked, and the rollup door is open. No cars.

It has happened. My daughter is hurt, dying, dead. What to do? Where to go? Where could Allison have taken her?

I run back to the house and dial 9-1-1.

"Nine one one. What's the nature of your emergency?"

I don't want to shout. I want to be clear. I try to speak slowly and carefully and logically, but I'm only partially successful because I can't catch my breath. "I'm at my daughter's house. The doors are open. There's no one here. I saw blood."

"What's the address?" the woman asks.

Shit. I can't remember. "Hang on." The phone is a cordless, so I take it from the kitchen out the front door. "Twenty-eight eighteen Linden."

"Are you injured?"

"Not me. My daughter."

"But she's not there? How do you know she's injured? Do you want me to send the paramedics?"

I realize she doesn't understand what I'm saying, what I meant to ask. "They must have gone to the hospital. Where's the nearest one? How do I get there?"

She's quiet, checking something, some sort of map. "Lodi Memorial is the closest to that address. Do you know where the park is?"

Where I met Allison. "I'm just east of there."

"All right. Go to the park, that's Ham Lane. Turn right and you'll go about a block. Just pull into the parking lot on your right."

I thank her and bang down the phone. Three minutes later I'm at Memorial.

THERE IS NOWHERE TO park sixty-five feet of truck and trailer hauling five boats, so I simply shut down the rig double parked in the street. Any cars between me and the curb are going to be there awhile. As I run toward the building, I spot the Emergency sign and veer to my right. I have to wait for the automatic doors, but mercifully there is no one in line at the check-in window.

"Amanda Clarke," I say, out of breath.

The nurse is cool and collected, used to half-crazed parents like me. She runs her finger down a sheet on the desk and says, "Relation?"

"Daughter. Father. I'm her father."

She stands and looks past me, I suppose to determine whether she can leave her station and show me where to go. "Come around through that door, Mr. Clarke. They're in number five."

Mr. Clarke. Mr. Stovall. Bassovich. Bass. It's no wonder I have problems.

Once I'm through the door, the nurse walks me to an area of cubicles walled on three sides by curtains, the common back wall being the solid structure of the building. We pass the first three spaces, which are exposed and empty, and then one more with the curtain drawn. We stop in front of the next space and she grabs a handful of fabric. When she pulls the curtain back, I see Amanda in bed, her head wrapped in gauze. Allison is in a chair next to her holding her hand. She turns toward us when she hears the drape slide. I see the bulge of her stomach and once again I feel a stab of envy for what her husband has.

"Jim!"

I nod and walk in, and the nurse leaves us alone.

I put my hand on Allison's shoulder and she covers mine with hers. "Hey."

She says, "How did you know?"

I'm not sure what she's asking. How did I know to come here? How did I know Amanda was hurt? Instead of pursuing her thought I ask, "What happened? How's she doing?" Amanda's eyes are closed and I wonder if she's unconscious.

"She's going to be okay," Allison says. "There'll be a scar, but her hair should cover most of it."

"But what happened?" I ask again.

Allison shakes her head. "I was just outside the door, but not right by her side." She's quiet again, gathering herself. "She must have climbed the little stairs, either to brush her teeth or get a drink, I'm not sure which. We only let her use plastic cups, but apparently she brought in a glass, and somehow in reaching and leaning, tipped the stairs over, the glass smashed against the counter and her head fell into the shards and then against the tile and then onto the floor."

Allison doesn't cry, but she's shaking. The skin on her arms is goose flesh.

"But she's going to be okay," I say. I inflect this as a statement, but it's really a question. I want to hear it again. I want her to repeat that Amanda will be fine.

Allison touches the left side of our daughter's head, just above her ear. "It's pretty deep along here, and back to here. Thirty-five stitches. Jim, it nearly cut her ear off." She practically shouts this last part. "I should have been there. I should have watched her closer."

There is only the one chair in the room, so I continue standing. I also leave my hand touching Allison because it seems an entirely appropriate thing to do. In silence we watch Amanda for several minutes, and then I ask, "Have you phoned Carl?"

Allison nods. "He should be here soon." And then she asks again, "How did you know to come? How is it you're here?"

I don't answer. I can't. Sometimes things just happen.

WHEN CARL SHOWS UP and I greet him, he doesn't act surprised to see me. I know it's because he's too upset about Amanda. Later, sometime this evening, it will occur to him how odd this is. I imagine the nurse thinks it's pretty odd too, a girl with two fathers named Mr. Clarke.

While Carl visits, I go outside and move the truck, which miraculously has been neither towed nor ticketed. I park at yet another supermarket lot, where I call Owen and tell him I'm going to be delayed coming home. Then I call Conrad with the same news. He's never fussed before about anything that's happened, but then I've rarely been late with a delivery either. He tells me the consignee expects the boats to be there this afternoon. My answer is, they'll have to wait. He knows from the sound of my voice this is the way things are, so finally he says he'll call them and make some excuse.

"What excuse?" I ask him. "Tell them my daughter was in an accident and I'm staying with her. Simple as that."

Last I call Niki. My bet is that of the three people I'm disappointing she will be the most hurt but also the most tolerant. She's a woman and a daughter herself, so she should understand. When I call, I only get her answering machine. I lay out why I'm here, that Allison's home was on the way and that I stopped to say hello to my daughter. I tell Niki what has happened, that I shouldn't be more than an extra day, which will still give us four days together. Finally, into the recorder I say, "I love you," which I now mean more than any time before.

I expect Amanda to be released the same day, but by early evening she is admitted, because the docs want to keep an eye on her. When I first saw her she was sedated, but now she seems pretty good. Pretty cheerful. It's heartbreaking, knowing she is hurt and still so brave.

"Hey, Punkin," I say. "How you doing?"

Now that she has her own room, we're all together; me, Allison, Carl, and Amanda. She is playing with a stuffed toy carrot supplied by the hospital. I can't imagine what this tchotchke is meant to promote.

"Good," she says. "I'm doing good." I'm certain her little voice is how angels sound.

From across the bed Carl looks at me. He and Allison are sitting on a small couch against the wall, holding hands. I'm sitting in a chair on the other side, not quite touching Amanda's hand, but close.

Carl says, "The doctor said she's lucky. Any lower, it would have taken her ear. A little deeper..." He shakes his head.

That's lucky? I think. Lucky would have been for it not to happen at all. And then the old feeling comes back. The feeling that there is no end to what hasn't happened yet. But instead of being terrified, I'm suddenly grateful that my little girl will have a scar hidden by her hair and nothing more than that.

"Why don't you guys go home and get something to eat?" I suggest. "Get some rest and come back later. Or don't come, if you're too tired. I'll just stay here."

"You're tired too," Allison says. "We'll take turns."

And that's what happens. I get dinner first, then Allison comes back at eight. Carl spells her at midnight. But I stay throughout the night, beginning to end, because really, there's no place I'd rather be.

SOMETIME BEFORE DAWN I wake with a start. My mouth tastes like it's full of mud. My neck and back hurt. I sit up in the chair and lean forward. "Hey."

"Hey," Carl says.

He's sitting on the opposite side of Amanda's bed and I imagine the noise of his chair scraping the floor is what woke me.

"How you holding up?" I ask.

"I'm doing all right. How about you?"

I say I'm fine and then get up to use the bathroom. When I come back, I look down at my daughter. Her hair is sweaty and stuck to her neck. I brush it back with my finger.

"You love her, don't you?"

"You can't imagine," I tell Carl. I sit down and look across the bed at him. "Ridiculous, isn't it?"

"What? That you love your own child?"

I shake my head. "Not that. I mean everything. Me here tonight, you married to Allison. The world, politics, the weather. The price of ice cream. Everything seems ridiculous at…" I look to a clock on the wall. "…three thirty-five in the morning."

Carl laughs at this and then I laugh, though we both keep our voices low. We're so tired it's like being drunk. And sometimes being drunk is a truth serum.

"How is it that you happened to be here today?" he says. "I mean yesterday."

I tell him about the delivery and that I was truly just passing by.

"Are you in love with my wife?"

This seems to have come from nowhere, except that his question doesn't surprise me in the least. In fact I've been expecting it for some time. And because it's three thirty-five in the morning, which is like being drunk, and being drunk is like a truth serum, I tell him the truth. "Yep."

"Are you going to be a problem for us?"

I stroke the back of my daughter's hand. "Nope." I cannot control the jumble of feelings when I touch her: ownership, responsibility, yearning, loss. "Don't worry," I say to Carl, "I've a got a girl. We're getting married. Maybe this weekend."

When I say this, it's like I've known the fact all along, just like I knew Carl would ask me about Allison.

He puckers his lips and nods at my answer. "Thanks," he says.

"For what?"

He shrugs. "Being honest about Allison. If you would have said 'no,' I'd know you were lying. Now maybe I can trust you."

I nod in acknowledgment, thinking about honesty. I wonder how I stack up against other people. I figure I'm not so hot, which probably puts me somewhere near the middle.

MID-MORNING, THE DOCS CHECK Amanda's injury and say everything looks good. They release her, and Allison prepares to take her home.

"You might as well ride with us," she says, so I leave the truck parked where it is and go with her to her car.

Minutes later we're in the alley behind her house. Allison punches a button on the visor, then drives slowly into the garage. Carl waits outside, his windshield wipers shucking rain, while I unbuckle Amanda and lift her from the rear seat. As I kick the door closed, she wraps her arms around my neck, lays her head on my shoulder. She's sleepy, and I'm ten feet tall.

"I'm going to skip the Sacramento meeting," Carl tells Allison after he parks. "I'll call George and tell him to go ahead without me."

"There's no need for that," Allison tells him. "We'll be fine here."

Carl looks at me. His expression is neutral, and I haven't forgotten his claim that he might trust me. I also haven't forgotten I told him I was in love with his wife.

I cover Amanda with the flap of my jacket as I head for the door. "I can't stay long," I call over my shoulder. "I still need to get those boats delivered. You may want Carl to stick around."

Not so surprisingly, this convinces him to go. After a half-hearted protest, he lets himself be talked into leaving and heads for the shower. By the time Allison and I get Amanda tucked into bed, he's off to his meeting, and we sit down for a cup of coffee. We're at the kitchen table, looking into the backyard at the slanting rain.

"Blowy," she says. "Cold."

"It's nice." Allison looks at me. "Nice to be inside where it's warm."

She's changed into a thick sweater and has her hands wrapped around the mug. She's in sock feet. "Thanks," she says.

"For what?"

"For being there. Being here. I was relieved when I looked and saw you at the hospital."

"I really *was* just passing through," I say.

"Yeah, well. I'm glad. And Amanda's glad too. She says she likes Mommy's friend Jim."

This kills me. Jesus, I think. I want to use this information to see my kid more often. Want to say, if she likes me, we should be together more. But I don't know the words to tell Allison how I hunger for our little girl. And before I can think of anything, the moment passes because Allison is talking again.

"You've made another fan as well. Carl." She looks out the window at the rain pummeling the grass in the backyard. I don't follow her gaze because I want only to look at her. "You can imagine he wasn't too keen on you at first. Now he says you seem okay. Decent and caring."

I think about our talk early this morning, and I conclude it is Carl who is decent. In his position I'm not sure I'd feel the same about me.

"And how about you?" I ask. "I could never figure you after... after I left. It seemed you encouraged me, to a point at least."

Allison sets her mug on the table. She rocks up first one leg and then the other to sit on her hands. Her face, which until now has retained some of the strain of the last two days, relaxes into sweet blankness. She is lovely.

"I was torn. I wanted to hurt you for hurting me. But for Amanda's sake I tried not to act it out. Then, once Carl came along, it made things easier between you and me because I had that extra support. He was somewhere I could go to be safe. He's so steady and reliable I knew I could count on him. And you have to admit I couldn't say the same about you. Even so, nothing will change the fact you're Amanda's biological father."

Allison may have answered my question, but not nearly in the way I'd hoped. I want her to say I'm welcome to come by anytime. I want her to leave off *biological* when she says *father*. Even with Niki waiting for me, I want to hear that Carl was second choice for Allison; that she picked him only because I wasn't available. The problem is, I know I've acted like a bum and therefore I'll always come out on the bottom of any moral comparison. Carl isn't really so great, I want to tell Allison; he's only great compared to me. But pointing out this fact doesn't seem the sort of argument to further my case.

So instead I say, "Sounds like I'm allowed here only because you have such high principles." I try to sound like I'm joking, but it comes out as bitter as I feel.

Allison cocks her head like an inquisitive puppy. "Excuse me for pointing out the obvious, Jim, but I didn't leave you. You'll recall it was the other way around."

The sting of this truth overwhelms her earlier statement of being relieved to see me. It overwhelms the notion that Amanda likes Mommy's friend. I'm embarrassed and I want her to make me feel better by saying she still thinks of me the way I think of her. Naturally, I choose the wrong way to get a response.

"But you did love me, right? When we were together and had Amanda, you loved me then?"

"Yes, Jim," she says. "I loved you then."

As promised, I'm home late Thursday. Friday morning I'm packing when I hear Niki's bug pull up outside. When she knocks I holler from the back room, "It's open," and I hear her walk in. "Almost done," I sing out.

I have a duffel and a suitcase; the suitcase is a gift from Mrs. G. It's old and shabby, which she said made her think I'd like it. She's right, I do. In addition to the normal latches, it has leather straps and buckles for extra security. It looks like luggage someone could have used on the Orient Express. Or the Titanic.

I pull the drawstring on the duffel, then come from the back of the trailer to see Niki standing just inside the door she hasn't bothered to close. I see she's wearing torn jeans and an old blouse, and although I didn't expect her to dress up, I did expect, I don't know, something a little more special.

She hasn't spoken yet and doesn't look like she intends to, so I say, "What's up?"

Niki looks to where two walls and the ceiling form a corner. There's a curious expression on her face, as if she's watching an intersection approached by three cars, none of which is slowing.

"I've been looking for something," she says, and I look at the corner too, wondering what she thinks she'll find there. "For a long time I thought you were looking for the same thing and together we'd find it. But we both know that isn't going to happen, don't we?"

I take a step toward her, but she stiffens and I stop.

"No," I say. "I don't know that at all. Let's just go and have a great time. We've only missed one day."

I want to make this conversation about the vacation. She wants to make it about something else. She goes to the table, picks up a cup, sets it down again. Looks at me.

"It isn't the one day. It isn't just this time," she says. "If it were, I could easily understand your reason for being late. But it's every time, Jim. I'm always last in line with you. I come after your business, after your beer-drinking buddy, and mostly I come after your ex and your daughter. For such a long time I've wanted to tell you, they were then, Honey. I'm here now. But you know what? That isn't true anymore. I'm not here now. I'm done."

Niki goes to the door and steps outside, though her hand is still holding the jamb. She pulls herself back in and says, "I hope your little girl is okay. I never had anything against her."

CHAPTER EIGHTEEN

I'M IN A HIGH meadow on a bright, clear day. At my feet, grass and wildflowers wave in a breeze I cannot feel. The principal sensation is of color—Easter greens and yellows, and dots of red clover like candy in dishes. When I walk through the flowers, their perfume stirs up so that I am nearly overcome by their sweetness and by the ache of too much beauty. I cannot carry such a burden alone.

I am at a great height, but in the distance are mountain peaks, higher still, covered in snow. The edge of my plateau is sheer and dangerous, and I know if I come to it I will fall. But here, away from the verge, I am safe.

I hear no sounds until there is a murmur I believe to be the wind in the grass or the hum of bees or the rush of water. I squeeze closed my eyes to listen more intently, realizing finally it is voices I hear. The whispers float toward me, familiar but undefined. I cannot distinguish individual words, but the tone suggests friendship. Laughter and goodwill. The conversation is among a small group; old and young, female and male. I want to join them, this community. These are the companions who will share my day. The ones who will help me bear this beauty.

Their voices grow louder; the people are near. I seek them among the reeds and flowers and grass, but they are never where I look. Their voices drift away behind me. I turn and run to where I hear them talking but find only trampled grass. They have gone.

The wind changes.

The sky is a bruise. The rows of mountains are gray-blue, towering above me. I sit low, as in the trough of a rising sea. Now I feel the breeze, which is a chill wind. Rain is coming. The flowers have gone dry, and then they are dead, and then they are dust. It is very dark.

I am alone.

CHAPTER NINETEEN

I T'S CHRISTMAS EVE MORNING. A great gift would be a return call from Niki; I've left messages on her home phone every day for the past week, but I haven't heard from her since she left my trailer that night. Maybe with time, who knows?

Still, I feel like talking with someone, so I call my mother. Her roommate, Mrs. Martin, answers.

"Hi, Jim," she says. "Happy holidays."

"And Merry Christmas to you. Is Mom there? I'd like to say hi."

I hear her take a sip of something. "She's at the Elks Lodge. Big to-do today. It's holiday bingo."

I know about variations in other games like midnight bowling, but I'm not familiar with this one. "How is that different from regular bingo?"

"I haven't the foggiest."

In a perfunctory way she asks how I am, and I do the same for her. Though I met her when I stayed with Mom, and though we've talked once or twice since then, we don't seem to find much to talk about now. Finally she tells me she'll have Mom phone later, so next I call my dad. But when he picks up, I realize I don't have much to say to him either. Less even, it seems, than to Mrs. Martin.

"Hey, Dad, it's Jim. Merry Christmas."

He doesn't answer, and I wonder if he's physically unable or whether he heard me or if he, too, simply doesn't know what to say.

"Hello, Jim," he says finally.

"I just, you know, wanted to see what's up with you."

"What's up with me?" he says, as if he's truly pondering what the answer might be. "What's up with me?" He lets that one drift away on its own.

"Well, you sure sound good," I tell him. "Your speech is fine. And Mrs. Trindle says you're walking with just a cane now. That's great."

But he's still on "what's up?" "Your mother hasn't called in weeks to see how I'm doing. On Christmas Eve she can't even call. I guess it's too much trouble for her. I guess she's too busy."

I'm struggling with what response I can give that he won't turn on its head. If I tell him I've called her and she's out, it will confirm her busy schedule. If I say I haven't heard from her either, ditto. If I suggest *he* make a call...well, let's give that a try.

"You have her number out there, don't you, Dad? I'm sure she'd love to hear from you. Why not give her a ring? And if she's out shopping or something," I add this as a hedge, "just try again later."

"I wonder if she even considers who paid for everything over the years," he says from some other, smaller universe. "The house, the food, her clothes. I wonder if she stops to think it was me who busted his ass, dressing in coats and two pair of jeans in the heat of summer just so I could stand in front of that furnace eight hours a day. Who got up for work at five every morning so she could—what? I don't even know. Sit around the house all day? And where does she think the money came from for that car she stole?"

I can't help it, I laugh. He can't mean these things. He can't believe them. "Dad, come on. She bought the car. And don't forget, she got up at four every morning to make you breakfast so you could leave at five. She ran all over town doing your errands, and fixed those jeans you wore, and watched us kids. She, she…" Why am I saying these things? They're too obvious.

Anyway, it doesn't matter. He's a train on a track, rolling downhill. He says, "That's what I get for making it all so easy for her. You make things easy for people and they don't appreciate it. She never did, that's for damn sure. Not one time. She has no idea how hard the real world is."

My father may have recovered enough to speak clearly, but it seems he can't hear. He can't hear her concern when she calls. He can't hear me defend her now, not that she needs defending. I'm just lost. I don't know what to do except try my best not to be him.

"Hey, Dad," I say as soon as I can get a word in. "I gotta go, but Merry Christmas, okay? I love you."

That's my gift to him this year, *I love you.* That, and my sorrow for his unhappiness.

WITH NO ONE TO share the holiday, I drive to the terminal and get to work. We don't have security fences up yet, so Owen and I keep the rigs at home like before. But whenever either of us is in town, we spend some time working on the place. By now the walls in the two smaller offices are sanded, and today I start to paint mine in an eggshell color. I tape the window trim and sill, but I don't bother to cover the floor because it will get new linoleum. Mrs. G says when we're ready she'll make us curtains, though my preference is blinds. I guess I'll hold my opinion until I see what she comes up with. Also she's keeping an eye out for desks and chairs at Saint Vincent's.

When the taping is complete, I start a pot of coffee and turn on the radio, which of course plays only Christmas music. Normally this would be fine, but today I'm not in the mood; it's seventy degrees outside and I'm by myself. I turn the sound lower but leave the radio on just to have some company. While the coffee drips, I pour paint into the tray, screw the roller handle onto a pole and begin with the ceiling. As the roller spins, it rains a mist onto my head and face and arms, but I don't care. With each pass the room brightens, and I do as well.

In an hour I've drunk the coffee and started another pot. I've heard "Rockin' Around the Christmas Tree" three times, which is two times more than I need per season. But at least I've completed the painting. The office is clean looking, and more importantly smells like a fresh start.

As I tap the lid back onto the paint can, I think of how I will decorate the place, though the word "decorate" is not the notion I have in mind. I want functional equipment, not foofy accessories: a dry-marker scheduling board and maybe a maintenance board and at least three file cabinets. There'll be a calendar on the wall over there by the window and one of those retro-looking-but-actually-cheap-knock-off coat trees in the corner. I'll have pencils in a cup on the desk. And a blotter. For sure I want a blotter.

I'm thinking of these things, which make me both excited and apprehensive, wondering what I've gotten myself into, when I hear a car drive up. I look into the parking lot and see Owen climbing out of his big Ford. He has on paint-spattered clothes, just like me.

"Hey, Bub," he says when he comes through the door.

"What are you doing here?" I ask. "It's Christmas Eve."

"That explains all those folks at the mall." He grins at me. "I see you've been busy."

"Done," I tell him. "At least with that room. Want to do yours?"

He spreads his arms as if to say, "You think I always dress like this?"

He's brought his own paint, a sort of an orange-peach color, pale enough not to be offensive, though I'd have never expected him to pick a shade anywhere near this soft. We start the process over again, taping the window trim, the door jamb, and he says, "You got plans for tonight? If not, come on over. We'll have some dinner and a snort. Open the gifts."

I'd gotten little things for him and Iris and for each of the boys. Nothing much, just thinking-of-you gifts. I'd handed these to him days ago.

"I'd like that," I tell him. "Thanks for asking."

I SUPPOSE BECAUSE OF the work I do, and also because of the person I am, I don't actually talk much with other people. I sit in the truck alone for hours and think as I drive. Or I go to the park and shoot hoops, mostly by myself, and I think there too. Or I listen to music or read. When I'm with Mrs. G, I answer when asked, but mostly she talks and I nod. The exception is when I'm with Owen. When we're together, we both talk all the time, like a couple of old hens.

Now while we paint his office, he starts telling me about the riding mower Iris got him for Christmas. He relates the horsepower and all the features he knows by heart—the speeds, gear ratios, the height adjustment—even though none of this has he actually seen yet. Still, he's convinced the machine is hidden somewhere because he's given her hints for weeks, and also they're now getting along great.

This brings us seamlessly to a discussion of rotary versus reel mowers, which then takes the odd leap to picking the best song of all time. This is not only a difficult exercise, it's pointless. Nevertheless, when he presses I come up with "Summertime" as my choice.

The word is hardly out of my mouth when he pounces. "Nope." I hear his roller make a liquid swish against the wall. "No, no, no. We're not going back to the dinosaur days. I mean something from this century. I mean the best rock song."

I don't bother pointing out that "Summertime" is, in fact, from this century—1934. I don't say anything, because even mathematics seem malleable under Owen's logic.

"Okay," he says. "I'll get you started. 'Great Balls of Fire.'The rockingest song ever recorded."

I'm painting the wall adjacent to the one he's working on, so my back is to him. Nevertheless, I can tell from his voice he has a smug look that says he's got me. He believes leading out with "Great Balls of Fire" is like going first in tic-tac-toe. He thinks he can't be beaten and probably not even tied, especially by me since I don't know rock from stone. Normally he'd be right, but not this time.

"No way," I tell him with conviction. "It's gotta be 'Tell Momma.'"

Ha! Silence! But then he says, "Which version?"

I hope this is a trick question because I only know one. "Etta James?"

Owen snorts. "Christ on a crutch. Where did you spend your youth? Best soul, maybe. Best rock? Not a chance."

All right, so I'm out of my element here. "Who then?"

"Hands down, no close second, best version ever is Janis Joplin live from the Fillmore."

I admit to him I've never heard it.

He says he wishes he'd known of my deficiencies before he signed on to be a partner. He figures he might have to reconsider the whole proposition. "I've got a tape," he says. "We'll listen to it tonight. She'll blow your damn socks off. Get you straightened right out."

Having decided that one, we move on to worst crashes actually witnessed, not heard about from another trucker. I tell him of a pileup on the Grapevine, where forty vehicles were involved and eight people died. Naturally the fellow who began it all was not one of them. He was an old hippie who'd been smoking dope and went from bright sunshine into a fog bank. He panicked, thinking he'd gone blind, and hit the brakes of his VW bus. The trucks started stacking up behind him, me among them, but I skidded off the shoulder and was spared.

By the time I finish my story, we're cleaning up. I'm washing the rollers and trays in the sink, and Owen is taking down the paper. He admires the carnage of my tale.

"That's a good one," he agrees from across the reception area. "But I've got the topper."

Of course he does, and I don't mind. Listening to him tell his stories, I'm carried away like a boy scout listening to the camp counselor around a fire. As I come from the bathroom into the reception area, Owen joins me, looking like he bathed in paint. I smile but look at the floor so he can't see. I slide my back down the wall and sit. I ache from head to toe, but it's a good ache like I've actually achieved something. I rest my arms along my knees and wait for him to begin.

"I'm on the 60," he says, "heading into L.A. Ahead is a guy with a dump truck, and we're both steaming, okay? All of a sudden what do I see but the bed of the dump starts coming up. Nothing in it, but she's going to full height, which must be sixteen, eighteen feet. Oh, Lord, I say to myself. Either he doesn't know what's happened, or he's trying do himself in, 'cause there's an elevated sidewalk a mile down the road and it can't be more than about fourteen and half feet high. So I pull into the next lane and start honking. I'm flashing the lights and trying to raise him on the CB. Nothing. I drop a gear and stand on it, full speed ahead, closing the distance between me and the dump, but he's closing on the walkway just as fast. I'm still behind, honking and cussing, trying to get beside the guy to flag him. Just before the bridge, I'm finally alongside and he looks over like I'm crazy. I got my thumb doing the hitchhike back to his dump bed, flipping my hand up like a mackerel. All of sudden he gets it. He checks the mirror, looks back at me with this *Oh, fuck* expression on his face, and..."

Owen stops here for effect and I think we *should* be around that campfire sipping whiskey. We'd hear the frogs croaking, the fire crackling. He slaps one hand against the other.

"Bam. Sixty to zero in one half of nothing. At least zero for the truck. The guy though, he busts out of his seat belt and through the window, and I swear this is true, he's flying beside me, right outside my window, for fifty feet or so until he starts to lose altitude. I lost track of him after that."

"Yuck," I tell him.

"Yuck is right."

We call it a day. Owen says to come by the house around six, six-thirty. We'll have something to drink, a nice dinner. Their big meal is tomorrow and he invites me to that as well, but I decline. Mrs. Garcia has already invited me to her Christmas dinner, and I'm looking forward to seeing everyone. I've decided I will not let my life be empty as my father's is. I'll fill it up with...I don't know. Work, of course. Friends.

Back in my trailer I strip down and throw my dirty clothes in a laundry bag. I step into the shower, hot as I can stand, and let it run a long time. When I finally get out, I put on dress clothes. Dress for me anyway. This will be a special evening and I want to give it the appropriate respect. I piddle around, chewing up time, but just before I'm about to leave, the phone rings. It's my mother. She says she stayed at the Elks until they threw her out.

"Did you call your father?" she asks.

I tell her I did.

"And how is he doing?"

I say he's doing fine. I suggest she phone him herself, even tonight. With the time difference, it won't be that late for Dad.

"The line runs both ways, you know." She says this with some vehemence. "I've called him plenty. He can call me for a change."

I figure that's a lost cause, so I ask something else that's been on my mind. It's about her outing today. "Bingo on Christmas Eve seems weird. Who doesn't have somewhere more important to be today?"

This is thin ice I'm treading, especially given how I've spent my own day. But I'm feeling pretty solid because I have a friend. I have a couple, in fact. With their help I'll figure a way to keep moving forward with my life and just see how things work out.

"Me for one," Mom says, sounding as happy to be alone as some adventurer who pities those unfortunates left home. "Actually there are lots of us. Harold Cruickshank, who lost his wife. The Shaver sisters, Eva and Joan, are old maids. Butch Johnston. We're all alone, but we're alone together. We're like family. And the main thing is, we had a ball."

I have to laugh at this. She has made the same decision as me. She's going to make a life with what she has.

"Did you win?" I ask.

"You bet I did. Twenty-five dollars."

"You can retire."

"And join the choir."

"That's your desire?"

"I do aspire."

"Then, may it transpire."

She laughs. "Merry Christmas, Honey. I love you."

"I love you, too, Mom."

I'm about to pick up my jacket when the phone rings again. To myself I say, Oh great, now what. But I mean it ironically because I'm pleased to get the call. Especially when I learn it's Allison.

"Hey!" I can't disguise how good it is to hear her voice. "Merry Christmas."

"And you," she says. Neither of us says anything for just a beat and then she adds, "I don't have much time. We're opening gifts here at home, and then we're off to Carl's parents."

There are four of them now; Allison and Carl, Amanda and Sammy, who's actually still on the way but much anticipated. They're the perfect little family, which normally would stab at my heart. But now for the first time I realize I'm not upset by their happiness. I may never get over wanting more from Allison, but I'm getting better at living with what I've got.

"Anyway," she goes on, "I've got a Christmas gift for you. At least I hope you'll see it like that."

"I'll check the mail," I tell her.

"It isn't that kind of gift. Remember I said Carl felt you were a decent guy? Well, I was thinking about that and I think maybe he was right. So we discussed it and decided it's time to tell Amanda about her other daddy."

My heart does one big BOMP. This is almost too much to take in. I look around my little trailer wondering if my daughter will think it's wonderful or ridiculous. I'm so happy, I protest slightly to check the reality of it all.

"I thought you were going to wait. I thought you or Carl felt it would be too confusing."

Allison sighs at this. "That's true, we both said it. At first it was mostly Carl's idea. Looking back, I think it's because he didn't like you very much. Or rather he didn't like the idea of you, you know, because of what you did. And I suppose I went along with him because it was a way I could control you or hurt you. Get back a little. It's not something I'm proud of now, but there you are.

"The truth is, young children absorb incongruities pretty well. If you think about it, two daddies are easy to understand compared to Santa Claus flying around the world in one night."

As she talks, I think of all the things that will be different from now on. I can take my daughter places, buy her things, worry over her. But somehow I think it will be a good worry. Like, is this school better than that one? Is this dress too low-cut for the prom? I look down at my hand and laugh. It's quivering like a butterfly.

"Can I be there?" I ask. "Can I be there when you tell her?"

"That's why I'm calling," she says.

"When?"

"It's up to you," she says. "We told her this special present wouldn't be with the others, that it's coming later. I wouldn't wait too long, though. She's easily distracted."

I don't answer right away because I'm thinking. Or maybe not thinking so much as feeling, since nothing in my head will resolve into a clear idea. I suppose it will in time, but for now there is just this sensation like sunshine in my body.

"Jim?"

"Uh-huh."

"Are you okay."

"Uh-huh."

"What are you thinking about?"

And then it comes to me, what this sweet, warm feeling reminds me of. "Butterscotch," I tell her. "Heated."

FOR A SMALL DINNER, Owen's table is mighty full. I wonder where they'll put everything tomorrow when they serve more. Tonight we have turkey and candied yams and rolls just out of the oven. There is a tossed green salad and a bean casserole and dressing on the side. The boys drink sparkling apple cider by the bottle.

"We're so happy you could join us," Iris says.

She's a nice lady, built sturdy, which is appropriate for her husband. But I don't know where their kids came from. The boys are both snake-hipped string beans, though Paul is not yet as tall as Aaron.

Owen hasn't mentioned much about his journey to South Dakota, so until now I haven't asked. But then he says to his wife, "Martha called today. She says to tell you hello and to let the boys know there's a gift on the way for each of them."

"Martha is your mother?" I ask

"Yeah," Owen says. "Tougher than boiled owl. Looks like she'll be around awhile." And then he says to me, "What happened between work and coming to dinner? You look like the cat that got the cream."

"What do you mean?"

Owen takes his index fingers and pulls the corners of his mouth into an exaggerated smile. "Eeee-eee-eee," he says.

I smile bigger still and shrug.

After dinner we open gifts. I got Owen a brass compass, and he got me a hula girl for the dash of my truck. When the kids have gone to bed, we three adults sit around talking about the future, how maybe we can get Terry to come work with us. We talk about salesmen we know from other firms and what sort of freight we should focus on. Iris takes this in for half an hour or so, then says she's off to bed. When she's gone, Owen finds cigarette paper and a pouch of tobacco. He rolls a smoke, licks it closed, and lights up. In his upholstered rocker he tips back and forth, heel and toe, next to the Christmas tree. The smoke rises up from his hand and tangles in the pine branches. Seeing him relax like this makes me think of Santa Claus on December 26th after all the work is done.

"Now that it's just you and me, Sport, you gonna to tell me what's this big secret?"

"No secret," I say. "Really."

"Bullshit," he says, smiling. "You're jumpy as spit on a skillet. Go ahead and go if you want. Do whatever it is you can't wait for. You won't hurt my feelings."

To prove him wrong I stay another ten minutes, sitting as quietly as possible until I say, "That was a great dinner, but I don't want to keep you up. I guess I will take off now."

Owen stubs out his cigarette in an ashtray, then crosses one ankle over the other knee. He laces his fingers in his lap and gives me a grin. "Gotta be a woman," he says.

"Not exactly," I tell him, grinning back. "But it is a girl."

ON THE WAY HOME I think about what I told Allison, that I'd leave in the morning and see them in the late afternoon. To get the car ready for my trip I pull into the Shell station for gas, check the oil and tires, buy some snacks. It isn't that late when I get to the trailer, maybe ten, and I'm not sleepy.

So then I figure I might as well pack, as long as I'm up. But that's done in about five minutes and I sit on the edge of the bench with my arms along my legs, looking at the floor. No way can I get to sleep. I stand up to put on some music, but sit down again because nothing seems right for the moment.

Then it comes to me, the one song that's perfect, and I find the tape it's on. But instead of putting it in the player I decide to listen to it in the car. Actually, what I decide is to listen to it while I'm driving.

I grab the packed duffel and throw it into the passenger's seat, padlock the trailer and pull the Duster into the street. I roll the gate closed and lock it too, and then I head toward the freeway and point north.

I save the music until I'm out of L.A., past Magic Mountain and up into the hills. The moon is high now, bright and cold. Its milky light makes the hills stand out in relief. I settle into the seat, relaxed, calculating time and distance. I figure I'll stop in a rest area along the way so I'm not too early, though even with the stop I can be in Lodi by ten. I'll call to make sure that's okay. I hope it is.

I push in the tape and adjust the volume. Not loud, not too soft. Just Barbara Lewis singing so sweetly to me. For me. Saying what it is I want to say. What I will say, tomorrow, to my daughter.

Hello, stranger. It seems like a mighty long time.